# The
# Edith Wharton
# Murders

**BY LEV RAPHAEL**

MYSTERIES

The Nick Hoffman Series

*Let's Get Criminal*
*The Edith Wharton Murders*

NONFICTION

*Edith Wharton's Prisoners of Shame*
*Journeys & Arrivals*
*Dynamics of Power* (with Gershen Kaufman)
*Stick Up For Yourself!* (with Gershen Kaufman)
*Coming Out of Shame* (with Gershen Kaufman)

FICTION

*Dancing on Tisha B'Av*
*Winter Eyes*

# The
# Edith Wharton
# Murders

## A NICK HOFFMAN MYSTERY

*Lev Raphael*

ST. MARTIN'S PRESS
NEW YORK

Library of Congress Cataloging-in-Publication Data

Raphael, Lev.
    The Edith Wharton murders: a Nick Hoffman mystery / by
Lev Raphael.
        p.      cm.
    ISBN 0–312–15519–0
    I. Title.
PS3568.A5988E35    1997
813' .54—dc21                                        97–7598
                                                      CIP

First Edition: September 1997

10   9   8   7   6   5   4   3   2   1

*For my sister*

"I hate authors. I wouldn't mind them so much
if they didn't write books."
—*ELIZABETH VON ARNIM*
*Enchanted April*

"*The only thing worse than not being published
is* being *published.*"
—*DANIEL MAGIDA,* AUTHOR OF
*The Rules of Seduction*

# The
# Edith Wharton
# Murders

# Prologue

T HE FIRST TIME I heard some Men's Movement honcho say that men desperately needed to get in touch with their Inner Warrior, I laughed because I was congested, couldn't hear that well, and thought he said Inner *Worrier.*

Hell, I didn't need any amateur-night shaman with a Kmart drum to draw me any maps for that kind of journey. I knew the way in my sleep.

Stefan says that what I do is catastrophizing. I call it planning ahead. But even I couldn't have predicted the Edith Wharton Murders.

My trouble began the very first day of fall semester when the entire Department of English, American Studies, and Rhetoric (EAR) held an "emergency" meeting in the conference room across the hall from the main office in Parker Hall. It was an old classroom remodeled sometime in the fifties or early sixties, when there was a lot of building activity here at the Michiganapolis campus of the State University of Michigan. The room might once have been pretty, but you could no longer tell. The ceiling had been lowered and was covered with those grainy off-white ceiling tiles extruding huge banks of neon lights that flickered and hummed and would have been more appropriate in an operating room or a morgue. Ugly beige venetian blinds obscured the filthy casement windows, hanging in dusty and uneven folds. The wainscoting had been heavily painted over and a metal-rimmed blackboard installed, the kind with the livid green writing surface.

Worst were the seats: horrible pedestal chairs with tiny curved arms that spread out into almost unusable gray-green minidesks. The seats were very hard, their lack of comfort exacerbated by fifty seats being crammed into a room that should have held no more than thirty. Not only was the fit too tight, but the chairs were bolted down—in case of earthquake, I suppose—so that if you tried turning around in one, you risked being disemboweled. The whole room had a grim authoritarian feel, with students forced to face the front, unable to interact with each other. You could almost imagine each seat linked to some electronic system of remotely delivered shocks for punishment and control.

We faculty members seemed foolishly out of place at the cramped and tiny combination chair-desks our students routinely suffered in. The air of crisis was heightened by the extra seats brought in to crowd the back of the room.

My partner Stefan, the department's writer-in-residence, hadn't come, because he had the luxury of skipping meetings now and then. It was an unspoken perk of his position, and one I envied, especially since EAR was divided into rival camps.

The department of nearly eighty had a core of twenty faculty who had once constituted the independent Rhetoric Department, which had been forced on English and American Studies about fifteen years earlier in a budget-cutting move. It was a transplant that had never really taken. The Rhetoric professors—surly, querulous, and underqualified—were consistently treated badly in EAR: their offices were smaller, their schedules less convenient, and their complaints ignored.

These professors acted like captives forced into servitude by the conquering armies of a brutal empire that had burned their capital city to the ground and sowed salt into the earth so that nothing would ever grow there again. They were beyond hope, beyond dreams, beyond nostalgia. Occasionally, though, they'd launch into bizarre self-immolating tirades at department meetings, making suggestions and claims that showed they had no grasp of university reality whatsoever.

The other faculty despised them, and the Rhetoric people didn't especially like me. Even though I taught composition, as they had been doing for years, I was an anomaly: I *enjoyed* it. But I also had a specialty in Edith Wharton and was likely to teach a Wharton seminar soon in addition to my other classes, whereas they were trapped teaching the same course semester after semester, year after year.

Standing at the front of the room, Coral Greathouse, the new chair of EAR, called the meeting to order in her diffident, disembodied way. Slim, blond, wide-eyed behind enormous thick red-framed glasses which highlighted her somber blue nun-in-mufti suit, she was pale, serious, intense—with the quiet conviction of a small-town librarian who knows where every one of her books is. Our last chair had been a blustering, loud, clumsy man, so it was also no surprise that the department had settled on a woman who was a bit of a cipher. Coral was almost affectless; her face barely changed expression and her small round mouth moved very little when she spoke. Was she tough, or a softy? Did people pay attention to her out of respect, or because they didn't think she mattered? It was too soon to tell.

"What poise that woman has," Serena Fisch muttered in the chairdesk to my right as we waited at the meeting for Coral to begin. Serena was Coral's opposite—extravagant of gesture, phrase, and looks. She was the department member most firmly rooted in the past, specifically the forties. I liked to think of her as the Lost Andrews Sister. That day, Serena's glistening dark hair seemed even blacker and shinier than usual, as if she had slathered on polyurethane sealer. Heavily made up in blocks of white and red, she had a sort of Kabuki-à-go-go look. She wore black sling-backs, seamed stockings, and a wide-shouldered, narrowwaisted black coatdress. A rhinestone peacock pin spread its tail up towards one shoulder, and all she needed was a snood.

Coral plunged right in: "You're all aware of the faculty complaints across the university that SUM is the State University of Males, that we don't have enough women faculty, that we don't hire enough women graduate teaching assistants, that we don't take women's issues seriously. Some of the state legislators have been echoing these remarks, and now the governor's chimed in."

There was facetious muttering and a great deal of eye-rolling. No matter that every year the legislature reminded us of its power to cut funding for SUM, which it almost always did, faculty members sighed wearily whenever the subject of the legislature came up, like employers dealing with importunate job-seekers. As if living a supposed life of the mind made them superior in every conceivable way. It was bizarre, high-handed, and self-defeating. But it never changed.

Coral almost smiled encouragingly, seeming to feel her very presence was proof of the stupidity of our legislators a few miles away in the capitol. Then she settled down. "How do we in EAR respond?"

Well, right then, EAR responded with a snarling roar of voices, demands, denunciations. Everyone had something to say now and they all started saying it. I tuned out because I knew this outburst would take a while to contain. I imagined I was watching a TV program with the sound off, and I just observed my colleagues around the room. Most fell into some clear categories. The older faculty looked as devoid of energy and life as week-old flattened roadkill. Too many student papers? Too many department meetings? Too many lies from the administration?

About half of the EAR faculty, forty in all, and mostly men, was given to decrepit tweed jackets and well-worn corduroy pants, in what I suppose they thought was deliberate self-parody. But their outfits had deconstructed themselves once too often. Balding, or with bad haircuts, it would have been a kindness to call them shabby. Their dowdiness was so oppressive and inescapable that the younger, more fashionably dressed faculty members came off as showy and inappropriate—as if they were reeking of perfume at a funeral.

Facing the raucous, clamoring crowd, Coral made a controlled moue of distaste. She could have been changing a particularly nasty diaper, and I started laughing. Serena joined me, and Coral nodded her gratitude at us as people shut up, trying to figure out what was funny.

"One at a time," Coral muttered. "Please."

The idea of including more women writers in syllabi was shot down by a curriculum committee member who said we'd done enough in that direction.

Les Peterman, the department jock, said, "How about some men secretaries to show we're not sexist?" He was booed and applauded. His field was the sixties, and for some reason he always joked about equal rights for women.

A new hiree asked, "How about a conference on Gender?"

There was a tentative silence as people looked around, trying to gauge each other's reactions. "Gender"—along with "PC"—was one of those terms that could ignite true and lasting hysteria on campus.

Serena drawled, "Lovely, then we could pay people to talk about their private parts."

Coral hushed the outburst of hilarity by simply shaking her head. "A conference," she said. "Why *not* have a conference? I don't mean on Gender, but on"—she hesitated—"a woman writer. An American

*4*

woman writer. The alumnae would approve, we could get Women's Studies to cosponsor . . ."

It made so much sense that you could have imagined everyone in the room was on time-release Valium, falling in with Coral's mood. We all nodded in slow motion, quiet now, trying to decide on whom to suggest.

"Anaïs Nin," Serena threw out.

"Oh, please!" That was Larry Rich, the shabby ex-hippie in stained cords and baggy sweaters. He taught Renaissance drama and poetry. "She's so passé."

Martin Wardell, the Victorian specialist who always returned his student papers late, seconded that. "Too much heavy breathing, too much straining for effect."

"She's not passé—she slept with her father," Priscilla Davidoff said reasonably, from over by the door. Priscilla taught genre fiction. "Incest memoirs are really hot right now."

There were shudders in the room, as if the suggestion was to put the whole department on the Geraldo Rivera show. Nin was clearly out of the question.

The predominantly male room similarly demolished Gertrude Stein, because she was a lesbian and therefore too controversial, and besides, "The Italians appreciate her much more than we do"—whatever *that* meant. Flannery O'Connor and Carson McCullers went down in flames as "too weird." Willa Cather was out because she was being done next year at that "other school" in Ann Arbor. Toni Morrison appeared to excite some interest, but was quickly dumped—though no one said it aloud—because there weren't any Black faculty members in the department. Cynthia Ozick likewise was axed because SUM didn't have a Jewish Studies program; the last thing EAR needed was to highlight the university's deficiencies. Besides, she was coming to campus in the President's Lecture Series in the winter.

The back of my neck suddenly felt cold, and I wondered if people were looking at me for some reason. I was right. Someone near the door called, "How about Edith Wharton?"

I whirled around; it was Carter Savery, the department's most colorless professor. One of the ex-Rhetoric faculty, he was a drab, bald, chunky, gray man whose face was consistently devoid of affect. The kind of man you see neighbors talking about on TV after a mass murder: "But he was always so quiet . . ."

Coral pressed her lips together as if possessed by the idea. Had that been her plan all along? "Comments?" she asked, looking like Lily Tomlin's phone operator with her pursed lips and squished smile. I shuddered while my colleagues blundered to comply with her request.

Listlessly, Carter said, *"Ethan Frome,"* as if that title explained everything.

People around the room nodded in dim recognition as their memories of being bored in high school by *Ethan Frome* drifted back.

"And look at all the movies they're making of her books!" someone else said, as if Hollywood's distant glamor would reflect on all of us.

"Wait—this is crazy!"

Silence. We all turned to Iris Bell, a tiny, red-haired woman with a loud, grating voice, whose every comment was so filled with roiling emotion you expected a breakdown when she said good morning. The corners of her mouth seemed to be yanked down by perpetual sorrow, as if she were possessed by the Mask of Tragedy. She was, of course, also a former Rhetoric Department professor.

"It's a fraud!" Iris leapt to her feet, her battered, elfin face twisted with passion, her hands clenched and arms outstretched as if she were begging us to see sense. "We should march to the president's office right now and protest this charade. We should demand real action, real attention to women's issues on this campus!"

In the silence that greeted Iris's remarks, you could almost hear the non-Rhetoric faculty thinking, "Yeah, right." And someone muttered, "Why don't they ever shut up?"

Coral Greathouse said smoothly, "Shall we vote on the conference?" and Iris sank back into her chair, meager shoulders hunched, her wan face clawed by defeat.

Like the moment in *Bringing Up Baby* when Cary Grant knows the dinosaur is going to collapse on itself, I realized there was definitely going to be an Edith Wharton conference at SUM—and I would be responsible, whether I wanted to or not. A vote went through before I could think of any way to stop it or protest. What could be better? Wharton was a popular but bland and uncontentious woman writer.

"And," Coral Greathouse summed up, with more than usual enthusiasm, "we have our very own Wharton scholar in this department."

"I'm just a bibliographer," I blurted.

But Coral waved that away: "We're *so* proud of you."

In the rush to escape, a decision about dates for the conference and actual planning was deferred, and people came over to slap my shoulder or shake my hand on their way out as if I'd won a prize, as if the department had *honored* me.

"Oh God," I muttered, as the room thinned out.

Coral Greathouse sailed up to me, her hand extended. I had to rise and shake it, feeling as if I were posing for a public portrait, with the photographers and press eager to capture my feelings and my face.

"I'm very pleased," she said in her faltering voice. "Very. It's the right choice. I know Dean Bullerschmidt will approve and support us. And you certainly have all the connections in the Wharton community."

"That's just it," I said. "There *is* no Wharton community."

She cocked her head at me as if she were a puzzled parrot trying to learn a difficult new word. "Sorry?"

I tried to think of a short way to explain what was a very complicated situation. "There are two rival Wharton organizations—and they hate each other. They hold separate conferences, they have separate journals. Whichever one we hook up with, the other will be outraged."

Coral considered that. "If there are two societies, invite them both." And she left, clearly buoyed by the idea of massive registrations.

I knew then that I was doomed.

Serena Fisch shook her head, surveying me with a wry smile. "Coral intends to make her mark with this shindig."

"You think so?"

Serena swung out from her chair, crossed her long legs. "I'm sure of it. If it flies, she'll claim all the credit."

"Wonderful."

"Good luck, dear. I hope you live through all the people phoning you because their names are misspelled on the program—that is, if your keynote speakers aren't stranded by an airline strike. Then of course there's always attempted rape at the cocktail party. Conferences are *such* fun."

"You ran one?"

"Yes," she said grimly. "I came down with walking pneumonia and bronchitis before it was all over."

"Carter did this on purpose!" I said through clenched teeth, and then I flushed. Serena Fisch was the former chair of the Rhetoric Department, and though she bore herself like a deposed (and jazzy) monarch, I was never entirely sure how she felt about her former subjects.

Serena shook her head. "I doubt that, Nick. Carter was just trying to be helpful."

"This is a disaster," I said, so only Serena could hear, even though we were alone in the room.

"I know." She nodded sympathetically. "I know. Everyone will expect you to do the work, while they get the credit, or get laid." Her eyebrows rose. "Or even both," she said thoughtfully.

"But you don't understand how terrible it is. You can't have a Wharton conference—you can't even have a Wharton panel—with both groups. They despise each other."

"On general principles? Or is there a history?"

I shrugged helplessly. It was too awful to discuss right then.

Serena ran a finger along her eyebrow as if coaxing an idea into light. "Can't you be the one to bring them together?"

"Listen, even Mother Teresa wouldn't try. It's like—it's like matter and antimatter. No—imagine Pat Robertson on a date with Madonna."

"Goody," Serena threw off. "Just what the university needs. Academic mayhem."

I shook my head.

"You should go right home," Serena advised, "slap a cold compress on your forehead, and lie down quietly in the dark."

Just then, Coral Greathouse bustled back into the room. "Nick, I think you should know that the pressure from the administration, especially Dean Bullerschmidt, is very strong. We have to do something right away. The conference has to take place *this* spring."

"That's impossible! You can't put together something that complicated in six or seven months!"

"But you've got the connections," she said with a grin. "That's what really matters. And remember, this will look very good when you come up for tenure in a few years, won't it?"

She left, and Serena shrugged at me.

"That was a threat," I said.

Serena nodded. "You look like 'Guernica.'"

"What do you mean?"

"Shattered."

ON THE SHORT drive home after the meeting that sealed my fate, I felt like I was trapped in one of those dream situations where you suddenly have to go onstage, but you can't remember your lines, can't even remember that you're in a play, have ever *been* in a play. The lights glare, the audience is hungry, dangerous, ready to humiliate you.

I felt a slight easing of tension pulling up to our house, which always reassured me. A center-hall brick colonial built in the 1930s, it seemed to offer so much stability, from the pillars flanking the front door to the large and airy rooms filled with our comfortable, overstuffed furniture.

Stefan, who had gone down to Ann Arbor to visit his father and step-mother, was back, and I almost cheered to see him. Hugging him, I spilled out my bad news, knowing that he would talk about how it had gone with his long-estranged father only when he was ready.

Stefan was surprised. "They asked *you* to run a conference?"

I nodded dumbly.

"I don't understand." He frowned. "Do they want to sabotage it? Don't they know how scattered you are?"

I started to laugh. Why is it that someone you love can openly tell you your faults and it seems funny, affectionate? Stefan knew I was one of the least organized people in the world, but I didn't mind him pointing it out.

We moved to the kitchen, where Stefan was preparing pasta puttanesca for dinner. A bottle of pinot grigio stood ready on the kitchen table, which was already set with pasta bowls and freshly grated Romano in a glass dish.

"Think of it," he said, mashing the garlic cloves, olive oil, and anchovies into a paste in the saucepan. "You could lose all the registration forms." I began to perk up. "Or invite Eudora Welty scholars by mistake—same initials, right? *EW.*"

I slumped. "I wish we lived near a volcano. That would make people think twice about coming."

Stefan added capers, chopped black olives, and seeded plum tomatoes to the simmering pan, and stirred. "Are you kidding? Nick, you

9

know what academics are like. Nothing would stop them from a tax write-off and time away from their classes."

"And Wharton people are the worst now that Wharton's so popular. They think it'll rub off."

Stefan nodded, checking the pan. It already smelled wonderful. He reduced the heat. "Basil tomato penne or spinach linguine?" he asked, putting up a pot of water to boil.

Is there anything better than a good meal prepared by a loving chef?

"The linguine. Spinach worked for Popeye."

"Why don't we sit down after dinner," Stefan said gently, "and start making some plans for the conference?"

"Why don't we call Dr. Kevorkian and have him put me out of my misery while I still have the chance?"

# Part One

*". . . her name had so long been public property . . ."*

—Edith Wharton, *The Touchstone*

# I

*"I* THINK I should warn you," I said, looking up from the layout of the Wharton conference schedule. "My previous office mate was murdered."

I didn't intend to say that to Bob Gillian the first January day we were both in our office that second semester. It just popped out. I do that a lot. I'll say something out of place just because the moment calls for the opposite. I guess you could call me quip happy.

Maybe it was a genetic mutation. My Belgian Jewish parents shared the French love of le mot juste; in me, it had degenerated into ill-timed wisecracking, or what my mother austerely called my *bêtises*.

Though Gillian's books, files, and Seurat posters had been unpacked, shelved, and hung before the second semester started a week before, I'd only seen the man himself in passing. I liked the posters, especially the one of *La Grande Jatte,* my favorite painting at Chicago's Art Institute.

I should have said something friendly and welcoming as he sat down at his desk opposite mine. But I was nervous. Gillian's wife, Joanne, was on the State University of Michigan's Board of Trustees. A local minister with her own church, she was an extremist given to frequent denunciations of "the gay lifestyle," and just the week before had declared that gays and lesbians at SUM were "unfit role models for our youth— just like devil worshipers, cannibals, and communists." She was a close friend of our conservative governor and there were rumors she was being groomed for state office. She was also running the university, since the current president—SUM's former football coach Webb Littleterry— was only a figurehead.

"Don't worry," Bob Gillian threw off, swinging around in his creaky desk chair. "I know all about what happened last year to your office mate, so I've already registered for a self-defense course and my will's up to date in case that's a bust."

And then Gillian smiled with the showy insouciance of a magician whooshing a tablecloth out from a fully set table without stirring a single candlestick, fork, or glass. In his midfifties, he was small, slight, and blond, bearing himself like a model, and his blue eyes, ruddy complexion, and thick wavy hair seemed like jaunty slogans in a successful ad campaign.

I smiled back. At least he had a sense of humor. And that made him more entertaining than Perry Cross, my previous office mate, who had plagued me more in death than in the brief time last year we had shared an office there in Parker Hall at SUM's Michiganapolis campus.

"I've been spoiled," I said to Bob. "I've had this place all to myself for over half a year."

"Why's that?"

"Nobody wanted to share an office with me, given what happened to my last office mate."

"But *you* didn't kill him, right? So it's not like you're dangerous."

"Maybe they think I'm cursed, or the office is."

Bob nodded. "That's it, then. Superstition. Bad vibes."

"Hey—in our department, bad vibes are the norm."

"I can see that," he said, looking around the office. "This place sucks. I used to have a great little office. It was modern—it was air-conditioned—it was *clean.*"

I could understand his letdown. The large office we were sharing was dark and gloomy, with wide-paned windows that rattled in the slightest breeze and were going crazy now in the winter wind; lots of oddly shaped exposed pipes; and a bewilderingly high ceiling that might have made sense if there was a fresco instead of flaking cracks. Over everything, there was that shabby, unpainted, uncared-for look of a department that the university doesn't take much notice of.

As for the rest of the building . . . The floors in Parker Hall buckled, the walls and ceilings were cracked and bulging, the place reeked of bug spray that didn't seem to faze the heroic squadrons of waterbugs, and the weathered sandstone itself looked ready to deliquesce.

Bob went on: "Well, I'm sorry you didn't get to keep your privacy.

I bet it was like being a freshman in a dorm and hoping you'd luck out and wouldn't get a roommate."

"Exactly! It wasn't much, but it was mine. I think we'll get along okay, though."

Bob shrugged genially. "We don't have much choice, do we?"

To change the subject a little, I said, "It must have been a bitch when the old provost shut your department down."

He shrugged again. "You know how it is. The administrators make speeches about how important freshman writing is, how dedicated we are as an institution, blah blah blah. Then they close the Writing Lab. Why? To save money. How much money do you really save by getting rid of the secretaries and the director? If they want to save big bucks they should dump half the paper pushers over in the Administration Building, those turkeys making over a hundred thousand a year. This place is top-heavy with those slugs."

Bob shook his head, and I admired his composure. He sounded less like a faculty member who'd been shafted and more like an ironic news commentator, pointing out social or political foibles that didn't touch him directly.

I would have understood angrier discontent. After two decades of working in the Writing Lab, he'd been cast adrift, washing ashore in EAR. Teaching composition for us, he was now at the very bottom of the pile, where before he'd had seniority and respect in his own unit. I taught comp, too, but I enjoyed it, and besides, Stefan was EAR's writer-in-residence, so I shared some of his status.

Bob Gillian certainly seemed very out of place in this shabby department. He was aristocratic-looking and as relaxed and offhand as someone whose private income had allowed him to follow teaching as a hobby. Maybe that was the truth, because his tweed jacket, his loafers and cords, his argyle sweater vest and blue buttoned-down shirt all looked very expensive. He drove a gorgeous if slightly battered old Jaguar, a car I imagined he was so sentimentally attached to that he would never sell it. When he'd come into the office, he'd dramatically peel off his expensive-looking driving gloves as if he were a dashing RAF pilot who'd just shot down a few German planes. Clearly, he loved to drive that car and wanted people to know it.

I was puzzled that being married to someone on the Board of Trustees hadn't protected Bob, hadn't yielded him a high-paying sinecure of some kind. Maybe that accounted for his trashing the administrators at SUM: he was angry he wasn't one of them. Just as I was trying to think of a subtle way to raise all that, Priscilla Davidoff strode from her office across the hall and knocked fiercely on our open door.

"Nick! You won't believe this." She brandished a glossy magazine at me. I could just make out that the text was not in English.

"What's wrong?"

Priscilla hesitated, and I assumed it was something she didn't want Gillian to hear.

"Your office?" I asked, and she nodded.

I followed Priscilla back across the hall into her plant-filled, richly carpeted office, where every chair was comfortable and inviting. In a building that was cracked, dirty, scarred, and ignored by the university because it housed departments that brought in little money, her office was a refuge: bright, fragrant, appealing. Maybe she'd ordered too many Bombay Company doodads and had overdone the potpourri pots, but I suppose that was her way to fight being ground down by Parker Hall's decades of neglect and decay.

Closing the door and lowering her voice, Priscilla said, "Doesn't Bob Gillian make your skin crawl? And his wife is the ultimate Christian Bitch. She's Anita Bryant on crack. The two of them make me sick—they're *evil*."

Priscilla's hyperbole bothered me. Since our enemies demonized us, I didn't think it was appropriate to sink to their level.

"Listen, I'm trying not to let that get to me," I said. "I have to share an office with him, right?"

"But all the stuff Joanne Gillian says about us, how we're sick, how SUM could never give us domestic partner benefits because that would undermine the American family, how it would send a message to students that anything goes at this university, even bestiality—doesn't that make you crazy?"

"Of course it does! But it won't help if I treat her husband like shit, will it? Maybe getting to know someone gay will help—"

Quietly, Priscilla cut me off. "Listen, Nick. That won't make any difference at all. Before you and Stefan got here, gay and lesbian faculty met with upper-level administrators in an advisory group for five years. And I chaired the Task Force on Lesbian and Gay Equality at SUM. We gathered research, had a conference, presented our findings, and this administration still hasn't done a thing. No domestic partner benefits, no gay studies major, no gay/lesbian coordinator. Nothing we recommended. They got to know plenty of us, but it hasn't made a difference. Even if we *slept* with them, nothing would change!"

"Well, I know what the problem is. Reports and advisory groups are a complete waste of time. The only way you can change things at this university for gays and lesbians is to seize the Administration Building and take hostages." I added, "And give them all fashion makeovers."

Priscilla grinned.

"Now, what's going on?" I asked. "You didn't come into my office just to remind me SUM's homophobic, did you?"

She flushed. "Look." She shoved the magazine she'd been holding at me, and I could see where her name was circled in red, the English spelling like a tiny bare island in a churning arctic sea of—what?— Swedish? Danish? I couldn't tell.

I sat by her desk; she thunked into her chair and slammed down the magazine as if she were a bailiff commanding the court to rise. Tall, dark-haired, and as striking as Geena Davis, she wore black boots and jeans and a heavy black cowl-neck sweater, with her hair in a ponytail. Despite her dramatic looks, Priscilla was ordinarily somewhat placid, even at department meetings where people's eccentricities tended to bubble over.

I had never seen Priscilla looking so furious. She was red, wide-eyed, tight-mouthed. But it was not a rage that sealed her off, because I somehow felt included, as if she were recruiting me to a cause.

"This," she spat, "is an interview in a Hungarian magazine—a *Hungarian* magazine!—with Chloe DeVore." She let the name quiver in the air between us as if it were a challenge to a duel. DeVore was a prominent bisexual writer whose work I didn't enjoy, but who was widely read and admired. It seemed clear that her popularity was a curse for writers like Priscilla, because the literary establishment didn't seem willing to praise more than one lesbian (or half-lesbian?) writer at a time. DeVore was *it*, and scarfed up the good reviews, the six-figure advances, the guest teaching positions, the awards and grants, the spots in anthologies, the TV appearances, the unctuous interviewers.

"And right in the middle of some comment about contemporary American literature," Priscilla went on, "she trashes me."

"How?"

Priscilla's eyes narrowed. "She says my work is artless."

I hesitated. "You're sure that isn't a compliment? I mean, like maybe she's saying you're not artificial, maybe she means easy, free, natural . . . ?"

Priscilla shook her head. "I was hoping that, but the woman interviewing her—Sophia, Sophia Nemeth—sent it to me. And Sophia's note said it was clear Chloe didn't like my writing. 'Artless' definitely means without art, lacking art, having no art, not artistic—" She faltered.

Before I could ask about the translation, Priscilla said, "I know someone in the Russian Department who's fairly fluent in Hungarian. I checked with him to make sure."

I nodded. "Have you ever met Chloe?"

Now Priscilla reared back. "You're trying to tell me it's personal?"

"No." I shrugged. "I just wondered."

Since I lived with a writer who was prey to bad reviews, late-night doubts, troubles with his editor, frustrations with his publisher's publicity department, and his own perpetually escalating set of expectations, the situation was very familiar. I'd learned the hard way that listening to an outraged or dispirited writer, whatever the cause, you have to be patient, soothing but not smarmy, and prepared to agree with the wildest assumptions, fantasies, and fears.

Anything else can lead to a blowup.

Eventually, you can move to a more tranquil place, but trying to calm them down too quickly—or even disagreeing—is a bitter mistake. Humor can also be useful—in moderate amounts.

"Priscilla," I began, "Hungarian isn't even an Indo-European language."

That threw her, and frowning, she put the magazine down on her neatly arranged wide desk as if she might need both hands free to deal with me. "What?"

"I mean, jeez, its closest linguistic links in Europe are Finnish and Estonian. It's not like this is an interview in French or German. How many Hungarians are there, anyway? How many would read this magazine, or read as far as your name, or even care if they did? What's the worst thing that can happen? Your name is mud in Budapest?"

Priscilla smiled wanly. Then she shrugged and shook her head. "I feel like I'm in junior high and I just found out people are gossiping about me, saying something terrible."

I nodded, remembering how awful that could be.

She leaned forward. "No—worse! Like third grade, and kids are saying your lunch box smells, when it doesn't! It makes me feel paranoid, and helpless. What's she have to attack me for? I've never reviewed her work, I've never said anything bad about her." Eyes down, she added quietly, "In public."

It seemed obvious to me that Priscilla's books must threaten Chloe in some way, but I couldn't imagine how, and I didn't bother saying it. It would be like telling your child after she'd been viciously mocked at school that her tormentors were not very mature, and obviously unhappy people inside. True, perhaps, but not very satisfying.

Suddenly, Priscilla's face changed and she looked pensive. "What do you think of Chloe's work?"

I wasn't a writer, just lived with one, but Stefan had warned me against dishing other writers because what I said could reflect on *him;* people might assume he shared my opinions.

"Well"—I hesitated—"it's . . . pleasant."

Now Priscilla grinned. "Beautiful," she said. "That is beautiful. You don't have to say anything more." But then she sighed, and I felt we had made no progress at all.

"The French are wild about Chloe," she said. "Don't ask me why."

"Hey, the French worship Jerry Lewis. The French test nuclear weapons in the Pacific."

Priscilla couldn't be deflected. "Chloe's even having an affair with Vivianne Fresnel! You know, the 'French Susan Sontag.' "

I shrugged. The name meant nothing to me, so Fresnel had obviously never written anything in my specialty, Edith Wharton.

"Nick, Chloe's work is available in French *and* Hungarian. Russian, German, Italian, Spanish, Dutch, Japanese, Hebrew, Portuguese, Swedish."

"How do you know that?"

She held her head up. "I checked," she brought out simply.

I nodded. That wasn't hard to imagine. Priscilla probably had a file at home, maybe more than one. Her Chloe files: interviews, reviews, advertisements, conference brochures, whatever she came across, all of it slow poison, weakening her confidence. I bet she had helplessly followed Chloe's career as if she were a losing general planting dispirited little flags on a map. I'd seen it with lots of writers; they can't stay away from the information—the magazines or book reviews, the phone calls or letters—that sickens them, that makes them despair of ever achieving success because so many unworthy writers do, thanks in part to the right connections, but equally to the unpredictability of literary life.

"My books aren't even available in *England,*" Priscilla said, eyes closed, clearly dragged down by this old grievance.

"I'm sure your publisher didn't try hard. And Stefan says the publishing business is terrible over there anyway."

She shrugged. It might have been true, but that didn't make it hurt less. Eyes down, she went on: "My last book didn't go into paperback."

We'd been in the same department at SUM for over two years, but this was the first time I felt really close to Priscilla, felt confided in, respected. It was very easy to sympathize with her because I was immune to the terrible disappointments and equally stunning excitement in a writer's life. Academics rarely make money on their books, which are most often stepping stones to tenure and promotion. We write and publish pretty much in obscurity, and the university press catalogues hawking our works are as meaningful as a glossy chain letter. But fiction writers always dream of a breakthrough, of a Big Book that will make the rest of their lives a little easier. I knew that for Priscilla, who wrote somewhat drab and rhetorical mysteries, the chances of making it big were nonexistent.

"What am I supposed to do?" Priscilla asked, hands tightly clasped in her lap.

I shrugged.

"You have no idea what it's like, Nick. People always ask me about her—at readings, or conferences. I'll be minding my own business, someone comes up and tells me that they love my work—and they love Chloe's too. It makes me sick. They ask if I've met her, and what is she like! She's this albatross—I can't ever get rid of her."

Suddenly Priscilla clapped her hands together. "Oh, Nick, I'm sorry,

I haven't even asked you about the Wharton conference. How are things going?"

It was my turn to feel plagued. "Fine, so far. No hitches yet." That wasn't really true, but I was desperate to change the subject.

"Isn't it pretty soon? Like next month?"

"No! Not until April—the first week of April." I said it slowly, as if casting a spell to protect myself. "I really don't want to talk about it right now."

Priscilla nodded sympathetically.

AT HOME THAT evening, I didn't mention Priscilla's confession about Chloe DeVore to Stefan because he'd been in a lousy mood for weeks. His latest book was not going into paperback because his publisher had been unable to sell it to any major trade houses, and even the smaller presses had said no. Stefan's agent told him it was the state of the market, and the influence of big book chains, and I don't know what else, but the plain fact was that for the first time, one of Stefan's books had failed. Stefan was humiliated, as if the *New York Post* had run a cover story: "PUBLISHERS TO STEFAN: DROP DEAD!" It was worse because the news was coming during the long Michigan winter, the time Stefan called "the envy months," when other people's good fortune could feel like a torment. Stefan was still smarting from one of the worst reviews he'd ever gotten for one of his books. We'd never heard of the newspaper, the *Bethesda Bulletin,* or the reviewer, Kevin Sapristi, but none of that mitigated the review's viciousness. Sapristi had willfully misquoted from Stefan's book, calling it "vomit." Was the reviewer anti-Semitic, antigay, or just plain stupid and mean?

It was the kind of deadly review an author might expect from a rival or an ex-lover.

The evening last month when Stefan got a copy of that review from his publisher's publicity department, I found him at his computer working on a letter.

"I'm writing to that reviewer," he announced, as if daring me to stop him.

I sat down at his desk, nodding. This was one of those moments Stefan had warned me about years ago, telling me to slap him if he ever embarrassed himself by responding to a nasty review. I bided my time, trying to keep my face blank. He typed, I sat.

"What I really want to do," he said as his fingers slammed at the keys, "is send him a bomb."

"Great. I married the Unabomber. Stefan, don't you know how hard it would be getting your work published from prison?"

He turned, frowning, on the edge of a smile—or outrage. I went for broke.

"Wait—maybe I'm wrong," I said. "It might be the best thing you could do for your career! Why don't we both kill this moron and do a dual memoir? I'm sure we could get on Barbara Walters from death row. I mean, memoirs are the hottest thing going—even your agent said so."

Stefan smiled wanly, looked back at the screen, shook his head, and switched off the computer.

That had been a few weeks earlier, and I think he had pretty much recovered from the review, but I didn't want to bring up Chloe DeVore and get him started on any train of thought that would lead back into his own little heart of darkness.

We did talk about Bob Gillian.

"He seems nice enough," I said.

Stefan shook his head. "He can't be nice if he married that she-wolf Joanne. They've probably got one of those relationships where she has all the permission to be vicious, and he's her foil."

I thought that over; it was an interesting theory. "Well, I'm gonna try to like Bob, because anything else will be too exhausting. I have to share an office with him."

Grading papers in front of the fire later that night, after Stefan had gone to bed, I kept thinking about Chloe DeVore, who I'd never met but now felt strangely inimical to because of Priscilla's revelations.

I had haphazardly followed her career. Chloe DeVore was in many ways a manufactured writer. She'd gone to Smith, and by the time she was nineteen had published several stories in the *New Yorker* because her father knew one of the editors. The stories were nothing special, but enough to get her a book contract, and she had a collection of stories out before her graduation. Reviews called *Angels of Light* "dazzling," "luminescent," "quiveringly intense," "radiant," "heavenly," playing inane variations on the title. Everyone noted her extreme youth and astounding maturity of vision. The book appeared briefly on the *New York Times* best-seller list and she won a Pulitzer.

Chloe DeVore was the first lesbian/bisexual author to be cosseted, even championed by the *New York Times*. When later books were occasionally hit hard by other newspapers, the *Times* always found someone to write a gentle review. Most reviewers mentioned her bisexuality in muted terms, which was appropriate, I think. In her writing, DeVore was bi in the most harmless and inoffensive of ways; her sexuality could have been a mildly eccentric hobby like bottle cap collecting. I knew from Stefan that gay male writers muttered about her success, but said little in public so as not to be branded sexist. From Priscilla, I had found out that lesbian writers thought even less of Chloe's work.

"Shallow," Priscilla told me was the consensus. "And nonthreatening—to straights. But you can't say that because it would mean you're undermining a sister, that you're male-identified, that you're a bitch."

With the success of her first book, Chloe DeVore also appeared in *Esquire, Vanity Fair, Interview,* even *People.* Slim, slight, completely unprepossessing, she was an oddly photogenic nullity in designer outfits. There was something almost freakish, exhibitionistic in the publicity that increased with her first novel, *Brevity,* and continued through another collection and a book of two novellas, *Drifting.* As she neared thirty, however, it apparently became harder for reviewers to find something remarkable about her—like those child prodigies who play the Beethoven violin concerto at ten years old and soon fade from the concert scene. Reviews were still full of praise, but it was softer, almost reminiscent. There were other stars to be dazzled by, and I noted that her reviews appeared further back in various book reviews, further from the front page, that imprimatur of significance. Had Chloe ever been remarkable—or was it just the American hunger for sensation, for youth?

I didn't think much of her writing, and I thought even less of her after Priscilla gave me copies of some of Chloe's interviews. She sounded as compassionate and thoughtful as Margaret Dumont in a Marx Brothers film. Asked about AIDS, she might ramble on about her "suffering brothers" and how her heart was "utterly, yes, utterly" with them—a statement that rang somewhat hollow when she delivered it lounging on a silk-covered Empire fauteuil in her apartment near the Élysée Palace. *And* when you considered that her greatest suffering seemed to have been a visceral dislike of the jacket art on her second book, a subject that drifted into every other interview like an ill-behaved little dog that won't stop pissing on the rug. "You want your readers to love your books, inside and out," she once explained, adding, "Inside *and* out," in case the interviewer had missed her subtlety of feeling. Equally as weird was Chloe's claim that she led "a hermit's life" in New York and Paris.

Which made me wonder how she had managed to wind up in so many gossip columns describing fabulous parties, and how she had snagged all the fabulous blurbs from well-known authors that glittered on each and every one of her books. They had to be her personal friends.

I was musing about all this when the doorbell rang and startled me out of my chair. I checked the mantel clock—it was after eleven P.M. A little nervously, I went to the front door, and saw Priscilla through the glass panel.

"I'm sorry," she said, as I opened the door. "I'm just so miserable about Chloe." Scraping her boots on the doormat, she looked pale, despondent. I reached for her parka, but she kept it on and followed me into the living room, headed straight for the chair by the fire. Priscilla had never dropped by before, never even called and said she would be in the neighborhood, and yet I felt no discomfort.

"Stefan's asleep," I said, pulling over a chair to sit opposite Priscilla. "He was pretty tired."

"He wouldn't understand," she brought out. "He'd think I'm petty and vindictive."

"Oh, I don't know about that."

But Priscilla was shaking her head. "A friend in New York just faxed me, actually a couple of friends. Chloe's new book is getting rave prepublication reviews. There's a film deal." She gulped. "With Sharon Stone!"

I whistled my amazement. "What's the book about?"

She sighed. "You know how some people think her work isn't sexy enough, and that she needs more range? Too much gentle Connecticut angst? The new book's called—get this—*Empire of Sin*. It's huge, seven hundred pages, in diary form. It's about Justinian and Theodora."

"The Byzantine Empire? Those guys? It sounds like a dud. What the hell would Chloe DeVore know about the Byzantine Empire?"

Priscilla shrugged. "I guess she spent a weekend in Istanbul once. But all the reviewers are saying it's brilliant, a rich tapestry of sex and fear and history."

That sounded like a quote. Priscilla was already memorizing Chloe's reviews!

"Do you want a drink?"

She nodded and I brought her some Cointreau. She peeled back her parka and sipped from the glass, looking as defeated as if the whole first printing of Chloe's book had landed on her house.

Priscilla breathed in and out heavily a few times. "Well, at least her girlfriend dumped her."

"That Vivianne Fresnel? How do you know?"

Priscilla grinned. "I don't think Chloe can buy a baguette in Paris without someone sending somebody a letter, a card, a fax, E-mail."

"Twenty-four-hour surveillance?" I asked. "Satellite photos?"

She laughed, and it made me feel good.

"So what's this about Chloe's girlfriend?" I asked.

Priscilla looked happier by the minute. "They had a big fight in the Tuileries Gardens—"

I cut her off. "Wait a minute—next to which tree?"

With mock dignity, Priscilla said, "I don't know that. Yet."

And we grinned like conspirators.

"She's also gained weight. They say she's looking puffy," Priscilla brought out with satisfaction. "And no, I can't tell you how much weight! But I heard she's wearing baggy sweaters." She nodded grimly, as if vengeance had been served.

I couldn't tell this to Priscilla, because it was too intimate, but Stefan and I had sat in front of the fire before, or in my study, or in restaurants, having similar conversations about writers he disliked and scholars I had no respect for. I was more intemperate than Stefan, who was usually fairly calm about other writers (not living in New York helped). But if he saw what he thought was unwarranted success or a review that was clearly rigged in the author's favor, that could start him spinning. And me, I always had outrage to spare. We could range freely from people's shoddy work to their shoddy personalities, implacable. It was like two nasty little kids mocking and mimicking their elder brothers and sisters who seem all but omnipotent.

"She really yanks my chains," Priscilla said, sounding apologetic. "It's not like I have a bad life, or that my books don't get published. It's just that—" She shrugged.

"It's just that Chloe made it so big, so fast, and doesn't deserve it."

Priscilla nodded, looking mournful, and then she made another quick switch, peering into the fire: "Do you think Chloe's written herself out?"

There was only one good answer to that question. "Written herself out? Honey, I don't think there was ever that much inside to begin with!"

Priscilla beamed. "I could grow very fond of you," she said. Smiling wickedly, she added, "I heard a wonderful story about her. A friend of a friend was in Paris and the subject of Chloe came up at a literary dinner. Someone had just had drinks with her, and was asked if Chloe spoke French well. The woman paused, and said 'Yes, but then she's boring in any language.'"

I laughed. It was the kind of casual put-down I could imagine my parents making. "Hey, why don't you put Chloe in your next mystery?"

"I've tried! But I can't calm down enough to do it right. Don't you think I'm dying to kill her off so I can get it out of my system? Give her some slow poison, or have her mangled in an accident and just hanging on before she croaks. Or a lingering disgusting disease . . ."

"Maybe you could commission someone to write a mystery *for* you," I suggested. "A freelancer. A literary hit man." After a second, I amended it: "Hit person."

"Wouldn't that be expensive? It's probably cheaper to have someone knock her off for real. Faster, too."

"Forget it. Think of the publicity. Her books would sell even better."

"You're right," Priscilla said, regretfully. She didn't sound like she had been joking.

"What's your new one called?" I asked.

Priscilla hesitated. *"Sleeping with the Enemy."*

"Like the Julia Roberts movie? Great title! It's due this summer, right? Or next fall?"

Priscilla didn't answer. She seemed distracted, but then I knew writers often didn't feel comfortable discussing books in progress.

"Nick, I know you said you didn't want to talk about the Edith

Wharton conference, but you've been so wonderful to listen to me about Chloe, I wanted to ask if I can help somehow."

I breathed in deeply, trying to picture the kind of calm and peaceful scene they ask you to think of on an imagery trip, but all I could come up with was an image of myself fleeing down the slopes of a volcano, the red-hot lava coming after me with supernatural malevolence.

"Really," she said. "I'd be happy to help out."

"I don't want to talk about it!"

Priscilla gulped, surprised by my vehemence, and I hurried to assure her: "I just can't talk about it now, *please.*"

"Fine."

Priscilla left soon after, and getting ready for bed, I thought about what she *hadn't* said. I knew that Priscilla was coming up for promotion to full professor next year, and that she was also turning forty. Both milestones would be enough to make anyone feel vulnerable, crazed, and diminished by a rival's undeserved success.

# 2

C YNTHIA OZICK CANCELED!"
Stefan rolled over in bed next to me while I tried to keep the phone from slipping into the covers from my sleep-heavy hand. "What?" I couldn't even remember hearing it ring, or having picked it up. I vaguely thought the radio alarm had come on, but it was Sunday, wasn't it? We should have been sleeping in—and when I made out the digital clock face, it read 8:15 A.M.

Stefan groaned and pulled a pillow over his head.

"Are you there? Nick? Nick?" It was Priscilla calling.

"I'm here. Let me switch phones." I found my robe on the floor, slipped it on and stumbled downstairs to my study, my feet cold, lifted up the receiver, and then went back to hang up the bedroom phone. Lucky Stefan was already snoring.

"This is horrendous," Priscilla moaned when I was finally on the line, and I felt she'd been talking into the phone even though I wasn't there.

I tried repeating her first comment, "Cynthia Ozick cancelled," hoping that would rub the magic lamp of our conversation.

"The President's Series."

It clicked. Once a year, a prominent author came to campus to speak and read. Ozick was due in a few weeks. She'd been invited because of a petition by women faculty to SUM's president to have more notable women speakers come to campus so as to "dynamite the rhetorical patriarchy" or something like that. It was part of a large drive to change the visibility of women on campus, which was also why EAR was hosting the Edith Wharton conference I was running.

But I didn't understand why I had to know that Cynthia Ozick wasn't coming, and why I had to know it so early on a Sunday morning.

"The provost just called me. He was so excited! They're bringing in Chloe DeVore!"

"Wait. She's not Jewish," I had to point out. "I mean, if they're trying to replace Ozick . . ."

Priscilla made an evil kind of sound that was part chuckle, part sneer. "You know how those administrators think—a minority's a minority. Woman, lesbian, Jewish, it's all the same."

"Don't tell that to Cynthia Ozick," I said. "I don't think she'd enjoy the company."

Priscilla's voice rose. "Chloe won't care! She's getting ten thousand dollars!"

I heard a faint ringing on Priscilla's end. "Oh, God, that's my fax," she moaned. And then her call waiting clicked in, so I let her go.

When I turned from the phone, Stefan was in the doorway, wearing his white silk pajama bottoms, and I felt immeasurably cheered up and awake. It doesn't matter how little sleep he's had—he always looks gorgeous in the morning. His dark, thick, curly hair can be parted anywhere or not at all, his skin looks taut and young, and though he may hunch over his breakfast and his morning paper, there's an aliveness in his muscular body that I envy and admire. He looked right now like one of those ruggedly handsome men you see in soap commercials, accessorized by a cute baby.

"What's happening?"

I told him to sit down, and I went to make some coffee. With the Royal Kona brewing, I explained everything that Priscilla had told me, while Stefan idly scratched his hairy chest, his arms, his shoulders, as if massaging himself more awake. During my recital, he nodded, closed his eyes in thought now and then, said, "Hunh" occasionally, but didn't interrupt.

"I'm surprised nobody asked for my recommendation," he said, sipping from his cup.

"Jeez, you're right." He was, after all, the writer-in-residence at SUM. But Stefan shrugged that off; he didn't like holding unnecessary grudges. And he wasn't at all concerned with status. That's why I let the matter drop—it wouldn't have done either of us any good for me to play a nagging Ann Baxter to his Yul Brynner as Pharaoh.

But I did start bitching about Chloe's enormous speaking fee. "She does not need ten thousand dollars."

Stefan laughed. "Who're you kidding? Everybody needs ten thousand dollars."

"But look at the writers they've brought in before! Toni Morrison. Jane Smiley. Philip Roth. Would you put Chloe DeVore in their category, either of talent or fame?"

"She is now."

"How can you be so calm about it?"

"Why are you freaked out? It makes sense that Priscilla is, but—"

"Because Chloe DeVore is one of the most overrated writers of the decade, and you know it. Because she gets reviews she doesn't deserve, because she's a star, because she's arrogant and believes her own press releases, because she's locked into the literary world like you'll never be and it makes me sick. It's disgusting—like watching a dog lick its behind."

Smiling gently, Stefan said, "She'll be taking questions when she's here. Why don't you ask her about some of that?"

I finished my coffee.

We had a lot of work that Sunday—picking up all the fallen branches that had been covered by snow until the previous day's sunshine—and I welcomed the release into physical concentration that blurred time and feeling. From time to time, I thought of Chloe DeVore coming to campus, and of the previous famous writers I'd heard here and at other schools. They were all both exciting and disappointing. Charming and witty, of course—and who wouldn't be, getting ten thousand dollars or more for a few hours' work?

Part of the excitement was simply hearing the author's words in his or her own voice, and storing that voice for encounters with their future books. Yet with each author, no matter how kind they seemed, you had the distinct impression that they were hiding their cruelly funny perceptions of your university, images and scenes that would crop up in one book or another. Talking to a writer like that left me intensely self-conscious. I'm sure others felt the same sort of embarrassment, which probably made the experience somewhat dull for the visiting celebrity. Last year at SUM, Philip Roth had looked out at us during the question-and-answer session like a bemused, dyspeptic hawk who finds nothing worth pouncing on. Even the self-styled provocative questions were clearly nothing new for him.

And when Stefan, a longtime fan, had handed Roth his card, hoping they might begin a correspondence, he was crushed by Roth's quietly withering comment, "I've never met a writer with a business card."

I told Stefan I wouldn't read anything of Roth's again after that, but Stefan didn't comment.

Stefan and I made steak Diane for dinner, with twice-baked potatoes, and watched *Laura* for probably the tenth time, as always hooting with delight when Judith Anderson says of Vincent Price, "He's no good—but he's what I want."

STEFAN'S EQUANIMITY ABOUT Chloe's upcoming campus visit did not last much past the weekend, because we got the word through Coral Greathouse that we had been chosen by President Littleterry to host the after-reading reception for Chloe.

Usually, these receptions were held at the president's campus mansion, which had been donated by a Ford relative in the 1920s after the original burned down during a homecoming parade. At the old center of campus, amid buildings dating back to the mid- and late 1800s, it was an impressive sprawling stone house with porte cochere, curving graveled drive, stone lions at the door, geranium-filled urns filing up the wide steps to the porch. Plopped in the center of campus, the house had the air of a movie set, and even inside, you kept wanting to touch walls to see how substantial they really were.

Apparently, it was deemed "more suitable" to have Chloe entertained at our house. Not a surprising line of thought, given that SUM's new president was its former football coach. And that since he was under Joanne Gillian's thumb, he didn't want to be publicity associated with Chloe, however much good publicity her presence might yield.

Stefan blew up. At me. "Because Chloe's a dyke! That's why! They'll bring her in, but they don't want her dining on campus—that's too much. So they dump her on the fags! Keep it all in the ghetto! And how the hell are we supposed to handle this *and* the Wharton conference?"

Stefan went on, storming around the living room, shouting his objections at the furniture. I watched him, feeling dazed detachment and lots of affection. With quiet people, it's sometimes scary when they lose their tempers, but it's also reassuring to know that rage *is* in there, somewhere.

I did not point out that Chloe DeVore was—according to her publicity—a bisexual, and not a lesbian. Or that actually *I* was the one handling the conference, and *he* was handling my hysteria. It didn't seem the right time for those finer distinctions.

Stefan eventually simmered down, and asked who we should hire to cater the party, because he refused to do any of the work, and I agreed.

I suppose I should have been stunned or outraged, but I felt disconnected from the whole situation. I was drifting along with the same sense of doomed detachment I had felt since the Edith Wharton conference had gotten started in the fall.

Stefan had been warm and sympathetic about the conference, but it was Serena who came to my rescue. Out of pity, she had quietly offered to run the conference for me, but only if I was the sole contact person. She'd arrange for the meeting rooms, the meals, the block of rooms at the campus center hotel, arrange for the calls to submit papers, find out about having the programs and name tags printed, and every other detail except selecting the papers. "But I don't want any publicity!" she said.

I was somewhat surprised by her generosity. After all, last year she realized that I'd suspected her of murder, and we hadn't exactly been collegial since then. But I was too desperate to question her motives. Even with her help, though, the flood of phone calls, queries, faxes, E-mail that only I could deal with had been stupefying.

The first call had come from Van Deegan Jones, president of the conservative-leaning Edith Wharton Association. He taught at Emory, and depending on whether you liked him or not, he was either pompous or magisterial. I found him stuffy—which I suppose put me somewhere in the middle.

"Nick, how are you?"

I was grading papers in my office when Jones called, and I told him so.

"Yes, it never ends, does it?" he asked with canned sympathy. It's the phony benevolence we overworked composition profs get from people like Jones who teach two graduate seminars a semester.

"Now, tell me, Nick, what's this I hear about a Wharton conference?"

He made it sound like it was a rumor, when he and everyone in both

Wharton societies had received an announcement calling for the submission of papers.

"What would you like to know?" I asked in my helpful bibliographer's voice.

"You're not serious," he said, asperity creeping into his tone. "Both societies? It's never been done."

I hadn't planned for this call, though I should have. Improvising, I said, "Think of the credit you'll get."

"I? Whatever for?"

"It's simple. You're president of the senior Wharton society. Your presence makes all the difference." Would he buy it? Hell, I wasn't sure yet what I was selling.

"That's true," he mused. "But you can't expect me to talk to those academic hooligans who have absolutely no respect for Mrs. Wharton. They're bandits, they're vulgarians, slashing something noble and fine. They loathe literature, and they can't stand to look up to anyone. They want it all reduced to the lowest common denominator so that Wharton is just another victim, just another suffering woman, when she, she was an *artist.*"

I was silent. I began to hope that he might work out how the conference could be used to his advantage.

He did. "Maybe it's time to attack them head-on," Jones said thoughtfully, and I cheered to myself. "To damn the tide of their pernicious nonsense." He hung up after warning me that I had to make sure things didn't get "out of hand" at the conference. "I'm not putting up with any crap," he said, his voice steely, and the unexpected use of even that mildest of swear words shocked me—as I suppose it was intended to do.

Van Deegan Jones meant business. So did his rival.

She called a few days later from Harvard. Feisty, sexy Verity Gallup had always struck me as a little too energetic to be an academic. It wasn't just her last name—she truly seemed more suited for the world of action. Not surprisingly, she got right to the point when she called.

"I always knew you were one of us!" she crowed. She'd reached me at home. It was late and I was already in bed. "Why didn't you say so? No, don't answer that. I know, you have to pretend you're neutral. You have to pretend you like all that tight-ass, boring, same old Wharton Association crap. That's history now, because we finally get the chance to demolish those suckers in person! I can't thank you enough!"

She went on and on like that, crediting me for having arranged the whole conference as an opportunity for her to win glory, as if I were a medieval pope calling for a Crusade. I could hear the clang of armor in her raspy voice, the shout of charging infantry.

I made the vaguest possible noises of agreement with Verity, letting her rave about how it was time to squash Van Deegan Jones's "hegemonistic stranglehold on Wharton."

This comment struck me as somewhat disingenuous. Gallup's group, the Edith Wharton Collective, had their own journal, their own presence at conferences, and professors situated at prestigious schools. Their voices had not been stifled by the patriarchy and were in no danger of going unheard. Hell, it was mostly women writers who'd led the Wharton revival starting in the 1970s.

But then Jones was just as out of touch with reality in his own way. He acted as if every article about Wharton he disagreed with was a personal slur, and chipped away at Wharton's solidity like that madman who hammered at the toes of Michelangelo's *David*. As the foremost Wharton bibliographer, I didn't think anybody's writing on Wharton could "damage" what was most important: the books and short stories themselves.

These opinions of mine were, of course, not for public consumption. Just as it would not be a good idea to point out that all those articles, essays, pamphlets, introductions, monographs, and books really weren't very important.

If the two Wharton presidents were happy about the conference, some of their standard-bearers were not. I got numerous faxes from people on both sides of the Wharton divide. Some accused me of being hungry for publicity, others of simplemindedness. Several announced the sender's intention to stay away. A few even seemed to make veiled threats to disrupt the conference, but I couldn't take such nonsense seriously. What would these academics do? Bombard me with hostile marginalia? Please!

Stefan was not impressed by what I considered skillful maneuvering with both Wharton bigwigs. But then he was keeping himself aloof from the whole business, or trying to, since he was an artist like Wharton herself.

All he would say was, "I feel sorry for Edith Wharton."

"What do you mean?"

He looked disgusted. "This is like watching scavengers fight over a carcass."

"Great! I've never been called a hyena before."

Stefan didn't apologize, and it left me sullen, which was a great mood in which to plan the damned reception for Chloe. Still, if I thought I was aggrieved, Priscilla had it much worse. Coral Greathouse had asked her to introduce Chloe at the reading.

"I WANT TO die," Priscilla said to me over lunch a few days after the news hit us. "I want to *die.*"

I shushed her. Given the contagiousness a suicide—or even the rumor of one—could have on campus, I didn't want any students or untenured faculty around us getting dismal ideas.

"It's my fault, Nick. I brought it on myself. I've spent so much time wishing Chloe evil that it's caught up with me, it's backfired."

"You really believe that crap? Karma—bad vibes—what goes around comes around?"

She nodded, and gloomily picked at her chicken croissant.

I bit hungrily into my cheeseburger. Michiganapolis might have lost its movie theaters, and might have fallen to the invading hordes of Arby's, McDonald's, Burger King, Crate & Barrel, Pizza Hut, Tower Records, and so on, but it still had Ted's. Ted's was a dark, smoky-looking restaurant with terrific burgers and the best jazz jukebox around.

I sat back and enjoyed Julie London singing "Cry Me a River." After a moment, I spoke up. "Saying it's your own fault is blaming the victim. It's retrograde."

"What?"

"Sorry—do I mean centigrade?"

Priscilla tried to smile. "I just feel cursed. I've spent all this time talking about Chloe, thinking about Chloe, dreaming about Chloe—and now she's going to be here. My phone has not stopped ringing. Last night I had *eighteen* messages when I got back from class."

"Who from?"

"Writers, editors, bookstore owners or managers, reviewers, creative writing professors . . ."

"And they all hate Chloe?"

Priscilla nodded. "Everyone's either commiserating or asking for details of her visit. You'd think the pope was coming, or Louis Farrakhan!"

I had an odd vision of a worldwide network of people armed with specially made seismographs that charted every movement, every twitch in the literary world related to Chloe DeVore. It was creepy, and fascinating.

"Nobody understands how she keeps getting these enormous advances for her books when they don't really sell," Priscilla complained.

"She must have a terrific agent."

"She must have a system, like gamblers at Las Vegas."

That made sense to me, since publishing really was a crapshoot.

"With all this interest in what Chloe's up to," I mused, "I'm surprised no one's stalking her."

She hesitated. "Don't be so sure."

IT WAS A relief to come home that afternoon from the hothouse of rumor and dread Priscilla and I were constructing. Now and then I had tried to tell myself that Chloe DeVore—whether she came to SUM or not—was nothing to worry about.

But how could I maintain my distance? Wasn't Chloe DeVore the very avatar of manipulation and fraud in politics and business risen triumphant in the world of literature? And so, while Priscilla was intimately stung by Chloe's success, for me the question was almost historical.

"Chloe DeVore is a Disturbing Development," I said aloud as I poured myself milk in the kitchen. Then I frowned. That much pomposity demanded an antidote. It was time to shovel the driveway. I changed into crummy jeans and sweatshirt, bundled into a parka, wool hat, and thick gloves, and armed myself with a shovel. I shoveled and scraped away all the snow that had drifted onto the driveway and walk overnight, enjoying the clang of metal on concrete. Then I swept snow off the front steps and felt as satisfied as if I were a shopkeeper laying out a pristine window display.

I heard Stefan's car in the driveway, but I didn't move until he came up behind me. Softly, he said, "Oh, yard boy, how 'bout something warm?"

Bob Gillian was surprisingly sympathetic when I complained about the reception, perhaps because he had seen how much time I'd been spending on the Wharton conference. I found him surprisingly easy to talk to, and couldn't help thinking, or hoping, that his marriage to Joanne Gillian was on the rocks, that they weren't at all close, that he must loathe her politics. He just seemed so damned friendly—and he knew I was gay.

"How'd the whole conference thing happen, anyway?" he asked one afternoon. "Are you doing it to make sure you get tenure?"

"Didn't you follow all the stuff in the fall about how sexist SUM is?"

"I was on sabbatical." He shrugged. "It was my consolation prize—they pulled some strings for me over in the Administration Building."

"Oh. Well, as if we haven't had enough trouble with budget cuts, shrinking enrollment, and—" I almost added "conservative pressure groups," but decided not to antagonize him. "There was lots of public criticism in the fall that SUM is insensitive to women's issues."

Bob snorted, "Bullshit!"

"What? You don't think that's true?"

"Of course it's true. This university is insensitive to everyone's issues, period. People don't count here and nobody higher up really cares about equity. Everything's done for appearances. I bet the only reason there was any fuss was because somebody must have gone public about women being underrepresented in the faculty and administration. Gone public in a big way. Am I right?"

Surprised at his insight, I said "Yes. How'd you know?"

"It's not clairvoyance. It's experience. This university never changes unless it's forced to. Somebody has to say or do something embarrassing and then the administrators rush to figure out how they can cover their asses."

"Well, what happened was that a few state legislators who'd been talking to women faculty here held a press conference."

"Don't tell me the rest. I bet SUM's been throwing women into highly visible positions. Kind of like a city that's besieged and they're filling the ramparts with teenage draftees. Qualifications don't really matter. It's all based on fear of lawsuits and meddling from the legislature."

"You're right on target. Every department was supposed to come up with an action plan."

Bob grimaced. "I know what that means! Do something showy but cheap to bail the university out. It's standard operating procedure around here. That must be why your new chair—sorry, *our* new chair—is a woman."

"That's part of it. Coral Greathouse got elected because she was a woman, but also because she wasn't too threatening, and there's no way she's going to generate any scandal like the last chair did. They call her Moral Coral—behind her back, that is."

He smiled. And I briefly wondered if I should have told him that.

"So anyway, we had a department meeting, and when the idea of a conference came up, I got picked to pull together a Wharton conference."

"I hate department meetings. They bring out the worst in people when they're about something minor—and whenever there's some kind of pressure."

"It was gruesome, all right! Like—" I hesitated. "Like Bela Lugosi in *The Island of Lost Souls.* You know, the scene where he leads all those creatures shouting 'Are we not men?' "

Bob nodded, but I wasn't sure he'd seen the movie. "Every few years at the Writing Lab they went through this big deal about making our services more accessible, staying open over the lunch hour, evenings, Saturdays. We'd do it and destroy everyone's schedules. What happened? None of the students took advantage of the new hours, so we stopped after a year. But different administrators kept coming back at us with the same tired idea, and even when we'd show them on paper that it wasn't a good use of our staff, they'd ignore us."

"What a waste of time."

"Well, look at it this way. The administrators have to justify their salaries, so they're always coming up with half-baked plans and reports and studies that drive other people crazy." Bob shook his head. "I've been at this university long enough to know that the shouting's going to die down eventually. There'll be lots of publicity, and bullshit about the university moving forward into a bold future, and they'll come up with a fancy name for whatever they decide to do, issue press releases, cook up stupid slogans to badger us with, and guiding principles, and new acronyms you can't remember that just rehash the tired old plans they tried before that never went anywhere, and then when we get a new president or a new provost, they'll come up with something else to pretend they're committed to."

"Wow." It was quite a mouthful, and pretty accurate, I figured.

"It's like communism," he said. "Designed to look like everybody's benefiting, but really it's about keeping a few people in power. Hollow. A complete fraud."

"Hey, at least the Soviet Union had the Red Army Chorus."

Bob chuckled and leaned back in his chair, hands locked together over his head. He stretched out his arms and cracked his knuckles.

"Do you think all universities are the same?" I asked. "Or is SUM worse—and if it is, why would that be?"

Bob considered that. "Some departments here do seem sick in a way. You know, departments are like cancers—they reproduce themselves. If there's something sick at the core of a department, that's how it grows."

I asked, "Well, how do you put up with it? I mean, you've been here at SUM over twenty years, right? Doesn't it get to you?"

"After a while it's just routine. You keep your head down, you do your work as best you can, and help your students."

"Have you ever thought of getting out of teaching?"

"Into what? The only thing this has prepared me for is urban terrorism." He stood up. "I'm going for coffee. Want any? No?"

I was dying to go home and tell Stefan how reasonable Bob Gillian was, how friendly, but he was in class, and luckily so, because a few minutes later, Bob revealed a much uglier side of himself.

Just after Bob returned with his coffee, Jesse Benevento, a student from one of my honors composition classes, knocked on the half-open door and wondered if he could see me. Jesse was one of my quieter students, and a bit sullen looking: tall and lanky, usually in black jeans and cowboy boots, black T-shirt, with multiple piercings including half a dozen earrings in each ear, and his thin oval face overpowered by thick spiky hair dyed dead white.

Jesse said very little in class, so I was somewhat surprised to see him of all people show up so early in the semester. Usually, most students avoid office hours unless they're in trouble with a paper or a grade, or if they're sucking up to you, or if you've specifically asked them to come in. I've learned that they would rather not talk to a professor without the protection of other students shielding them from the possibility of humiliation. They're awfully afraid of being seen as stupid—and that's for asking *any* kind of question—so they stay away. A similar question in class could more easily be laughed off, but alone in your office, it would be too revealing. Who would change the subject? Who would back them up or explain what they "really" meant?

It's frustrating to know that students need help but are too ashamed to ask for it, and at the beginning of most semesters and even through the middle, I've sat in my office like the one kid no one picks to be on the softball team, waiting.

Anyway, I waved Jesse in to sit by my desk in the comfortable well-padded armchair my students enjoy, whether they say it or not. At least they don't squirm, and that's a relief for *me*.

"How can I help you?" I asked Jesse, leaning back.

Quietly, as if put off by Bob Gillian working at the other desk, he said, "Well, it's nothing, really. I wanted to talk to you about something you said last class about our next paper."

I waited for some harmless question, getting ready to reassure him. I assumed he was nervous about the assignment. But what he said shocked me.

"Right at the end of class, Dr. Hoffman, when you told us to make sure we relaxed before starting on the paper, you said, 'Go to the gym, take a walk, have sex, whatever.' "

I smiled. "Did I? I guess I did. And?"

Leaning forward a little, with his large, long hands clasped in his lap, he said, "Dr. Hoffman, sex is the most sacred thing that can happen between two people. It's not something to be treated lightly. Never. It's one of God's gifts to man. It's not a joke. I got together with some of the kids in class, and we figured you probably didn't mean any harm, you were just joking." And his silence seemed to add *"this"* time." He went on, "But we're not like you, and we don't want anyone pushing sexual immorality on us."

I stared at him, waiting for more, but he didn't say a word, and I felt absurdly threatened and on the defensive. I managed to thank Jesse for coming in. I did not apologize, as he must have expected, and he rose with a dissatisfied frown on his pale, long face.

"You should read this," he said, handing me a shabby xeroxed pamphlet titled "The New Chastity: Virginity in the 90s." He left.

When I assumed Jesse was far down the hall, I ripped the pamphlet up and turned to Bob Gillian. "Can you believe it?"

Gillian shrugged, looking right past me as if speaking to a hidden camera. "You have to be careful with students."

"It was a joke, something to make them relax! You know how kids are anxious about their first big paper." Just as Gillian had worked quietly at his desk while my student was there, helping me out in that unspoken understanding you have when you share an office, I had expected him to commiserate with me about Jesse's arrogance. That was part of being a professor—the war stories, the anecdotes you traded as if you were old-timers rocking on a back porch describing some terrifying storm of fifty years before, or an almost forgotten train wreck. It brought you together in a community of survival and complaint; it made you appreciate who you were. But Gillian just peered at me, as if he had never played that game before and certainly wasn't going to try it now, with me.

"I guess he didn't think it was funny," Gillian brought out, with finality. "It's not. Sex is serious business."

"But I wasn't really talking about sex."

He frowned. "You were," he said primly. "And you shouldn't have been."

We both went back to work at the same moment, turning our backs to each other as if by plan.

He was obviously a lot more like his wife than I had wanted to believe, and I had better watch what I said around him. Bob Gillian might be charming, but not someone I could trust.

In the tense silence I thought, Wonderful. A fucking conference, a reception, and now Newt Gingrich's spy in my office.

It was worse than that, however, because Jesse's father was the chairman of the History Department, which shared Parker Hall with EAR, and I could just imagine Jesse complaining about me to his father, who'd mention it casually to Coral Greathouse. Trouble.

Bob gathered up his papers soon after and left, nodding good-bye. Was that a sign? Was he offended?

It seemed that thousands of people were offended these days, on our campus, and across the state, which seethed with political and social pressure from the Christian right. Every other day there was news about a local school board trying to ban "un-Christian" books or activities—like yoga, which its opponents believed to invite the Devil to take over people's souls.

Self-esteem programs aimed at young children were being attacked for supposedly encouraging social anarchy and undermining family values because students taking them would think "too well of themselves." A number of state legislators had come out in favor of an initiative overturning gay rights ordinances in the more liberal Michigan towns like Michiganapolis and Ann Arbor.

The ferment on campus now was taking similar form. Rabid, snarling students on a local cable show regularly denounced gays, Democrats, environmentalists, and minorities in language that was as extreme and offensive as their outraged expressions. I couldn't stomach more than a minute of watching, because in their braying I heard the flames and cheers of centuries of hatred and intolerance.

There were a growing number of student letter-writing campaigns aimed at SUM's Director of Libraries complaining about "obscene" books or magazines in its holdings. The campus paper was constantly being accused of a liberal bias, even though it was filled with letters that called for gays and lesbians to be put to death—by the government. Pat Buchanan had been brought in that fall as a speaker by Students for a Decent America, and his speaking fee came out of university funds, until there was an investigation and the money was withdrawn and made up by unnamed private donors.

Several times now, there had been incidents that temporarily shut the newspaper down—vandalism, bomb threats. The university administration couldn't do very much about any of it, because President Littleterry was a dishrag and Joanne Gillian didn't seem to care whether we had a newspaper or not.

I decided I needed to get as far away as possible from the conservative miasma, so I packed up and headed for a stop at the gym before going home. Surely I'd be able to escape there and forget about Joanne Gillian and everything she represented.

# 3

B REATHE!!" THE COMMAND was husky and urgent. It came from
somewhere off to my left.

I got up from the chrome and black plastic bench on which I'd been
trying to do bicep curls and studied the source. Two guys, as grotesquely
muscled as Bluto in the Popeye cartoons but with vacuous and unre-
vealing faces, were doing bench presses with enormous amounts of
weight. That is, one was on the bench and the other stood behind him,
spotting. They almost looked like twins in their torn and sweaty gray
T-shirts, black cross trainers, and baggy white Champion shorts.

*"Breathe!"* came the command as the awe-inspiring barbell dipped
and rose. I wondered if someone who needed that kind of reminder
should be allowed to lift that much weight.

"Focus!" said the spotter. "Don't listen to your mind. It wants you
to think your body's tired. Come *on,"* he growled, with the kind of intonation I've only heard in gyms and porn movies.

The adjurations kept spilling out: "Come on, yeah, it's all you, do
it, you got it." It was oddly erotic. Maybe my shaky workouts would
change with that torrent of grim encouragement.

They switched places. The same motions, the same supportive chanting, the same red face, the same grunting and release.

Finally the bar and weights were racked and they moved on, with
the heavy drifting grace of whales idling underwater. They were the only
other people working out this afternoon, and it was a pleasure to be
alone in the neon-lit wilderness of free weights and Nautilus machines
that rose about me like altars, tombs, and monuments in a crowded old
cathedral, each battered icon with a history, a life of its own. I was not
in a particularly worshipful mood, nor did I want to be drawn out of

myself, exactly, I just wanted to escape SUM, and The Club was proving the right place to be today.

The Club is an enormous and startling facility perched on the eastern edge of campus, a sort of gateway to the exclusive suburb of Michigan Hills (which is completely flat, of course, in this flat central part of the state). A concrete and glass behemoth, The Club reeks of money and newness and is so lavish with space it seems like a sort of health mall. It's built on several different levels and linked by wide, impressive staircases. There's a large restaurant and equipment shop, a banquet/conference hall, an indoor track, and such a profusion of tennis and racquetball courts, aerobic studios, pools, and cardiovascular equipment rooms that I've seen friends from the East Coast practically quiver with envy, picturing their cramped little gyms back home where space is at a premium and you're so crowded you can *hear* other people sweat. I imagine petty monarchs in the eighteenth century felt something similar when they first came upon Versailles.

But for all the ostentatious use of space, there's a stinginess of color—everything gray, black, white, steel blue—which for me heightens the air of fantasy. The "weight room" is so long and wide that it's sometimes almost like being in a dream where you reach and reach across a table that always grows vertiginously beyond the length of your arms.

I found it comforting, in a way, and it was certainly a good place to escape. Most SUM faculty members worked out on campus or at various area health clubs, and you usually only ran into students on the weekends, when I was least inclined to go. When I did work out, I wasn't there to check anybody out, and I wasn't there to meditate on my own perfection or even show off that I could afford the pricey membership, like the people who came no closer to exercise than the glass-walled restaurant on the main level, which was almost like a control tower with a dazzling and minatory view of most of the facility. Drinking beer there, you could watch other people grunt and sweat down in the weight room, on the basketball court, across in one of the aerobics studios, or in the room jammed with treadmills and Nordic Tracks. It was like watching a nature special where the side of an anthill had been cut away and you marveled at—and felt superior to—the ceaseless activity. The Germans have a word for enjoying the pain of others—*Schadenfreude*. I wish they'd invent one for enjoying other people's workouts. We need one.

It was also good being almost alone there that afternoon because sometimes I feel utterly foreign at the gym. I watch and listen to the trainers and their friends, people who call each other "Bud" and "Big Guy" unself-consciously, and marvel at how different a world they inhabit. I live in the world of words—in and through books, magazines, newspapers, plays, films. I get restless when I'm not reading or hearing words, and often dream of glowing, crowded bookstores and libraries, always with fondness and affection. I mark stages in my life by whom I was reading: "That was my D.H. Lawrence time." "I was just getting into Jean Rhys when I took my GREs."

But these men at the gym with their sculpted bodies and sculpted lives exist in a universe dominated by action. They work out, play tennis or racquetball, swim, golf, shoot hoops, play baseball in neighborhood or business leagues, ski—and move through the year talking about and watching football, basketball, baseball, hockey. It's not just another life, it's another language, and their gym clothes match. I see them in a bewildering array of T-shirts, tank tops, shorts, biking pants, gym shoes, socks, caps. It's a colorful, absorbing pageant full of display, symbols, tradition. And I feel there like I feel in France—I can get myself into a conversation, but usually get lost on the way out.

More than once, Stefan had told me, "You think about all that too much. Forget about it. Just go and do your workout."

"But it amazes me. Those guys have been jocks since they were little kids. And they're the *real* Americans. The real men, anyway."

"You don't believe that, do you?"

"Sometimes."

Stefan shook his head, but looked suspicious, as if expecting me to grin and say, "Just kidding!"

Having done some surprisingly good work on my arms and chest today, I went upstairs to spend some time on a treadmill, but didn't get to one.

Up on one of the Stairmaster machines, striding away and covering the platform and the moving steps with sweat, was Jesse Benevento. In a soaked T-shirt and running shorts that bared sinewy dark legs, he looked driven. Hell, he *was* driven. He was doing the Gauntlet with a ten-pound dumbbell in each hand. Jesse had headphones on, and because he was alone, he was singing loudly along with what seemed to be a rap song. Christian rap. I heard the words "victory in Jesus."

I fled for the locker room, showered, and went home to brood about the Wharton conference.

Just in case I needed any more lessons, Joanne Gillian was on the evening news. In a surprise meeting of SUM's Board of Trustees that afternoon, she had been elected chair, with the previous chair stepping down because Joanne "was more qualified." It was obviously some kind of coup which showed that the radical right had won control of SUM's board.

That evening, Joanne was getting an award from the Michiganapolis Women's Family Council. Stefan and I heard part of her speech: she called for women across Michigan "to use their pure spirits to fight depravity, indecency, and perversion."

I slept badly, troubled by Joanne's new status, and her speech, so when the phone rang after one AM, I grabbed it right away. A muffled voice answered my "What?" with "I hope you get AIDS" and the line went dead.

Now I was completely awake. I put down the phone as if it were in danger of exploding, shook Stefan awake, and told him what happened.

"It was that student," I said. "Jesse Benevento."

"You recognized his voice?"

"Of course not—it was disguised! But who else would it be? I told you he was at The Club. He's harassing me."

"Coincidence," Stefan said through a yawn.

"Aren't you upset?" I wanted to really shake him hard.

With his eyes closed, he said wearily, "Nick, students do all kinds of things around here that are terrible." His words came out slowly, as if he was under anesthesia. "You don't even know the call was for you, or for us. But if it'll make you feel better, talk to the police. If you think it's worth the time."

Stefan was so calm I wanted to yell at him, but I knew he was right. The call could have been random, and even if it got into the newspaper, wouldn't that encourage the caller to do it again?

Stefan was snoring.

Somehow, amazingly, his calm possessed me, and I fell back asleep as easily as he did.

I DIDN'T NOTICE any hostility from the class Jesse was in the next time we met, not even from him. That made me wonder if perhaps he'd been trying to bully me in my office. Maybe there wasn't anyone else in the class who was upset; maybe he was doing a freshman Joe McCarthy. And maybe the phone call was no big deal either.

I forgot all about what he'd said, since the reception for Chloe De-Vore was hurtling closer, and so was the Wharton conference, which was not getting enough registrants, even with official recognition from both societies.

Serena tried calming me down.

"Listen. People always send in their registrations late, as late as they can. It's because they're petty academics. They're pushed around by more senior professors, by their chairs, their deans, especially administrators, so they take it out on whomever they can. On students, and anyone who wants something from them."

Bob Gillian walked into our office just then, and I tried to shush her, but she went on. "When I organized my conference, half the people registered in the last few weeks. It was agony, but that's the way it always goes."

Bob busied himself at his desk, acting as if he wasn't taking in a thing, but I felt him recording each syllable for possible use against me.

"How about some coffee?" I said, rushing out the door.

Serena followed, amused, and grabbed my arm halfway down the hall. "Why are you letting him intimidate you?"

"Because of Joanne Gillian—I'm sure he tells her everything. I don't want her to know the conference has only a few dozen people registered!"

Serena shook her head. "So what if Joanne Gillian knows?"

"She hates gays, and she'll turn it against me somehow, I'm sure."

Serena took my chin in her hand, and made me look her right in the eyes. "You have to relax," she said. "It's only a conference."

But it wasn't. This conference was supposed to show how concerned EAR was with women's issues, and so the department's reputation was riding on its success. It had to be very successful, or I wouldn't get tenure, and Stefan and I would have to leave SUM.

*"You* can talk about relaxing," I brought out heavily. "You're a full professor. If it bombs, there's not much they can do to you."

Serena looked away, embarrassed by the truth.

As IF I didn't have enough to worry about, Joanne Gillian continued flying her broomstick. Somehow, she had gotten wind that a number of the critics registered for the conference were—in her view—perverted, having published papers like "Clitoral Rage in *Ethan Frome.*" She'd announced she was going to attend "to see how the university spends money supporting filth."

So I not only had to share an office with her husband, who I'd been deeply suspicious of ever since our talk about Jesse Benevento, but Joanne Gillian would probably be spying on me during the conference, ready to pounce on anything that would feed her hatred.

She would certainly be spoiling for a fight. A few days after her election to chair of the Board of Trustees, gay student activists at SUM protested the university's refusal to grant domestic partner benefits to gay and lesbian faculty and staff. SUM OF US, the campus radical queer student group, interrupted a Board of Trustees meeting at the Administration Building, chanting and shouting. The meeting couldn't go on, and Gillian called the Campus Police to drag the protesters away. One of the gay students called Joanne a fascist. Under her orders, I assume, our nitwit President Webb Littleterry denounced the gay students as "vicious hooligans."

The next day, President Littleterry and Joanne Gillian got telephone death threats, which she publicized in the *Michiganapolis Tribune* as "evidence" of the "deep moral rot" at SUM. Obviously, she claimed, these students were spurred on by gay and lesbian faculty and staff, which proved they couldn't be good role models for SUM students.

I was enraged by Joanne Gillian's accusations and slurs, but there was nothing I could do. If I brought up the crank phone call *I* had received, to show there was intolerance on both sides of the issue, it would be dismissed as bogus because I hadn't reported it right away.

I fully expected Joanne Gillian to take out her anger about the meeting on me.

And I was annoyed that Stefan wasn't being more sympathetic. We'd argued about the conference more than once.

"You didn't have to take it on," he said.

"I'm an assistant professor without tenure! I can't afford to say no. I don't have that luxury."

Stefan shook his head. "You're too accommodating."

"No—I'm too scared. And don't get psychological on me. It's not helpful."

Well, that set him off.

We were sitting by the fire on a nasty wet February evening, and Stefan looked like he wanted to hurl his drink into the fireplace, or at me. But he got very quiet, like that moment in the jungle movies when the madly beating drums stop, and the silence is terrifying.

"You know what?" he began. "I'm sick of Edith Wharton. You spent five years traveling around the country, faxing, photocopying, stinking up the house with all those photocopies, writing and calling all over the world to track down the tiniest mention of that second-rate writer in print—"

"She's not second-rate!"

"Spare me. Virginia Woolf was a genius. So was Jane Austen. Wharton doesn't compare. And I had to listen to you complain about archivists and librarians, complain about copying machines, complain about unhelpful scholars, complain about computer programs, complain about how expensive it was getting stuff translated from Indonesian and Czech, complain about doing the indexes."

I was chilled by his subdued, measured anger.

"Four—fucking—indexes," he said, eyes drilling me. "Did I ever say to you that I didn't want to hear the plot of Wharton's stupidest short story? Or hear about the time Wharton turned to Erik Satie and asked how his roses were doing? Or what Henry James told Bernard Berenson that Wharton told Steven Crane about walking sticks? Did I ever complain about a single idiotic Wharton anecdote you told me—even when you told them to me twice?"

Chastened, I brought out a hushed "Never."

"And it wasn't enough for you to get books from libraries, you had to *own* everything that was in print on Edith Wharton. And then you started collecting her first editions."

Guiltily, I thought of the ranks of Wharton books in my study.

"You spent thousands of dollars on that Wharton bibliography, and even if it's a library best-seller you'll never see a dime in royalties. I've been living with Edith Wharton for years. I'm sick of her and I'm sick of this conference." Stefan stalked from the room and I didn't follow.

How could I argue with what he said? I loved Wharton's writing, but devoting myself to working on her had been a tremendous financial drain and was turning into an emotional burden as well.

I did not need anything coming between me and Stefan now. Last year he had helped an ex-lover, Perry Cross, get a job at SUM in our own department, because he was confused, wondering if he was still in love with Cross. While Cross was now out of our lives forever, he'd left plenty of damage behind him. Stefan mourned his having lied to me, and he easily slipped in and out of being depressed. On those days, I'd come home to find him listening to Gorecki's *Symphony of Sorrowful Songs,* or worse, lugubrious, android, synthesizer music by Gary Numan. He played one song—"Remind Me to Smile"—over and over, probably because of the line "This is detention." I'm sure that's how he felt.

For me, sleep was still a problem. There were nights when I'd wake up thinking about Stefan and Perry. They hadn't slept together last year, but they were ex-lovers from graduate school, and the idea that Stefan had been trying to choose between us haunted me. After all our years together, the idea that my contract might come up for renewal had never occurred to me!

And though I knew that I had forgiven Stefan for bringing confusion into our lives, I wasn't entirely sure I could trust him again.

I wanted to.

CHLOE DEVORE HAD sent word to SUM that she didn't like "being social" before a reading, so on the evening of her reading, there was to be no pre-event dinner. Thus we missed the usual uneasy hour or so in which faculty members and large contributors to the university show off their culture while the writer is expected to be relaxed, funny, fascinating, and very human—all of it effortlessly, and without spilling any wine or dropping food on the floor.

The guest writer is supposed to glow and inspire, like some relic unearthed for a yearly parade, but also to enchant and charm like a Victorian hostess at the tea table. Names of famous writers should be dropped, but lightly.

What a burden. You have to be a star but not act like one, and also make everyone at the table feel important. No wonder some writers turn cranky or sullen at such dinners. Who needs the hassle?

I guess I understood Chloe's reclusiveness, but Priscilla held it against her.

"A visiting author is supposed to be accessible to faculty, to students, to the whole community. And *she's* playing Greta Garbo!"

We were huddled over coffee in Priscilla's office a week before the reading. The weather had turned brutal, with wind chills below zero, and given the howling winds and insanely rattling windows, Parker Hall felt like an unseaworthy ship in a gale. I had a brief fantasy of the building sinking, and the two of us fleeing to the roof, waving for help . . .

I shook my head to get rid of the image and refocused my attention on Priscilla. I certainly wasn't going to defend Chloe DeVore in any way, so I just sat there quietly while Priscilla ranted a little. Listening to her, I thought how lucky I was not to be mired in writer's envy.

I was the only living bibliographer of Edith Wharton, and scholars all over the world looked up to me, or at least they needed me. Every day brought letters, E-mail, even faxes from people working on Wharton who were trying to locate various articles, or had questions for me, or wanted my approval of their work. There was simply no one to compare myself to, no one whose success seemed to diminish or even challenge my own. I was king of a very small hill.

"You know what I heard last week?" Priscilla asked, grinning. "Chloe was being photographed for some exhibit of foreign writers who live in Paris, and she was reading a book while she was being photographed!"

I didn't get it. "As part of the pose?"

Priscilla chortled. "No. She wouldn't talk to the photographer, so when he was in between shots, she picked up a book and ignored him. Is that arrogant or what?"

I nodded, wondering how much of what Priscilla heard about Chloe was actually true and how much was apocryphal. I imagined there was a tremendous hunger for nasty anecdotes about Chloe DeVore.

"YOU SEEM OKAY," Stefan said to Priscilla warily, as the three of us drove to SUM's Arts Center the night of Chloe's reading in late February.

In the back seat of Stefan's Volvo, Priscilla shrugged. "It's like that thing Henry James said. You know, 'Here it is at last, the distinguished thing.' "

I objected. "He was talking about his stroke!"

Priscilla's head went down. "Oh," she said quietly. "I didn't know that."

Embarrassed for raising my voice, I reached behind me and tried to pat her shoulder sympathetically, but I missed as the car turned and I ended up poking her in the ear.

"Ouch!"

"Sorry—sorry!"

I felt like we were at the beginning of a Feydeau farce, where energies are about to be unleashed that will send the characters hurtling across and after each other in a spiraling set of improbabilities.

We parked and managed to leave the car unscathed. Outside, I felt suddenly energized by just being there. Our Arts Center is an amazingly beautiful Georgian-style little hall of fifteen hundred seats. Modeled inside on Carnegie Hall, it has the best acoustics and sight lines of any theater in Michigan, and is a plush jewel box of royal blue and gold, as improbable on this sprawling midwestern agricultural campus as an opera house in a decayed Brazilian provincial capital.

The three of us checked our coats and plunged into the mass of people dressed in the usual campus mix—everything from sequined jackets and flowing skirts to fluffy white socks, Birkenstocks, and jeans. Priscilla headed backstage.

"Hi, Professor Hoffman!" I turned to smile at a former student, Angie Sandoval, who'd been tangentially involved in helping me investigate last year's murders on campus. I was very fond of her.

"Do you read Chloe DeVore?" I asked.

Angie grinned. "Never heard of her! A friend gave me his ticket. Seeya!" She slipped off and before we moved on, I made a mental note to tell that to Priscilla. She'd love it.

Stefan and I had dozens of quick conversations in the lobby as we pushed through to the lofty main hall, avoiding a sullen knot of ex-Rhetoric professors including bland Carter Savery and woeful Iris Bell.

Our seats were almost dead center, twenty rows back, and while Stefan lingered to talk to colleagues, I waved and smiled once I'd gained my seat, knowing that I wouldn't have much chance to sit down at the reception. I was relieved to know that the caterer was at our house right now, setting everything up.

The hall was packed and noisy when Stefan joined me and I felt as indolent as an emperor waiting for a gladiator's certain defeat. The evening started on time with the house lights dimming at eight o'clock sharp, leaving the stage and miked podium gracefully lit. Priscilla came out onto the stage and up to the microphone, glamorous in her deep green floor-length dress with a wide rustling skirt. She looked pale now, but otherwise handled the introduction beautifully, I thought, giving a smooth mix of Chloe's reviews, awards, and career, but going light on her own commentary. Finished, she smiled as if inviting Chloe had been her own idea.

Hearty applause as Priscilla walked off stage right, and Chloe came on stage left.

Chloe had indeed gained weight that the frumpy dark blue suit couldn't disguise.

"What a bizarre outfit," I said in Stefan's ear.

Her dark hair was in an unflattering bun. The navy blue suit and pumps, the white blouse and Chanel scarf made her look like any one of dozens of drab businesswomen you'd see in London around St. James.

"What'd you expect," Stefan whispered, "Dykes Are Us?"

"She's bisexual," I said. "That makes her a byke."

Someone a row back shushed us.

Obviously standing on some kind of small riser, Chloe smiled, said she was glad to be at SUM, opened up the book that had apparently been waiting there for her, and began to read with almost no explanation.

Since Chloe had started off her visit rudely by not wanting to have dinner with anyone beforehand, I expected her to be awful: boring and obnoxious and vile. I was disappointed. Chloe wasn't personable, but she wasn't a bomb either, and I knew at once I couldn't expect her to humiliate herself.

But then even if she had, would I have been able to savor it? I was calculating times: how long it would take me to get to my coat when this was all over, then to the car and back home to finish setting up for the reception. I was in the middle of my own little film, running through each action obsessively, as if somehow that would make everything work out well—and more importantly, go faster.

From what I could make out while Chloe read, her new book was the diary of a married Byzantine noblewoman in love with Empress Theodora, and the section Chloe read was a meandering set of reflections on the theme of fidelity. I glanced at Stefan over the next half hour while she read, trying to rouse a smirk, but he had his public attentive face on: chin up, eyes fixed. He looked just right, which convinced me he thought the reading was crap.

How do you explain the impact of Chloe DeVore's writing? On the surface, it's smooth, assured, decorative. Yet after a while, it doesn't add up; you feel you're listening to a sonorous bore who assumes every one of her sentences is elegant and wise. I guess it's really like the Monty Python skit in which Eric Idle keeps elbowing a man, saying, "Nudge, nudge, know what I mean, know what I mean?"

I drifted off, thinking about one of Chloe's worst but most widely anthologized stories, about a daughter caring for her mother who's dying of breast cancer despite a radical mastectomy. In a Bonwit's somewhere, the daughter hands her mother a revealing negligee, and they laugh as they finger the intricate silvery lace. The portentous last line was something about "finding herself revealed at last." It made no sense . . .

When Chloe's dry little voice wound down, I was shocked by the heavy applause. But then we live in a culture where people give standing ovations to the dreariest Broadway play, so I guess I should have expected the enthusiastic response.

The first question came from an EAR graduate student I vaguely recognized. "Ms. DeVore, since you live in Paris, are you planning a novel about Americans abroad?"

Chloe pursed her lips. "I couldn't imagine anything more boring. It's been done to death. Paris is crawling with budding writers soaking up impressions. The sound of all those tapping fingers on"—she shuddered—"*laptops* at cafés can be deafening. I think every one of them should be turned back at the airport, forced to go someplace more unusual. Tashkent. Montevideo. Ann Arbor." She paused. "Well, maybe not Ann Arbor."

Hundreds roared at the reference to the rivalry between our school and the University of Michigan an hour away in Ann Arbor, and from that moment on she was a victor: a little haughty, perhaps, but in a conspiratorial way that turned the audience into her confederates. It was quite a show as she talked about her success, other writers, her writing habits. She kept things light, entertaining. I wanted to dislike Chloe's confidence, but I felt swayed and bombarded as if she were a particularly hypnotic televangelist who never has to shout to make a point.

People kept rising from the audience to gush: "I love your work." Chloe bowed her head a bit each time, as if receiving a laurel wreath, reminding me of Ronald Reagan's "Aw, shucks" routine. Corny, but decidedly effective. And I was impressed, even humbled a little. I've always admired writers who interacted well with their public, the way Stefan did.

"We have to go," I whispered to Stefan when it was clear that Chloe would be fielding questions for a good while longer.

He nodded grimly and we annoyed everyone in our row by standing and making our unsteady way past all those knees to the aisle, then rushing out to grab our coats. The speed of our exit made me wish we were fleeing the state, not heading home.

STEFAN HAD INSISTED on not hiring a bartender, so that he'd have something to do all night that would keep him away from Chloe and anyone else he didn't feel like talking to. Most of our department was there, plus dozens of administrators and community sponsors of the President's Series. It was so crowded you could barely see the complex, thrusting flower arrangements, and it was almost impossible to reach the food: cheese puffs, eggplant caviar, tiny shrimp egg rolls, smoked salmon pâté, leek and mushroom miniquiches, and scallop mousse.

Chloe barely moved from the chair by the fire (the best chair, of course, the most dramatic), as if she were content to gather adulation to her, like a sea anemone sweeping food inward with its lovely tendrils. Me, I circulated like a restless fish in one of those huge round tanks at an aquarium, moving from kitchen to living room to study to sunroom, smiling, patting backs, trying to enjoy the air of festivity. It was as if Chloe's success had less to do with her than with the university, as if *we* had polished her to a brighter sheen than usual.

Bob and Joanne Gillian came late, and I was a little surprised that they'd come at all. Surely they knew Chloe was bisexual and a bad role model.

Bob and his wife made such an unlikely couple. It was the first time I'd seen them together. Bob was so debonair in his camel's-hair coat and driving gloves, but Joanne looked as dowdy as Chloe, with a face just as narrow-eyed and unsmiling. In fact, they were almost the same height, with similar dark hair. From a safe distance, I watched Stefan greet them at the door and tell them where they could put their coats.

Joanne's eyes narrowed even more when she came back from leaving her coat in the guest room, where one of the posters was of the Robert Mapplethorpe exhibit in Chicago—just one of his erotic-looking flowers, but the name alone was probably enough to give her palpitations.

Bob caught my eye and gave a half-nod that clearly acknowledged he didn't want to greet me but since it was my house and my reception, he didn't have much choice. I understood that he was here because of the EAR connection, but why had Joanne come too? How could she set foot in the home of avowed sodomites?

Coral Greathouse, unusually buoyant tonight, sailed over just then and took my hand, telling me how impressive the reception was, and that Stefan and I had a lovely home.

Two points for me, I thought, hoping she'd be even more impressed by the Wharton conference.

"Have you seen Serena Fisch?" Coral asked, and I realized then that not only hadn't Serena come to the party, I hadn't seen her at Chloe's reading.

"Maybe she's not feeling well," Coral continued. "The weather's been so nasty." We chatted about the weather for a while, boring each other intensely.

Priscilla kept trying to snag me that evening, but I avoided her. I knew she'd be depressed now that her introduction was over, and I didn't have the energy to deal with her despair, fatigue, or whatever.

Eventually Priscilla cornered me in my study, where the lights burned as furiously as if in a crisis center. I turned some lamps off, some down, wondering who'd been in there.

Priscilla sat at my desk, nodding. "It's not so bad," she said.

"What!"

"Honestly, I mean, you dread something so long, then it happens . . ." She looked at her watch. "This time tomorrow night, Chloe will be back in France, or at least gone."

But Priscilla kept looking at her watch, and when I heard a raised voice out near the front door, she stood up attentively. "What's that?"

I followed her out to the front hall.

A woman, a very beautiful woman, was talking rather loudly to Stefan, who held what I took to be her coat. She was slim, with masses of thick auburn hair that looked as perfect as if her stylist had followed her to the front door, making last-minute adjustments. Green-eyed, oval face perfectly made up, she was in a black woolen sheath and crimson stiletto heels, with what seemed like pounds of silver jewelry at each wrist. She looked French to me—assured, chic, flawless, like many women I'd seen near the Place Vendôme in Paris, where Stefan and I had stayed several times. As soon as she spoke again, I knew she *was* French.

"Where is she? I must address her."

Stefan looked nonplussed.

"That's Vivienne Fresnel," Priscilla whispered behind me. "Chloe's ex," she added even more softly. "Remember?"

Stefan seemed to want to hold Vivianne back, but she pulled away from him and strode into the party with the poise of Audrey Hepburn approaching the throne in *Roman Holiday*.

"What's she doing here?" Stefan said, still holding her coat. "Who invited her?"

"I want you to know," came the clear ringing voice from our living room. The party hubbub faltered, then stopped when Vivianne repeated herself. "I want you to know that I intend to sue you in a court of law."

I pushed forward to see Vivianne standing a good two or three feet away from Chloe. People had cleared back as if at a saloon gunfight.

"How did you know I was here?" Chloe demanded.

Vivianne tossed her beautiful head of hair, but didn't answer.

Chloe smirked. "You're drunk," she said. "Go and sleep it off."

"I was drunk, once. With you."

I heard someone in the crowd sigh at the sound of those romantic French-accented words.

"You *made* me drunk," Vivianne said. "And you stole my treasure."

This struck me as embarrassingly like a Silhouette Romance, but I understood in a minute how wrong I was.

"Chloe, you are a liar, and also a thief. *Empire of Sin* is *my* book, not yours."

Chloe was pale and frowning.

Stefan said flatly, "This is incredible."

"It was my idea from the beginning. I talked to you about it for months. You can't deny it. You have stolen my thoughts!"

Chloe shook her head as if to say, Prove it.

"I have my notes," Vivianne said. "I have my friends. They know it was my idea, not yours."

Chloe sighed like a parent faced with a contemptuous adolescent, wondering if the child will ever be likable again.

In the eerie silence it seemed that everyone was waiting for even the most attenuated act of violence—a smack, a drink splashed up into someone's face, a broken plate. But Chloe and Vivianne just stared at each other, and then, amazingly, Chloe shoved past her, muttering, "You're just hungry for attention. Jealous." She plunged out of the room. From the door we all heard Chloe shout, "Whoever set this up will regret it!" before the door slammed.

Someone I didn't know said, "I'm her wheels," and disappeared after Chloe, brandishing her coat, apparently to give her a ride back to the Campus Center hotel.

The room was as frozen as one of those moments in an opera just before the chorus is about to burst into full-throated clamor.

"Excuse the outburst," Vivianne announced gracefully, with a huge smile. "Please enjoy yourselves."

And of course, even though the guest of honor was humiliated and gone, the party continued with renewed excitement. Some faculty members recognized Vivianne, and soon they were locked in a roiling conversation, half English, half French, which seemed only partly to concern Chloe's malefactions.

I stayed away. Maybe because of my parents' disappointment at my poor showing in high school French classes, I always felt a bit embarrassed around a group of people setting off conversational flares in that very showy language. Every time I didn't understand a word or idiom, I could feel my parents staring at me in wonder. They had spoken French to me as a little child—how could I have forgotten so much?

Off in a corner, Bob and Joanne Gillian seemed to be having a very intense discussion, the kind where every word crackles with the rage behind it and the energy of keeping your voice low.

Joanne's face was red, and I was sure she was on the verge of denouncing me and Stefan as immoral monsters or something like that. Maybe Bob was calming her down, telling her that it would be unseemly in my own home. She pushed him away and made for the guest room. He followed, and they left a moment later, both looking disgusted. Great, I thought, Joanne will probably make some new accusation on the news, or write a hate-filled and dishonest letter to the *Michiganapolis Tribune,* painting the reception as some kind of grotesque orgy.

Stefan was still holding Vivianne's coat, and he looked down at it, shook his head, and headed for the guest room to lay it across the huge pile. I followed.

He rolled his eyes at me. I giggled once, nervously, and then took his hand. "Couldn't we leave, too?" I asked. I was thinking of our cabin up north.

Stefan grimaced. "People will be thirsty after the floor show." We headed for the kitchen, where Stefan returned to his duties as bartender.

Priscilla was there knocking back a big glass of something, looking as tired as a marathoner.

"Come over here," I said, motioning her closer. "What's Vivianne whatever-her-name-is doing in Michigan? Doesn't she live in Paris?"

Priscilla looked off into the living room, where Vivianne was surrounded by even more admirers than Chloe had been. Later I heard that she told wild stories about shopping with Derrida at Galeries Lafayette in Paris and water-skiing with Hélène Cixous.

Priscilla turned to me, looking composed. "It wasn't secret that Chloe was speaking here on campus."

"Okay. But how did she know where the party was?"

Priscilla flushed.

"You told her!"

"Shh!" Priscilla glanced around us. "I wrote her an anonymous note."

"But how'd you get Vivianne's address?"

Priscilla shrugged.

My mouth must have been hanging open, because Priscilla tapped a hand under my chin. Smiling tentatively, she said, "It turned out rather well, don't you think?"

Soon, Vivianne ended up thanking Stefan and me for our hospitality. I was so bowled over by her chic that I said, "We were in Paris last year," like a trick-or-treating little kid bursting out to a neighbor that he had a new coat.

"Yes? Where did you stay?"

"The Hotel Vendôme."

"Oh, but that's lovely." Her eyes glittered as if I'd just presented her with the column at the center of the Place Vendôme. "You must phone me next time you're over."

And she swept off, without, I realized later, having told us if her number was listed or not.

Priscilla was in the bathroom during this interchange. She stayed on after everyone else was gone, to help clean up, and after the dishwasher had finished a second load, she, Stefan, and I sat in my study. I felt insulated there from the evening's chaos, as if the walls of books, the heavy drapes and deep carpet were the thick steel-clad walls of a bomb shelter.

We were drinking icy glasses of Diet Coke, which seemed to penetrate the fog. I told Priscilla about chatting with Vivianne, who had held my arm and confided that what Chloe hadn't just stolen from *her*, she had lifted from Procopius's book on Justinian and Theodora, *Secret History*, but without acknowledging her source.

"Isn't that plagiarism?" Priscilla asked, delighted.

"I don't know," I said. "Procopius has been dead a thousand years or more. I don't think it matters. I'd just call it being lazy."

Stefan was silent.

Priscilla gloated. In various ways she kept saying, "Chloe is finished." She could have been a religious Russian exulting in the miserable fall of the Soviet Union.

I disagreed. "You should never have gotten involved."

"Why?"

"You can't control what happens."

Priscilla shrugged, disdainful now, relaxed.

"He's right," Stefan said, surprising both of us, rumbling into life like a brooding drunk at a bar. "He's right. This won't knock Chloe out at all. People like that never fade."

Indulgently, Priscilla said, "So tell me the future."

Haggard now, oracular, Stefan complied, his eyes closed as if it were all coming to him. "Okay. The plagiarism suit? That's going to make newspapers across the U.S., England, and France. In publishing, it'll be gripping and creepy, like Court TV. Most people will dismiss Vivianne as a bitch, as a scorned lover, as overemotional—you name it. But none of that matters. Chloe's bound to triumph. She'll probably confess to Barbara Walters that she really *did* steal the book—or most of it—and she didn't know what she was doing because she was addicted to diet pills. She'll settle with Vivianne out of court for half a million dollars, she'll go into a clinic in Zurich, come out three months later with the manuscript of a confessional book written in English but with a catchy French title like—" He hesitated. "Like *Je M'accuse*. The critics will love it. They'll call it a gritty, devastatingly self-flagellating exposé. After a year it'll be translated into twenty-seven languages, and it's bound to hover on the *New York Times* best-seller list for three months just above *Men Who Were Run Over and Bitten by Women Who Run with the Wolves*."

Finished, Stefan got up and stumbled from the room. Priscilla gave me a baleful, frightened look.

Stefan was wrong, because he was drunk. None of that happened.

It was all a lot worse, especially for me.

# Part Two

*"It is less mortifying to believe one's self unpopular than insignificant . . ."*

—EDITH WHARTON, *The House of Mirth*

# 4

I SHOULD HAVE known that the Edith Wharton conference was doomed the morning I read a front-page student newspaper article headlined "Chaos at Campus Center."

SUM's conference center/hotel was a characterless fifties red brick and concrete building that had been haphazardly added to every decade since, creating a small labyrinth of hallways and wings in which people often got lost. Chaos was nothing new there, nor were problems with the physical plant.

The trouble this time was pipes that had broken overnight, flooding various corridors, and the prediction was that repair work and remodeling might take several months, given the extensive water damage. This was where the conference was supposed to be held—would we have to relocate to a local hotel?

I couldn't imagine the reshuffling involved, and, even though Serena Fisch would probably not quail at the task, I was panicky.

When I called the Campus Center to find out how the repairs would affect our meeting rooms and everything else, an "events secretary" cheerfully told me that there would only be "slight inconvenience."

That's just as comforting as a surgeon talking about "a minor procedure" and I hung up feeling miserable. I decided to dash over to the Campus Center to take a look, which was a big mistake. I discovered that whole corridors were roped off, their walls and floors stained brown, and, in some cases, the walls had cracked and the floors buckled. Workmen were busy cleaning up the mess, which as far as I could tell involved making an even bigger mess: ripping out sections of linoleum-tiled flooring and sodden plaster hunks of wall.

And the smell: like a dirty wet mop that's been allowed to ferment in its own pail of filthy water . . .

I left, feeling even more dejected. I'd been up late the night before anyway, worrying about the registration, which was still at only a few dozen with the conference just a month away. Part of the problem was that the country's leading Wharton experts, Cynthia Griffin Wolff of MIT and R.W.B. Lewis of Yale, weren't attending the conference. Wolff was teaching in Australia this semester, and Lewis, retired, was leading a scholars' tour of Tuscany. That meant we'd instantly lost what Serena called the "Chapstik contingent"—that is, the academics who'd only show up so that they could kiss ass and hope to accrue some advantage from it.

As for those who'd come whether there was a Wharton star or not, Serena kept reminding me that academics always register late—it's the revenge of the powerless, she said. And in fact, I knew I had been guilty of just that crime myself. But if she was wrong, poor attendance would not help the EAR department, which meant it certainly wouldn't help *me*. The chair would blame me for making the department look bad.

I WAS FULLY expecting another crisis when I heard Serena Fisch call my name down the hall from my office a few days after I read about the Campus Center's busted pipes and went over to inspect the damage.

She stormed into my office waving two scholarly journals I recognized right away, since I'd lent them to her. She shouted, "This is nuts! This is absolutely nuts!"

In her royal blue beaded-neck dress with the square neckline, hair in a French twist, and flushed under her heavy makeup, she looked like an irate forties chanteuse.

Serena smacked the two journals together like cymbals, and fell heavily into the chair nearest me, crossing her legs and angrily swinging one foot. "Nuts," she muttered. As always, I was struck by the retro way she dressed—it was weird, but it made an impression.

"I've been so busy working on the nitty-gritty of the conference," she said, "that it wasn't until last night I sat down to read these. It doesn't add up. You read the articles and you come away thinking there are two completely different Edith Whartons. One's a powder puff, and the other's a carnival sideshow act! What the hell is going on here?"

66

Serena brandished the two Wharton journals at me as if she were a cop giving me the third degree, threatening me to spill the beans or else. So I sang.

"Didn't I tell you there were two different Wharton societies with two different journals and that they loathe each other?"

She nodded.

"Well, it's like an academic version of the old *Star Trek* show—you know, parallel universes, and when they come in contact, there's disaster. At the Modern Language Association conferences, each Wharton society has a separate Wharton panel, and even then there've been incidents."

"Like what?"

"People have been forcibly ejected from meetings because they heckled speakers—quiet little academics going nuts! I'm surprised there hasn't been *real* violence by now."

"You're kidding, right?"

"Listen—these Wharton folks are just like gang-bangers, only they dress marginally better and they don't have drive-by shootings—they try to destroy each other with sarcastic footnotes."

Serena grimaced. "Footnotes can't hurt anyone."

"They sure can. Humiliation's like dying if all you care about is your reputation. And if the *intent* is murderous . . ." I shuddered, having read more than my share of venomous criticism. "They're just like Conan. There's that scene when someone asks him how he would define happiness—"

Serena's eyes glowed. "Oh, yes! I've seen *Conan* three times." And then, in a passable Austrian accent she quoted, "To crush your enemies, drive them before you, and hear the lamentation of their women."

Looking at Serena's slightly feverish eyes, I thought that she was someone I had better not ever offend.

"So tell me more about these societies," Serena said.

I complied. "The older group is bigger and fairly conservative, that's the Edith Wharton Association. They publish *Edith Wharton Studies.*"

Serena waved their journal, which had a beige cover and beige contents.

"Actually, it used to be the *Journal of Edith Wharton Studies,* but that kept getting abbreviated as JEWS, which made people nervous. For these guys," I explained, "Wharton's basically private property. Their thing is that she wasn't really a feminist, etc., etc. They want to make her safe and dull, and slam feminist critics while they're at it."

"Dull is definitely their forte," she said.

"The head of the EWA is Van Deegan Jones. I'm not crazy about him. He's mildly anti-Semitic."

"How so?"

"He's got this weird tic. I've heard him at conferences when somebody's name comes up, somebody he doesn't like, and he'll always say 'Jewish, isn't he?' He's almost always wrong, but that's his automatic assumption when he doesn't think much of the person."

Serena frowned.

"He's a very distant cousin of Wharton's. I think that explains his society's sense of ownership. They make a show of elections every few years, but he's really president-for-life with no chance of a coup. It's a mostly male bunch, and they treat Wharton sort of reverentially, but with a tinge of contempt. To them, she's a minor Henry James, you know? A Lady Writer. It's really like Wharton's some stuffed bird under a Victorian bell jar. Quaint, but useless."

"I saw that! Some of the articles call her *Mrs.* Wharton. *Un*-believable!" Serena snorted with contempt.

"Right. Now remember, I would never say any of this in public, so you have to keep it to yourself. I'm a bibliographer. My job is to be humble and helpful and stay out of the politics."

Serena shrugged as if to say she understood the ways of the academic world. "What's with the other group?" She flapped the second journal at me, *Wharton Now!* On the glossy, neon-colored cover, Wharton's head was dripping off a bookshelf like a Salvador Dali watch.

"That's the Wharton Collective." And here I couldn't stop myself from grinning, because if the Wharton Association was boring, its rival was almost too interesting.

"This bunch is wild, way beyond feminism, deconstructionism, or postmodernism," I explained. "They're pretty funky scholars, a lot younger than the EWA people. Most of their writing is highly speculative. They're going for shock value and they're desperate to say something new at any cost, no matter how crazy. The conference paper and article titles they come up with, God, they're like headlines from the *Na*-

*tional Enquirer:* Edith Wharton was bipolar, anorexic, a lesbian, she sexually traumatized Henry James, she was a Nazi sympathizer, she was an incest survivor. You name it."

Frowning, Serena leafed through the issue of *Wharton Now!* "Here's one that's really disgusting," she said, stopping at a title page. " 'Edith Wharton's Petophilia.' Yuck. It's about her dogs!"

"That's going to be a full-length study next year," I said.

"Goody."

"About all that's left is saying Wharton had a love child with Clemenceau, or she's been spotted eating ribs with Elvis, or that she appeared in the skies over the Ukraine while peasants wept and fell to their knees."

"And who's in charge of this lunatic asylum?"

"The leadership rotates. Right now it's Verity Gallup."

Serena said, "Verity Gallup? What a bizarre name!"

I didn't mention that some people might find "Serena Fisch" worthy of comment.

"Verity was a former graduate student of Jones's, but completely different. Wait till you meet her. They loathe each other. Years ago, after she started teaching, she submitted an article to *Edith Wharton Studies* which he rejected as soon as he saw it. He didn't even bother sending it to any readers. Verity was furious and started her own journal."

Serena nodded. "I know you said it was oil and water, but I didn't realize the differences were so big. It's not just a schism, it's personal."

"Exactly."

"But what about the major Wharton scholars you mentioned once, Lewis and Wolff? Which side are they on?"

"Well, they don't have to get involved in the politics because they're so big and both sides want them at their conferences."

"And everyone else is a fanatic of one kind or another. Wonderful. We're hosting a conference of academic militia members." She grinned. "Isn't that just what SUM needs? More dissension, more invective? Now I know why you haven't wanted to talk about a keynote speaker," Serena said, sitting up sharply and letting the two journals slip to the floor. "It'll never work. Even if you have one person from each society, like the presidents, whoever goes first, the other side will feel insulted."

A sudden gust of wind rattled the enormous rotting window behind me, and I thought that if this were a book or a movie, it would crash in and we'd have a visitation from some maleficent spirit, warning us to turn back.

We sat in a strange silence, Serena unusually quiet and subdued. Having laid out the territory for her, I felt oddly peaceful, almost as if I were a messenger bearing bad news and relieved to have discharged my mission. We had to put on a conference with two warring clans; choosing a keynote speaker was impossible—yet I felt momentarily free.

Was that hysteria?

Serena suddenly leaned forward. "Nick, I've been wondering about something. Last week Joanne Gillian was complaining about Wharton 'perverts' registered for the conference. That must mean some of the Wharton Collective-ites. But how did she know who was coming? You and I are the only ones with the registration forms. Did she dig up a copy of *Wharton Now!,* and what would have made her do that?"

We both turned to Bob Gillian's empty desk at the same time, obviously thinking the same thing.

"Jesus," I breathed. "I've left all kinds of conference stuff on my desk and gone out for coffee or to check my mail when he was here. I never thought that could be a problem."

Still staring at Bob Gillian's desk, I had no trouble picturing him checking the hallway through the open door while I was out, and stealing over to my desk, rifling through my papers to see what he could find that would be ammunition for his wife.

"You have to be more careful," Serena said.

I felt like an idiot, and started to turn red.

But Serena wasn't paying attention. Head up, eyes half-closed, she was suddenly muttering about the keynote speaker as if she were at a seance trying to contact her spirit guide.

"Who can we get—who can we get—who can we get?"

I thought it was worth a try, so I did the same thing, but she stopped and glared at me. I shrugged an apology.

"Maybe," I said, "maybe we can find someone who doesn't belong to either society—at least for the first evening." But Wharton scholarship was sharply divided, and I knew where everyone belonged. I wildly thought of inviting some actor or actress who had appeared in a Wharton movie or play, but that would be too expensive, and our conference budget was not generous.

"Wait a minute, Nick. What about that awful woman who was in *People* magazine last week? The romance novelist?"

"Oh my God. You're a genius. We can invite Grace-Dawn Vaughan!"

Known for best-selling bodice rippers, Vaughan was doing a big trade biography, *Passion and Pain: The Loves and Life of Edith Wharton*, for which she had just received a six-figure advance from a major publisher. The idea of her having anything new or important to say about Wharton was ludicrous, so I hadn't even read the article (though I knew it would have to be included in a revised edition of my bibliography).

"Serena, this is great. She'll offend everyone," I said, cheering up for the first time in days. "She's not a scholar, and she's rich. They'll all hate her, and that'll bring them together."

Serena grinned. "I'll take the heat for inviting her, if you want."

I thanked her, and asked what she thought was the best way to contact Vaughan. But before Serena could answer, I jumped to my feet. "Priscilla teaches romance novels in her genre course. Maybe she even knows Vaughan."

I dashed across the hall and knocked on Priscilla's office door and felt like a lottery winner when she opened it and then told me that while she didn't know Grace-Dawn Vaughan, she had Vaughan's editor's name—Devon Davenport—and his phone number.

I explained what I was up to, wrote down the information she gave me on a Post-it note, and scooted back to my desk to make the call.

Serena stopped me. "Invite the editor too," she suggested. "That way we'll change the focus a little at the beginning of the conference. It'll be publishing in general and not just Wharton."

"If this works—!" I shook my head, dialing the New York number, thinking it might take days to get in touch with Vaughan's editor.

It only took a few minutes, and I was soon sorry it was that easy.

Davenport was as hoarse and loud as a trucker, and snarled at me after I explained myself.

"Let me get this straight," he said. "You want us to come all the way out to Nowhere, Michigan, to some half-assed conference and there's no speaker's fee for me or my author? Is this a joke? I've never even heard of you *or* your school."

I didn't get defensive, didn't remind him that it was a university, just said, "We can pay your airfare, of course, and take care of the hotel and the registration fees."

I glanced at Serena—who kept all the budget figures in her head—hoping that was true. She nodded encouragingly.

"You've got an airport out there?" Davenport asked with mock surprise.

"This would be a wonderful way to generate publicity for Ms. Vaughan's biography," I said. Serena nodded and gave me two thumbs up.

"We're gonna have all the PR we need," he said, but I knew that no publisher would turn down free publicity. Davenport was hooked, or at least interested; I could hear him chewing his cud for a while. "Okay. Fax me some info and I'll get back to you." He barked out his fax number and hung up.

Hushing Serena so I wouldn't forget it, I quickly jotted the number down, then told her what Davenport had said. We pulled together the conference information and registration sheets and went downstairs to the EAR office to fax them off to Devon Davenport, both of us feeling the conference had a chance now.

Serena headed to her office to get ready for her next class.

As soon as I got back upstairs to my office, I heard wailing from across the hall. It was Priscilla Davidoff, and when I hurried to her open door to see what was wrong, I found her slumped over her phone fax. I was terrified she'd had a heart attack, since I didn't know CPR.

She looked up at me, her face ravaged and pale. She held out a few pages that must have come right off the fax, hand trembling as if they were her death sentence.

I took the pages from her and read a letter from a colleague in England. It was all about Chloe DeVore and Vivianne Fresnel.

They were back together again. The book they had argued about at my house last month had just been published with Fresnel listed as coauthor and was making the international best-seller lists.

It got worse: Chloe had set off fireworks in the publishing world by announcing she was going to write a memoir revealing everything about her supposedly wild bisexual past. The book was being described as "Joan Didion meets Joan Collins."

Priscilla stared at me in desperation, as if willing me to say she'd misread it all, but she hadn't.

The final blow? Chloe and Vivianne were coming to the Wharton conference.

Now it was my turn to wail. "That's impossible! Neither one of them has ever published anything on Wharton!"

"It's not Wharton," Priscilla moaned. "It's me. They probably guessed I sent Vivianne the letter about your party. They're out to get me for trying to break them up. It's going to be like *Fatal Attraction.*"

"Get a grip, Priscilla. Nobody's going to boil your bunny or shoot you in a bathtub. If Chloe and Vivianne really are coming to the Wharton conference—and we haven't gotten registration forms from them— then I'm the one in trouble. I'm the conference chair, remember? And the party for Chloe was at my house. It's me they're after."

Priscilla perked up a little. "You think so?"

Stefan wasn't interested in hearing my woes that night, so I stayed up watching TV until four A.M., crawling from one dreary cable channel to another. It was the first time I noticed a strange linguistic development. Speaker after speaker—whether on infomercials or the news—weirdly emphasized the prepositions in what they said. Like: "One *of* them—" At first I thought I might be tired, but I soon realized it was stationwide. It sounded so ugly and inappropriate. Or was it me? Was I becoming hopelessly cranky?

That morning I also learned all about diamonique, ab machines, and *real* live psychics. I felt like I could use all three.

REGISTRATION FOR THE conference picked up within a few days after Priscilla got the news (or rumors) about Chloe, but unfortunately, Chloe and Vivianne were indeed SUM-bound. Chloe was being courted by many publishers, and she'd announced that she intended to reveal her choice at the end of the conference. We were all going to be upstaged—but there was nothing to do about it.

Yet even a terminal pessimist might have felt hopeful as the conference rolled around the first weekend of April. Most of the remodeling and repairs at the Campus Center were done except for one wing near our meeting rooms, but we wouldn't be bothered. And after another visit, I was actually pleased. The lower half of the walls were almost all redone with gorgeous polished granite tiles that were midnight blue, heavily flecked with orange. This was the kind of granite you see decorating the exteriors of office buildings, or used for floors, and these tiles were twelve by twelve inches and half an inch thick. I know because they were stacked in some unfinished hallways and I picked up one to take a better look. It was surprisingly light.

A Campus Center workman, youngish, with a goatee, came up right next to me. "Nice stuff," he said. "Solid granite. Indestructible. Expensive."

I put the tile down guiltily. "I'm a faculty member," I blurted, and he nodded suspiciously, as if faculty members had already been caught pilfering these lovely granite tiles.

I slunk away, mortified, but the beautiful weather immediately changed my mood, and I wondered about possibly redoing our entryway floor in those same granite tiles.

We were having a glorious early spring, and SUM's campus was wild with forsythia, redbuds, and crocuses of every hue. Soon, you'd notice that whole streets were lined with flowering lilac bushes, each a different shade from a white that seemed almost gray to deepest purple, as if a painter were showing off the refinement of his palate.

Already there was on campus the air of festival and reprieve that people in warmer climates can never know. Even Stefan seemed a bit calmer about the Edith Wharton monkey on my back. "I hope things go well," he said at breakfast the morning of the conference.

As for the conference itself, there were enough people registered to make sure we turned a profit, no flight delays, no problems with reservations or name tags, no typos on the program. Joanne Gillian had also fallen silent for a few weeks. I'd been avoiding her husband, switching my office hours around, and all in all, if I wasn't exactly whistling a happy tune, I sure wasn't sunk in Buster Keaton frowns.

And I thought my first official act as conference chair that Thursday would likely be the hardest, making the rest of the weekend seem like an Aegean cruise by comparison. I was picking up both Van Deegan Jones and Verity Gallup at the airport—at the same time. There were so few flights into Michiganapolis (despite it being the state capital), and they were usually routed through Detroit, so it wasn't an unlikely coincidence.

But it was hellish for me.

Jones came down the beige walkway before Gallup did, sixtyish, portly, beautifully dressed and manicured as always. Round-faced, blue-eyed, and bald, Jones had a vaguely hieratic and sinister air about him, as if he should have been some Renaissance cardinal who could order an assassination with the flick of a jewel-heavy index finger.

He nodded as I approached him through the drifting crowd, handing me his heavy black leather garment bag, the bag practically jerking my shoulder out of its socket. Holding on to his attaché case, Jones proceeded towards the escalator, paying no attention to anyone or anything around him.

"We have to wait," I said.

He turned, one eyebrow up. "Can't *she* take a cab?"

I wondered how close together their seats had been on the plane.

Verity Gallup strode over to me, eyes narrow. All she had was a bulging backpack slung over her heavily buckled black leather jacket, which she kept, eyeing the garment bag I held with wary amusement.

It got very quiet around us, and Gallup smiled languorously, enjoying her role as showstopper. She wore tight jeans, heavily stitched cowboy boots, and a tight black turtleneck sweater that looked like cashmere and was working overtime to cover her *Baywatch* breasts. Her black leather biker's jacket bristled with so many buckles she could have been an amulet-draped shrine in Spain.

Her white-blond hair was cropped even shorter than usual, and with the large round-framed blue glasses, she looked like a brainy European terrorist.

Neither one of them directly acknowledged the other, and we must have made a very odd trio heading out to the parking lot, because people stared. I kept up mindless conversation about the conference, desperate to fill the ugly silence between them.

When I unlocked my new spaceshiplike purple Taurus, Jones opened the back door and slid inside like a potentate. Verity Gallup sat in front, tucking her backpack between her feet, and I kept yammering about the conference while I stowed the garment bag in my trunk, relieved that I had washed and vacuumed the car that morning.

As we drove off, Gallup drawled, "Frankly, I'm so tired of Edith Wharton." She sighed, sounding like Alexander the Great lamenting that there were no more worlds to conquer. So that's why she'd declined doing her own talk.

Van Deegan rose to her bait. "What?"

Verity shrugged gracefully, but didn't turn around to him. "I think we pay far too much attention to dead writers these days. If we're to live, our authors should be alive, too."

"It's easy to get bored when you have nothing to say," Jones spat.

Verity laughed. "Well, boredom's one thing you know about."

I wondered how I could keep violence from breaking out in the dismal fifteen-minute ride to campus, but they both shut up.

THE TENSION DIDN'T end there. The cocktail party reception that kicked off the conference that Thursday evening was as strained as the dance in *West Side Story*. Members of the rival Wharton societies had instantly formed separate clusters, staring suspiciously at each other.

Wharton Association members were uniformly dressed in sober-looking suits, while the Wharton Collective constituents were given to New York black. A number of them had chic eyebrow piercings that made me shudder because I assumed they signaled more private, discretionary holes.

Van Deegan Jones had switched to pinstripes; Verity Gallup had the same outfit on but with an oversized blue blazer that made her look even sexier, though in a daunting, heroic sort of way. Like Delacroix's bare-breasted woman with the French flag.

I guess it didn't help that we were in a fairly featureless conference room with black and blue carpeting and drapes. Great, I thought. If there's a brawl, the bruises will mix right in.

We were all supposedly admirers of Edith Wharton, and lots of the sixty-five or so people there were carrying paperbacks of their favorite Wharton books, or copies of critical studies and biographies. They looked a bit like priests with missals.

A local bookstore, Ferguson's, had set up a small table in one corner with dozens of books by Wharton and her critics. Serena had insisted we have Ferguson's in charge, since it wasn't a chain store but the last independent bookseller in the area. The people who weren't drinking or chatting were browsing through the books. Some even made purchases from the clerk, who seemed to be having trouble with his credit card machine.

The clerk was a former student of mine, Cal Brendon, a sweet, soft-spoken Michiganapolis boy whose father taught economics at SUM and whose mother owned one of the better jewelry stores near campus, Beau Geste. Cal had graduated last year, but wasn't sure what he wanted to do besides be around books. And though he was a graduate, he still looked like a student, wearing what I thought of as "the" haircut right then, since half my male students had it: shaved on the sides and back, thick English schoolboy waves brushed straight back but tumbling free every time he moved. A high-maintenance haircut that he was always adjusting. He had shaved the optional goatee, however.

"Having fun?" he asked, as I drifted over at one point.

"Check with me when it's over."

I noticed that a few academics were jealously inspecting books at the table to see if their rival's work was there, and the *really* envious ones were looking at publication information on the copyright pages to see how many printings the books had gone through.

Every now and then, I saw Jones and Gallup glare at each other as if ready to duke it out. Each time, I turned away, wishing that Stefan were there to remind me that none of this was really very serious.

Serena Fisch kept up a sarcastic commentary for me, resplendent in a shimmering white silk pants suit that seemed very Jackie O. She was even wearing large sunglasses, and I wondered if she was trying out a new image.

"You should have had a metal detector at the door," she whispered at one point, while I watched people circulate warily through the room. "This crowd could get ugly."

I whispered back, "They *are* ugly."

Behind me, I heard some fuddy-duddies from the Wharton Association savaging *The Buccaneers,* a recently published unfinished Wharton novel that had been rewritten and completed by a minor Wharton scholar who wasn't at the conference. The men were quite hostile, angrily quoting from a Book of the Month Club ad that said the book was "finished in the Wharton style." The line struck me as waiter talk; you know: "The roast goose is finished by a reduction of port wine, goose stock, and an infusion of butter."

Suddenly the whole party seemed to be talking about *The Buccaneers,* though still with clear boundaries between the two groups.

One reviewer had called the book "literary necrophilia," but it had been made into a PBS movie, and the "author" had probably earned more money than anyone in the room would ever make from their writing on Wharton.

"They're envious," I said quietly to Serena. "Underneath the bitching, they wish they'd thought of the dumb idea and gotten some idiotic publisher to pay for it."

Serena roared, "Why stop there? Why not rewrite Wharton's *finished* novels? That's the real challenge. Some of her books are such downers, like *Ethan Frome.* Do we really want our children reading that kind of stuff—in high school?"

I shushed her because I couldn't afford to seem unprofessional, but around us, a few men and women nodded appreciatively at Serena's salvo. Even Verity Gallup and Van Deegan Jones looked amused, though they became poker-faced when they caught each other smiling.

Where was Priscilla? She'd promised to come and help me feel less isolated and desperate, and I needed as much support as possible.

Just then, Grace-Dawn Vaughan made her entrance, and the mood in the chattering room turned dark again. Vaughan was the only truly popular and successful writer at the conference. The "Wharton boom" in books and movies hadn't made money for any of the army of critics working on Wharton, though they would all kill to get the kind of attention and money that Vaughan had earned for her forthcoming biography.

In cruel contrast to her hyphenated first name, she seemed neither garceful nor liable to inspire an aubade. In fact, she was rather troll-like: short, glowering, beady-eyed. Dressed a bit like Cher in her gypsies, tramps, and thieves period, Vaughan was followed by Devon Davenport. Serena had picked them both up at the airport and when I'd asked her before the reception what they were like, she would only slyly and melodramatically quote Joseph Conrad: " 'The horror, the horror.' "

Stefan had explained to me about Davenport: he was one of the best-known editors in publishing, both for being a star-maker and for his cruel rejection letters. Tall and thin, Davenport was as leathery and wrinkled as someone who'd spent his lifetime in the Australian outback rather than a manuscript-ridden office.

I sailed over to Davenport. "Welcome! I'm Nick Hoffman."

"I know that," he snapped, and he steered Vaughan to the bar manned by a student in the hotel management program. The Campus Center was almost entirely staffed by these generally eager but hopelessly young-looking kids. I couldn't hear what passed between Davenport and the student bartender, but it couldn't have been pleasant, since the kid looked stunned when Davenport snatched a wine glass from him.

With amusement, Serena and I watched Davenport hold rude court. He leaned back against the portable bar with a sneer on his wizened old face. Various professors drew closer, apparently trying to suck up to him, but all were brutally rebuffed as if he were a crime boss who'd never do a favor for even the most obsequious supplicant. I'm sure there were some men and women in the room who'd had their book proposals mockingly returned from him in the past. Academics often mistakenly think they can "dash off" a popular book and get themselves on the bestseller list—after all, how hard can it be?

Loud enough for everyone in the room to hear, Davenport said to Grace-Dawn, "Authors! They're all scum! Except you, sweetie."

I moved through the room trying to do some damage control, but even though everyone I spoke to was friendly enough, I couldn't get much of a conversation going anywhere. Maybe it was my fault. I was nervous, wondering when Chloe and Vivianne would show up, and vainly hoping they hadn't made it. And why couldn't Stefan have cancelled his evening class to be there and help me?

Turning to get a refill on my rum and coke, I froze when I saw Joanne Gillian enter the room with the air of someone in the Woman's Christian Temperance Union about to take out an axe in a saloon. Bob Gillian was by her side, even more dapper than usual in contrast, though that wasn't hard, given Joanne's unflattering dark blue suit. What an odd couple they were—they barely seemed connected to each other. He had that dashing Jaguar and she was a troglodyte.

Joanne surged over to me, looking as large as life—in Oscar Wilde's phrase—but only half as natural. Bob followed in her wake, flicking his driving gloves against his side like a riding crop.

"I want you to know," she announced in a fishwife's voice, "that I protested the choice of Chloe DeVore as a guest speaker. She's foul and degraded, and her work is poisonous. Bob couldn't even read it."

Bob nodded severely, and I wanted to deck him. Chloe DeVore as the Marquis de Sade of contemporary literature? It was ludicrous!

"I did everything possible to see that this purveyor of filth was un-invited, but I failed." Her eyes narrowed. "You people are very power-ful—sometimes. But evil cannot triumph in the end." She stalked away, having delivered her sermon. Bob followed, without any comment.

Whatever happened to being polite to your host, I wondered, try-ing to make conversation with conferees. And which people did she mean? Bibliographers? That's right, I wanted to yell at her, the bibliog-raphers are plotting to take over the world—and *bore* everyone to death!

I kept glancing at the door as people passed in the brightly lit hall-way, hoping that I'd see Priscilla. From where I stood, I could see a large backlit map of Michigan. That main hall of the Campus Center was lined with several of these, along with maps of the campus for visitors, blown-up photographs of scenic parts of campus, and Michigan travel posters (our tourism industry brings in well over a billion dollars an-nually).

Suddenly, there was a loud cry of "Bitch!" outside the door, and two women were snarling at each other, but in French now. I could tell that one voice was a native French speaker's, the other clearly American-accented. Oh, God, I thought, it was Chloe and Vivianne, it must be, and they were creating a scene!

Everyone in the room fell silent and we stared at the door as expec-tant as science-fiction movie earthlings watching a flying saucer land.

I made out a few words in the vicious argument: *"salope,"* which meant whore, and *"espèce de con,"* which meant cunt.

One or two people in the room gasped in surprise or disapproval, though a few chuckled.

The shouting stopped as unexpectedly as it had erupted. And then lustrous Vivianne Fresnel walked into the reception, head high, cheeks red and a striking contrast with her beautifully tailored lime-green suit.

She gave me a little wave and mouthed "Hello, Nicholas," with a wry smile, as if we were old friends.

My name isn't Nicholas but it sounded good—it sounded *right*—when she said it.

Fresnel headed to the bar and I heard her ask for champagne, which I was sure was unavailable, even that Freixenet slop.

A moment later, Fresnel was followed by the rather dowdier Chloe DeVore, wearing the same frumpy outfit she'd done her reading in a few months earlier. Most of the Wharton scholars didn't recognize Chloe and Vivianne, though they all stared at the two actors in the strange little hallway drama.

But a few people seemed not just to know them, but know them well. Crane Taylor, of the Wharton Association, stared for a while, looking sweaty and white-faced, and then he darted out of the room as if he were going to be sick.

Gustaf Carmichael, a Wharton Collective member, raised his glass to Chloe ironically, but she ignored him.

Even stranger, Grace-Dawn Vaughan looked very upset to see Chloe and Vivianne. She gulped down whatever she was drinking and turned her back on them. Devon Davenport put his hands on her shoulders as if to calm her down, and then he made a beeline for Chloe, taking her aside and whispering to her urgently.

Her memoir, I thought. He wants to publish her memoir. Chloe shook him off.

"He's going to have a stroke," Serena said behind me, instantly captured as I was by Davenport's contorted, shocked face. We both heard him mutter, "You'll never get away from me."

What the hell was going on here?

I turned to Serena and found her glaring angrily at Chloe over the tops of her sunglasses. This wasn't the outrage of a hostess saddled with a bumptious guest; Serena looked as if she had an old score to settle. When she found me studying her, she turned away.

As if that wasn't enough, Verity Gallup and Van Deegan Jones, at opposite ends of the room, were staring at Chloe as if she were something horrible your dog had rolled in on the beach. The Gillians showily turned their backs on Chloe, but I doubt she noticed or cared.

I didn't have time to think about any of the peculiar reactions to Chloe and Vivianne, or about their public and embarrassing altercation. It was almost nine o'clock, and Serena and I had to shepherd everyone down the hall to the next event: the keynote addresses by Grace-Dawn Vaughan and Devon Davenport.

"Hurry up, please, it's time," I said, quoting T.S. Eliot, because the tired old line never failed to make academics who recognized it smile. "The auditorium is down the hall to your left," I called, waving my hands in what I hoped was a convivial manner.

People slowly surged to the doors, slower than usual at a conference because like little kids afraid of getting "cooties," members of the different Wharton factions avoided brushing against each other.

I brought up the rear, and out in the hallway, Priscilla rushed up to me, breathing hard as if she'd been running. But even red-faced, she looked vibrant and glamorous in a black sweater dress and black boots, her thick hair drawn into a loose ponytail.

"Oh, Nick! I'm sorry! I was just so—"

Serena was down the hall, waving me along. "Come on, Nick."

Chloe and Vivianne were arm-in-arm in front of Serena, and they both turned at Serena's voice, catching sight of Priscilla, who broke off talking.

With a haughty smile, Chloe descended on us. On Priscilla, really. And even though she was a foot shorter than Priscilla, she proceeded to dress her down—sweetly.

"I know you arranged for Vivianne to find out about my reading here back in February. But you see, it didn't work. You think a pipsqueak like you can break up a bond like ours? You can't write worth a damn, so why did you think you could plot against me? It wasn't even an original plan, darling. It's right out of one of your crummy little mysteries. Dabbling with death?"

I had no idea what Chloe DeVore meant by those last comments, but Priscilla was dumbfounded, and looked on the point of tears.

Priscilla clearly couldn't reply, couldn't even think, I bet, and Chloe serenely headed away from us. Bob and Joanne Gillian were arguing quietly nearby, and Joanne moved away from Chloe as if she had a contagious disease, heading off to the auditorium by herself.

Serena waved impatiently to me, and strode away.

But I turned from the crowd to take Priscilla's hand, and squeezed it. "You okay?" She shook her head and proceeded down the hall like a zombie, clearly beyond my help right now.

Chloe and Vivianne were sitting on one of the many couches lining the central hallway of the Campus Center, looking perfectly relaxed together, as if they hadn't been yelling at each other only an hour ago. Maybe they weren't going to attend the keynote speeches—wouldn't that be great? Vivianne smiled and headed for the ladies' room, I think.

Suddenly thirsty, I walked over to a water fountain but the cool stream made me head for the men's room instead, where I splashed my face with cold water a few times to calm down. I breathed in and out, willing everything to go right.

After all the drama, when I walked into the cool auditorium, it was a shock to me even though I'd been there before. Such a pretty little room, with its 150 gold velveteen seats, lovely blue, burgundy, and gold carpeting, warmly stained oak paneling, and the stage as intimate as a setting for private theatricals in an English country home. I paused in the doorway, taking it all in.

The hall was far too quiet, ominously so. Here, too, as during the reception, the Wharton Association and the Wharton Collective sat apart on opposite sides of the center aisle, or as much apart as possible. Verity Gallup and Van Deegan Jones across the aisle from each other in the third row, both very straight in their seats as if they were standard-bearers for opposing armies.

The Gillians were in the last row, and I saw Priscilla not far away, arms crossed and neck bent as if she were trying to stay warm, or comfort herself.

I trooped down to the front row to sit next to Serena, smiling at Grace-Dawn Vaughan a few seats down from us. She simpered. "Where's Davenport?" I asked her. She shrugged.

I quietly apologized to Serena for taking so long, but she was intently studying large index cards for her introduction of Grace-Dawn Vaughan. "We're running late," she muttered. "I hate that." Serena's sunglasses were off, and when she asked a bit testily if she could get things rolling, I nodded.

Serena was true to her name. With no sign of annoyance, she strode up the low side staircase to the podium that was fixed center stage, smiling benevolently at us all.

She introduced Grace-Dawn Vaughan with so much warmth you'd never have guessed she'd called Vaughan "that awful woman" a few weeks back.

The applause was heartier than I would have expected, but maybe people were just glad to hit something, if only their own hands. Vaughan wafted up onto the stage with her many scarves billowing and her New Age earrings and bracelets clattering. Serena's more graceful and much quieter exit as she passed in the other direction seemed an ironic comment on all the noise.

Vaughan yanked the microphone down closer to her mouth. "Edith Wharton," she announced in a hortatory, evangelizing voice, "Edith Wharton has never been truly understood!"

Most of the people in that auditorium stiffened a little, since there was hardly a soul there who hadn't written a book or an article about Wharton with the firm belief that he or she alone knew what made Wharton tick, and could give the truest interpretation of her work. I knew—I'd read every word anyone had written on Edith Wharton.

"She wasn't complex at all. She was simply a woman in love, a woman of many loves, a woman of passion and pain," Vaughan said rhapsodically, and you could feel waves of hostility beating at the stage. "And only a woman who has loved with her passion, her desperation, can know Wharton's core."

Out of the side of her mouth, Serena muttered, "That would have been a good song cue for Marlene Dietrich and 'Falling in Love Again.' "

I tried studying the audience behind me as surreptitiously as possible. Davenport still wasn't there. Men were squirming, and some of the women smirked at each other. But it didn't last, because Vaughan drifted into talking about her own "passional life" (which seemed largely imaginary) as a template for reading Wharton's.

I tuned out. I'd been absolutely right that Vaughan didn't have a damned thing new or interesting to say about Edith Wharton. She was just turning Wharton into a Harlequin Romance cartoon.

"Marvelous," Serena said next to me, sotto voce.

Vaughan blathered on for only ten more minutes, making me glad we hadn't been able to give her a speaker's fee. She ended with a plug for her book, and then bowed her head for the expected applause. It came, but only out of strained politeness. I'm sure if someone had suggested a lynching right then, there would have been plenty of volunteers.

Vaughan then introduced Davenport as "one of publishing's most influential editors," and her "personal friend." I turned to see him bounding down the aisle from the back of the hall. Thank God he'd finally made it, I thought, when he moved to the stage. Vaughan grinned as Davenport took the steps like an eager valedictorian. While the podium changed hands, so to speak, I could hear people leaving the auditorium, some grumbling aloud.

Vaughan drifted back down to her seat, looking very pleased with herself. I suppose she was happy to insult all the academics who she must have known thought she was a fraud.

A fraud with a six-figure advance.

Davenport surveyed the auditorium with a disgusted mien. "Most of you are academics," he said. "And you can't write for shit."

There were outraged cries throughout the hall.

Davenport upped his volume. "You've got such a hard-on for your own rhetoric that you can't be understood by intelligent readers. And the rest of you are just plain, old-fashioned bores."

I tried not to grin and refused to look at Serena, who I knew was eating this up. If we had wanted to unite the two Wharton groups, these two outrageous speakers were bound to do it. But I could imagine Stefan asking me: At what cost? Even though Serena had said she'd claim responsibility for the choice of speakers, I knew I'd be facing bitter complaints.

Had I been too cavalier about unleashing so much hard feeling in a public place? Was the damage repairable, or would the conference burst into flames and crash?

"What the hell do *you* know?" someone shouted from the back of the auditorium, and for a wild second I thought he was yelling at me, not Davenport.

So the question-and-answer session was starting early—and with naked hostility, instead of the customary disguised brand. Before I could rise and ask for quiet, and before Davenport could lash out at his opponent, there was an ear-splitting woman's scream at the door.

Joanne Gillian staggered into the auditorium, sobbing, white-faced, wringing her hands. "There's a woman out there! I think she's dead!"

# 5

RUSHING UP THE aisle along with Serena to the doorway where Joanne Gillian had appeared, I noticed with concern that the back rows of the little auditorium were completely empty. Grace-Dawn Vaughan and Davenport between them had certainly done quite a job.

Serena reached Joanne before I did, grabbing her arms and quietly demanding, "What's going on?" Serena was like an experienced, unflappable nurse, and the cool force of her question—or maybe her grip—seemed to instantly calm Joanne Gillian down. She pulled Serena out into the hall and pointed across to one of the darkened corridors where the construction work was still unfinished.

I followed, feeling the press of conferees behind me.

Voice unsteady, Joanne Gillian said, "There." She broke away from Serena and fell into her husband's arms.

I could barely make out a body lying at the far end of the very dim hallway, head down near a pile of those polished granite tiles being used to reface the lower part of the corridor walls.

Serena and I exchanged a blank look, and then without thinking, I headed into the shadowy corridor.

That's when I could see it was Chloe DeVore.

One of her arms was outstretched as if she'd been trying to grasp something, and I felt drawn closer as if by a tractor beam. Nothing could have kept me back.

"No!" Serena called. "Don't touch her! Don't touch anything." Someone else cried out for a doctor, and I heard confused voices shouting in the crowd that swelled in the hallway behind Serena.

I stooped down to feel for a pulse in Chloe's wrist. It was still warm, but lifeless, and I set her hand down as gently as possible. That's when

I noticed a bloodied granite tile not far from where she lay. Taking a closer look at Chloe's body, I could see that her face was grayish-blue, and that her skin looked waxy.

I closed my eyes and backed away, praying that this was some kind of accident. She'd slipped, I thought, or had a heart attack, and hit one of those tiles the wrong way. It couldn't be murder. I couldn't be involved in *another* murder—how was that possible?

"No need for a doctor," I said to Serena when I was out of the hallway. "It's Chloe DeVore, and she's dead."

"I didn't do it!" Priscilla shouted from the middle of the conferees. "I didn't!"

I stared at Priscilla, and so did everyone else as she burst into tears. The astonished crowd erupted in a jabber of questions, opinions, and exclamations.

I heard several people ask with pique, "Who's Chloe DeVore?"

I felt both frozen and amazingly clear-sighted. Vivianne was nowhere in sight and I imagined her shock when she heard that Chloe was dead. A number of other people weren't there either: Grace-Dawn Vaughan and Devon Davenport, who had probably beat a retreat to avoid being harassed. Van Deegan Jones and Verity Gallup were missing, too. I was surprised that the two Wharton society leaders hadn't stuck around to rally their troops after the inflammatory keynote speeches, or at least to take me aside and say they were very concerned with the tone being set at the beginning of the conference.

Bob Gillian supported his now-tearful wife with surprising tenderness. Serena was quietly talking with the Campus Center manager, a balding, thin man who looked stunned. He was nervously pulling at his beardless chin and I heard him say the Campus Police—who had jurisdiction over all crimes and disturbances at SUM—were en route.

"Back off!" came a loud voice with a Grand Rapids twang, and I was suddenly being shoved away from the corridor entrance by a burly campus cop with the angry red face of a drunk and the swollen muscles of a bouncer. Several cops spread through the area, cordoning off the corridor and herding back the crowd of Wharton conferees and everyone else who'd gathered to stare: students, staff, hotel guests.

I had learned last year that the Campus Police, with its staff of close to sixty, were not the dregs I'd imagined them to be. Many had master's degrees, and the job was considered a plum for people in other Michigan law enforcement agencies like the state police.

Someone said "Dr. Hoffman" behind me. It was not a voice that I was glad to hear.

I turned to face Detective Valley. "Surprised?" he said, reading my face too well.

We'd met last year under unpleasant circumstances that hadn't gotten much better. There were a dozen detectives on the Campus Police force—why did I have to run into *him* again?

"Are *you* surprised?" I asked. Then I wondered why I couldn't have just said hello.

"Not really." Detective Valley didn't look like a Campus Policeman or any kind of policeman. He was more like a salesman you'd find in one of those furniture slaughterhouses, not the eager convivial kind, but the subtler, nastier ones who seem to quietly mock you for not having enough money or taste to shop somewhere else.

Tall, thin, freckled, with curly red hair, I imagined he might have been the caustic kid in junior high who could imitate all the teachers with devastating accuracy—but only when he wanted to. All that sarcasm was just under the surface in the adult, ready to bubble up.

"Has anyone disturbed the scene?" he asked, and I said I'd tried for her pulse.

Valley stepped carefully down the corridor to Chloe DeVore's body to inspect it and the area, jotting notes in a small pad as he squatted by the corpse. He took out a cellular phone, made a call before he walked back, and then ordered the excited, confused mob to be quiet. "Does anyone know who the woman is? Who found her?"

Joanne Gillian meekly held up her hand, and Valley waved a cop over to take her aside. Bob Gillian followed and I saw the three of them move down the hallway to a seating area where the policeman could, I supposed, take her statement without interference.

I told Valley that the dead woman was Chloe DeVore, a well-known writer who lived in Paris. He didn't seem to have ever heard of her.

Again, Valley addressed the crowd that looked on with the dumb eagerness of bystanders coming upon a movie being filmed right in the middle of their city. "Did anyone notice anything suspicious? Did anyone see this woman enter the hallway, or see anyone follow her or leave the hallway?"

Some of the conferees looked frustrated, as if they wished they *had* been witnesses and could grab some attention. But no one came forward or spoke up.

Valley shook his head. "Nobody leaves," he ordered, "until we get statements from everyone, or your names and phone numbers." There were annoyed sighs, mixed with the expectant murmur of people about to ride a truly fiendish roller coaster.

Valley called over the manager, who he seemed to know, and asked for some rooms on this floor to be set up so that he and other Campus Police could interview everyone on the scene.

He beckoned me away from the crowd so we couldn't be overheard. I asked him if it looked like a stroke or a heart attack—or an accident. Valley hesitated, and then seemed to relax, as if there was no point hiding what he'd observed. He told me he'd noticed a head injury which looked suspicious.

"Suicide?" I asked, a little desperately.

"Not likely. Now, what's this got to do with you? What are you doing here? Was she your dinner guest?"

I ignored his nasty reference to the murder I'd been involved in last year.

"We're having a conference and I'm the chair," I said, gesturing at the dozens of people in the hallway. "A Wharton conference."

"What's that?"

"You mean who, not what. Edith Wharton."

He looked right at me, expressionless.

"Edith Wharton's a writer," I explained. "A famous American writer." Silence.

"You know, *Ethan Frome, The House of Mirth, The Age of Innocence?*" No response.

Exasperated, I said, "Michelle Pfeiffer! She was in the movie of *The Age of Innocence.* Just a couple of years ago."

"Okay. And this Edith Wharton wrote the screenplay?"

"Wharton is dead," I snapped. "She died in 1937. She's a major American writer."

But even the mention of Michelle Pfeiffer didn't seem to convince

Valley of Wharton's stature. Why should he believe me? I'd claimed that Chloe was a well-known writer and her name hadn't registered, so why should Wharton's? I wondered if he even knew of the writers who made it onto the best-seller list, or did they only get his attention if their books were turned into big-budget movies?

Serena sidled over and introduced herself as cochair of the conference. Valley wordlessly inspected her and nodded as if she confirmed his jaundiced idea of the kind of woman who'd work with me.

Serena bristled when Valley said he'd get to her after he was done asking me some more questions, but she left us alone.

"How'd you get involved in this stuff?" he asked.

"I'm a Wharton scholar. A bibliographer, actually. I published a book, a secondary bibliography, describing what other scholars have written about her."

Valley's eyes widened slightly as if he couldn't believe anyone would pay for something like that. He wasn't far off—not that many people had, and lots of them were at the conference. Academic writing is like poetry; it's read almost exclusively by the people who write it. And secondary bibliographies of authors are about as specialized as you can get.

"You could say that I know where the bodies are buried," I dropped, and instantly regretted it.

"What?"

I blushed at how unfortunate that line was. "Sorry. It's just a joke I sometimes make—"

"What does it mean?"

How was I going to explain this to someone who wasn't an academic? "Well, I'm an expert on Edith Wharton. I've read everyone's work on Wharton, *everyone's*, dead or alive. All the books and pamphlets and articles and introductions and prefaces and passing references in other books and pamphlets and articles— You get the picture. So I know who's borrowed ideas from someone else without proper attribution. You'd be surprised what's out there."

"That's stealing, isn't it?"

"Plagiarism," I corrected.

Valley asked me if that might have a bearing on the case—if Chloe DeVore had in fact been murdered, that is.

But all I could share was my confusion. "Chloe DeVore wasn't a Wharton scholar."

"Then what was she doing here?"

I did not want to tell him anything about Chloe, Vivianne, and Priscilla. It was all too murky and made Priscilla look bad. Especially since she'd called so much attention to herself already.

"If anyone was going to be killed," I mused, "it would have been one of the Wharton presidents. The groups hate each other."

"Why's that?"

"They see Wharton very differently."

"And somebody's gonna get killed over that?" Valley shook his head, having just been given more proof of the idiocy of academics.

Just then, the Campus Center manager walked up to tell Detective Valley that several rooms off a nearby corridor were at his disposal, with pitchers of water and coffee urns. I was surprised that Valley thanked him, and even more surprised when he said that since I knew the Wharton scholars and their work so well, he wanted me to sit in while he questioned witnesses or whatever they were. I assumed the cops in the crowd were separating out the people they thought had something to say.

"But you're first," he said, after conferring with one of his men. We entered the nearest of the rooms set aside by the manager. It was like thousands of such rooms in universities across the country: neon lights too bright and carpet woven in drab colors that matched the worn-looking, cheap drapes. The tables and chairs were functional, but nothing more. And the saddest part was that it was all fairly new.

I found myself wishing Stefan were there to lend his calm insight to what had happened. But maybe he couldn't find that strength right now—at least for me.

Valley sat on the edge of the conference table at the front of the room and waved me into a chair a foot away.

"Okay. How was the body discovered?"

"There was screaming—Joanne Gillian. It interrupted the second keynote speech. That was about ten-fifteen, I think." I tried to recall when we'd begun, and told him he should check with Serena to be sure. But I thought it was close to nine-thirty. Which meant that Chloe had died somewhere between nine and ten P.M. I'd read enough about death to know she'd probably been dead about half an hour, given what I'd observed.

I told this to Valley, who said, "Moonlighting as a Medical Examiner?" and ignored me.

Valley wrote Serena's name down, and asked who else I thought he should speak to after Joanne Gillian and Serena. I mentioned Vivianne Fresnel, and had to spell it for him.

"And she—?"

"She was Chloe DeVore's lover, on and off. They had a fight tonight before the reception."

But when Valley's eyes looked greedy, I rushed to counter what I'd blurted out. "They seemed fine an hour later."

Valley almost smirked, and I was sure his mind had settled into a precut groove about Killer Lesbians.

"What did they argue about?" he asked.

"I don't know, since it was in French and they were talking too fast."

"You understand French?"

"If it's slow, and quiet."

"So they were shouting?"

I shrugged. "It was an argument."

Valley went to the door, called for one of the dark-blue-uniformed cops and asked that Vivianne be found and brought to him for questioning, and also asked where Joanne Gillian was. I stood and pulled a chair off to the side where I could watch Valley and whomever he questioned.

Joanne appeared moments later, pale, eyes down. Bob Gillian accompanied her into the room, insisting to Valley that he had to be there with her, "because of the shock." Gillian helped his wife into a chair and sat by her.

Maybe I'm superficial, but it always puzzles me when good-looking men like Bob marry plain, even homely, women. There was something so squashed and unappealing about Joanne Gillian. She seemed the kind of bland, angry woman you could imagine having been laughed at as a teenage girl when she stuck an overly ornate barrette in her mousy hair. Who did she think she was, her mocking peers would have jeered, and she lived every day of her life haunted by that amphitheater of derision.

Bob was being so solicitous, I half expected him to coo at Joanne and stroke her hand. This intimacy was quite a change from their mood at the reception, when they'd seemed distant from each other. I could imagine Stefan pointing out to me that maybe the shock of finding a body had brought them closer together. He's less quick than I am to make snap judgments about people.

Joanne Gillian wasn't too overcome to glare at me and order Valley to kick me out. "He has no business here!"

I confess I admired the way Valley just ignored the outburst.

"Mrs. Gillian, what were you doing in that corridor?" he asked quietly. "It was dark and under construction."

"I told that policeman already."

"I want you to tell me."

"I'm the chair of SUM's Board of Trustees. I pay your salary."

"The citizens of Michigan pay my salary."

Joanne squared her shoulders, her round face assuming an air of hauteur that seemed slightly ridiculous under the circumstances. Who did she think she was, Marie Antoinette facing a Revolutionary tribunal?

"I was looking for a ladies' room. I got confused."

"Lost," her husband added.

Valley silenced him with a curt wave of his hand. Gillian sat back in his chair as if he'd been smacked, but he didn't stop talking. "Joanne sometimes has trouble making out signs—she's dyslexic."

Valley glanced at me as if for confirmation, and I nodded; I'd heard about Joanne Gillian's dyslexia from someone I know in the provost's office.

"Why are you asking *him?*" Joanne said, her face contorted by disgust. "Ask my doctor!" She gave Valley a name and phone number, which he wrote down, unflappable.

"I cannot believe you'd have that sodomite here while you're questioning me!" Joanne was in her public address mode: head high, voice round and clear like God had just charged her with a mission to save the world from itself. I was sure people heard her out in the hall. "This murder is exactly the kind of thing you can expect at SUM after all the open promotion of perversion! What's next? Bestiality? Witchcraft?" Her face was as hateful as any other finger-pointing Sunday morning TV preacher's.

I tried to stay calm.

"We don't know it's a murder, Mrs. Gillian. The Medical Examiner will tell us that." And then Valley zapped her, quietly. "Are you implying there's some satanic cult at work here?"

"Of course not! But instead of harassing decent people, why don't you find out why that woman, that tall woman with the ponytail out there, started crying when she heard the DeVore woman was dead—and said that *she* didn't do it?"

"What woman?"

Joanne Gillian tossed her head impatiently—why should she have to remember anyone's name?

"Priscilla Davidoff," I said, reluctantly.

Valley turned to me, clearly annoyed that I hadn't mentioned Priscilla. I tried to look apologetic but innocent, like I'd simply forgotten. I don't know if I succeeded.

"What do you know about Chloe DeVore?" Valley asked them.

"I'm glad she's dead!" Joanne shot. "She was evil, a pornographer."

"Evil," Bob said in a mindless-sounding echo.

Valley was clearly uncomfortable with their vehemence and seemed to be thinking it over. "You've read her books?"

"I tried," Bob said. "Joanne finished one."

"And have you ever met her before?"

Joanne laughed scornfully. "Mix with someone unclean?"

"Not everybody's born with religion," Valley said sagely, but Joanne just gave him a haughty look. "What did you do when you noticed the body?"

"I called. I asked if she was—all right."

"And she didn't answer?"

"Of course not!" Joanne was more and more indignant. It was clear that being challenged in any way pushed all her buttons.

"But how did you know she was dead?"

Joanne looked at Bob, then turned rapidly back to Valley.

"How did you know she wasn't just unconscious?" he pressed.

"She seemed dead," Joanne barked. "She wasn't moving."

Valley nodded, and I wondered if he was really probing or just trying to annoy Joanne. He went on asking Joanne and then Bob what they knew about Chloe DeVore, but didn't learn anything significant that I could see. He let them go.

After they'd left, he pointed out to me that from behind, Joanne Gillian and Chloe DeVore looked somewhat alike.

"Huh?"

"Figure it out. About the same height, same hair color, both wearing dark blue suits, black shoes."

Stunned, I said, "You think *she* was the target? Joanne Gillian? That it was a mistake?"

"If Joanne Gillian is really dyslexic," Valley reasoned, "and it's fairly well known, then maybe someone at the conference was hoping to take advantage of her condition in some way. I have to consider the possibility."

I felt sick. If someone did want to kill Joanne Gillian, and that could be proven, then she'd have another weapon to use against the gay community at SUM. Even if it wasn't true, Joanne Gillian could try riding that horse to the finish line. She was clearly not a woman grounded in reason and fact.

"Now, I want you to tell me the truth," Valley said, and I was sure he meant to ask me about Priscilla's bizarre declaration. "What's this Gillian lady got against you?"

I relaxed a little. "She's chair of the Board of Trustees."

"She said that. And?"

"Don't you know what she's been doing at SUM?"

"I don't follow politics, especially campus politics."

Reluctantly, I explained to Detective Valley what had been happening on campus regarding domestic partner benefits and gay rights in general, insisting that none of this could have anything to do with Chloe's death.

Valley was noncommittal, just taking it all in. "So you want to be treated like you're married?" he asked.

"Of course!"

"But you're not married, so how does that make sense? It's not fair to people who *are* married."

"What's not fair is that we *can't* be married."

He nodded a few times, clearly unconvinced, and I did not feel this was the time to pick up a megaphone.

Valley went to the door and asked the cop waiting there to send in Serena Fisch. Out in the hallway, the hubbub was dying down. I assumed that most of the people not directly involved had already scattered, their names and phone numbers recorded just in case.

Serena came in smiling graciously, as if she were a celebrity granting a chatty at-home interview. Maybe she did think she was Jackie O. in that white pants suit, even though she'd put away the large sunglasses. But it seemed a very strange attitude for someone being questioned in connection with a sudden death. Or was I being too picky? And given Serena's usual "Boogie-Woogie Bugle Boy" aura, who could say what attitude of hers *wasn't* strange?

Valley didn't hesitate. "What do you know about this Chloe De-Vore?"

"She was here in February to do the President's Series, and was a guest at Nick and Stefan's party afterwards."

Valley glanced sidelong at me as Serena went on. "Another dinner guest?" he asked.

Serena continued. "And I met her once before that, years ago when I was a guest lecturer at Emory University. In Georgia. Chloe was the writer-in-residence there, but we didn't really have much contact."

This was the first time that Serena had ever said she'd met Chloe before. Why hadn't she mentioned that to me? Putting it together with the way she'd stared daggers at Chloe during the reception, I felt deeply uncomfortable. I didn't look at Serena, because I was sure that she was lying—about something.

"What are you doing at this conference?" Valley asked her.

"Running it," she said, a bit smugly, and she flushed when he glanced my way.

"I thought that Professor Hoffman was the Wharton expert, and he was the one in charge."

"Oh, he is. But pulling off a conference like this takes—it takes a team, working together." She nodded, satisfied with her answer, and she smiled at me as if to say, "See? I gave you credit."

"And you had no interest in seeing Chloe DeVore again?"

Serena flared up. "What the hell does that mean?"

"You tell me," Valley rejoined, voice soft.

"I don't know what you're talking about. I met Chloe years ago, I met her again at the party, and that's it. There's no other connection between us."

She was so vociferous I was convinced the truth was the exact opposite.

Valley seemed to think so, too, but even when he rephrased the question, she kept repeating her denial.

"Where were you between the reception and the speeches?"

Serena closed her eyes briefly to remember. "We all drifted out into the hall. I told Nick to hurry up but he was talking to Priscilla Davidoff. Then I was in the auditorium. Everyone saw me. That's the only alibi I have."

"I wasn't asking for an alibi."

"No? Then why are you questioning me?"

"Because we have a death here of undetermined cause."

Serena gave him a silky grin. "Well, if it's murder, I'm not in the habit of killing campus guests. I have a little more school spirit than that."

Despite himself, Valley cracked a smile.

"Can I go now?" Serena asked.

Valley looked annoyed, but he nodded, and she left us, looking very disgruntled.

Vivianne's entrance was quieter than Serena's exit, but more dramatic. Valley was surprisingly intimidated by Vivianne's beauty and her chic. She was still wearing that gorgeous lime-green Chanel suit and reeked of self-confidence, and even the ugly chair she sat in gained some elegance from her presence. I'm sure Vivianne was not his idea of what a lesbian was supposed to look like. I suppose she might have vaguely fit his *Basic Instinct* file, but there was nothing predatory about her.

And right now, she seemed strangely unemotional to me.

Valley first asked her what her relationship was to Chloe, and I know he didn't expect the offhand reply, "Well, she was my wife."

Had Chloe seen the relationship that way? I wondered.

Poker-faced, Valley asked, "Where were you when her body was found?"

"I assume upstairs. I went to our room to take aspirin." She gave a very Gallic shrug. "Headache, boredom."

But the last time I'd seen Vivianne before the keynotes, out in the hallway, she had been smiling, with no sign of a headache. She was on a couch with Chloe, and then left—for the ladies' room, I had thought.

"Why didn't the deceased come with you?"

Vivianne raised an eyebrow. "To help me take aspirin?"

Valley hesitated, looking down at his notepad.

"Did anyone see you go to your room? Do you remember talking to anyone in the elevator?"

Vivianne gracefully shook her head.

"Why were you at this conference? Professor Hoffman says that your . . . that Chloe DeVore was not interested in Edith Wharton."

"True, but this is such a beautiful campus and we simply took advantage of the opportunity to enjoy it again. We thought we might also explore your lovely state."

Valley was disarmed, as Michiganders usually are when foreigners (like people from New York) praise their state. It's so unexpected. And me, I was charmed just by listening to Vivianne's English. Her pretty accent graced her speech as beautifully as a sachet sweetening the contents of a drawer.

"Tell me about your previous trip here."

"Chloe flew ahead to make her address, and I followed on a later flight." She shrugged as if to say there wasn't anything more to it.

But I knew that Vivianne's charm was covering up a great deal. I couldn't believe she didn't mention the confrontation at my house about the book, and Priscilla's role in setting it up. Vivianne smiled at me, as if trying to tell me not to mention it myself. I looked away.

"Did she have enemies?" Valley asked.

"Of course not! She was so loved."

I could see Valley wasn't buying that.

"But you and she had a fight, an argument of some kind, right? Before the reception."

Vivianne shrugged. "When you love, it is easy to hate."

Valley was silent, waiting for her to add something more, but Vivianne clearly had nothing she wanted to say.

"So if she was loved, then she was hated, right?"

Vivianne eyed him coolly, but Valley didn't give up. "What was the argument about?"

"Who can say?"

"I'm told it was very heated."

"Of course." She smiled. "It was, as you say, an argument. One raises one's voice to make oneself heard." She seemed to enjoy deflecting him, and she wasn't doing anything to hide her enjoyment.

"You don't remember what you said?"

"There was no time to take notes, I'm afraid."

I tried not to laugh and turned away when Vivianne glanced my way and muttered in French, *"Quelle barbe!"* What a drag!

Looking frustrated, Valley told her she could go. She thanked him, nodded at me, and made her slow way out of the room.

When Vivianne was gone, Valley turned to me. "No enemies? None?"

"Bullshit. People hated Chloe."

"Did you hate her?"

"I didn't know her. But other people did."

"Like who? And how do you know?"

I felt trapped and tried to squirm out of it. "Chloe's got a bad reputation for screwing people over on her way up. That kind of thing gets around, so you hear about it, even though you don't have specifics."

"Right."

Priscilla was next, and she was more distraught than I'd ever seen her, eyes red and unfocused, hands clenching and unclenching. Her black sweater dress and boots made her look even paler.

"Why did you say that you didn't do it when Chloe DeVore's body was discovered? Do what?"

"Kill her," Priscilla whispered.

"Kill her? What made you think it was murder?"

Priscilla shrugged helplessly. "She was dead. I just—"

"Why would people think you had a reason to murder her?"

I was amazed at what followed.

"I hated her," Priscilla said forthrightly, but her eyes wandered. "I hated her more than I've ever hated anyone. I loathed her."

Valley took that in greedily.

"She's been my nemesis," Priscilla continued without prompting. "She's had the success I wanted, but she doesn't deserve it. And she's attacked me in print."

"You're a writer?"

Priscilla nodded. "Mysteries."

Valley looked like that one word made him wonder if he could take Priscilla seriously. Or was I misreading him?

"So you were jealous of Chloe DeVore?"

Priscilla said, "Absolutely. Just like the cliche: insanely jealous. But I didn't kill her. I couldn't have."

"Why not? You're bigger than she was. It wouldn't be hard."

Now Priscilla fixed him with her gorgeous dark eyes. "I couldn't have done it because I wasn't anywhere near that corridor. I went right down the hall to the auditorium just like everyone else. And how could I murder someone with all those people around?"

"Good point," Valley said. Then he leaned forward so that his face was very close to hers. "But if she was murdered, *somebody* killed her with all those people around."

Priscilla slumped, seeming to cave in on herself as she realized that he was right. I thought of mysteries I'd read where murderers had taken great risks. It was daring, but it wasn't impossible, given the animosity between the two Wharton groups. I'm sure the conferees were paying more attention to their ill will for each other than to what was happening down a dark corridor under repair in a building none of them were familiar with.

"Unless someone was with you every minute, and can swear to that—" Valley left the sentence hanging there as he moved back. He then asked Priscilla who else hated Chloe.

"Everyone, I guess. I've never met anyone who liked her."

"What about that French woman?" I wondered if Valley couldn't remember how to pronounce Vivianne's name.

Priscilla rallied. "Vivianne felt sorry for her, that's all. It wasn't love, it was pity."

"How do you know that?"

"It's obvious." Priscilla rubbed at her eyes. "It *was* obvious, I mean."

Valley considered that, then told Priscilla he'd want to talk to her tomorrow after the Medical Examiner's report, and she trailed out of there like a schoolgirl expelled for cheating on an exam.

Valley stood up, clapped his hands, rubbed them together as if facing a roaring fire, and seemed ready to call it a night.

"Wait," I said. "There were other people at the reception who acted weird when Chloe arrived. The keynote speakers, Devon Davenport and

Grace-Dawn Vaughan. And Davenport took a long time to get from the reception to the auditorium." I also told him how Crane Taylor and Gustaf Carmichael had behaved, one leaving the room, the other raising his glass in mocking salute.

Valley sent for them all.

Devon Davenport arrived first, with Grace-Dawn Vaughan on his arm, looking very proprietary. They were a very odd couple, him grizzled, arrogant, and dressed so conservatively, her looking like a slightly moth-eaten hippie. Davenport seemed unaccountably flustered. Maybe he'd had too much to drink by now.

"Why don't you make all those ghouls go home?" he demanded, pointing out to the hallway. "Vampires. It's a fucking zoo out there."

Davenport had been loitering out there too, I thought.

As with Joanne Gillian, Valley ignored the fussing and went right to what he wanted to know. "Did you have a reason to dislike Chloe De-Vore?"

"I hate all authors—or most of them. They're scum!"

"Was she better than most? Or worse?"

"She's dead," Davenport rumbled. "Who the fuck cares?"

Valley snapped his fingers right in front of Davenport's nose. It was so unexpected, Davenport jerked back with a little yelp.

"I care," Valley said calmly. "And you better care, because I am conducting an investigation here and this is serious. You're not in New York. You're on my turf and I'm not putting up with your bullshit."

Davenport gobbled a bit, but said nothing.

"Now. What did you know about Chloe DeVore?"

"Just what everyone in the business knows. Nothing special."

Grace-Dawn looked down, and I was sure she knew that Davenport was lying.

"The memoir," I said.

Davenport glared at me.

Valley asked, "What memoir?"

I explained that Chloe was working on a sensational memoir and a lot of publishers were interested.

Valley turned to Davenport, who gave me a particularly ugly look. "Is that true? And where do you fit in?"

"It's true, but it wasn't any sweat off my balls who published her memoir."

Valley persisted with Davenport, but all he got was more canned abuse about writers' iniquities. Grace-Dawn Vaughan was more open about her feelings when Valley tried her.

"DeVore was a viper. She satirized me in her novel *Brevity* many years ago and I've never forgiven her."

"That was you?" I asked, remembering the nasty portrait in that book of a showy, dumb writer called Ann-Marie Tyree.

Grace-Dawn preened a little, enjoying the attention.

"How much contact did you have with her?" Valley asked.

"None. Not until this conference, that is."

"Did she know how angry you were about being satirized?"

Grace-Dawn hesitated. "I didn't keep it a secret. She probably heard about it from one author or another."

"Where were you between the time of the reception and the time the body was found?"

"In the auditorium, I presume. Giving my speech."

"And you?" he asked Davenport.

"I gave a speech," Davenport threw off.

"But he was late," I blurted, earning a nasty stare.

Valley waited for Davenport to explain himself, but he just said, "Don't remember where I was every minute."

Valley said sharply, "You'd better remember," and then he dismissed them both after a few more listless questions.

Crane Taylor was the next to face Valley. In his late forties, wan and beady-eyed, Taylor made an instant bad impression on Valley. Taylor was the kind of nose-in-the-air academic who gives teaching a bad name: arrogant and dismissive.

Crossing his thin legs in a parody of gentlemanliness, he was as belligerent in his own way as Devon Davenport had been. Everything about him, from his well-cropped beard to his shiny loafers, seemed showy and aggressive: Look how sharp I am.

"What's your problem with the dead woman?"

"I detest writers who act like celebrities. I'm a scholar. That's why I didn't want to be in the same room as Chloe DeVore. She stinks."

Valley shook his head.

Taylor said, "It's true."

"You always walk out of a room if someone doesn't meet your standards?"

Taylor smirked. "Not always. Sometimes I stay, out of morbid curiosity. But Chloe was beyond the pale."

"Why's that?"

"She was going to publish a trashy memoir."

"You read it?"

Taylor frowned, "No, but—"

"Then how'd you know it's so bad?"

"I know Chloe. Her work, that is. What else could it be?"

I thought this was an exaggeration. Grace-Dawn Vaughan was a writer of trash; Chloe's work didn't have enough sincerity to be truly awful.

"So it was just a question of taste for you," Valley tried.

"Not just. Taste and discrimination aren't anything minor." Taylor sounded as if he was lecturing a dim acolyte.

Valley pounced. "You really hated her, didn't you?"

"No!" Taylor's denial didn't seem at all authentic, and that was so obvious, he wilted.

"If you're lying, and you're involved in her death—"

Taylor almost blubbered, "I haven't done anything!"

I couldn't believe his sudden shift from hauteur to vulnerability.

Disgusted, or perhaps pleased that he'd broken Taylor down so quickly, Valley dismissed him. "What a prick," he muttered when Taylor was gone.

"Amen to that," I said, wondering why Chloe's memoir would matter so much to Crane Taylor, and why he seemed to think her as terrible a writer as Grace-Dawn.

Gustaf Carmichael was the next person Valley interviewed. Carmichael gave me the creeps. He was that new academic type: the "punk" professor with big gold earrings in each ear, tightly trimmed goatee, and shaved head. I expected him to blather on about Derrida and Foucault when Valley asked him why he'd raised his glass to Chloe.

His answer was smooth. "I wanted to honor the triumph of sleaze."

"Say what?"

"Her memoir. She was going to be all over TV, *People,* the whole shmear."

"How'd you know that?"

"It's inevitable these days."

"And you read her book?"

"I don't think anyone's read it yet."

"You've got a lot of attitude about a book you haven't seen."

"Detective." Carmichael grinned. "Detective, I just have a lot of attitude." He was so pleased with himself I had the urge to smack him. I caught Valley's eye and he seemed to feel the same way.

A uniformed officer interrupted to tell Valley that they were all done at the crime scene, the body was being removed, and the Medical Examiner would be meeting them at the morgue.

Valley thanked him, and wearily dismissed Gustaf Carmichael, who seemed annoyed. "That's all you had to ask me? Everyone else was in here longer."

Valley eyed him up and down. "If you're feeling left out, I suppose we could arrest you and keep you in jail overnight. Would that do?"

Carmichael blushed and departed. When he was gone, Valley asked if there was anything else I could tell him. I thought a moment, and then remembered that Verity Gallup and Van Deegan Jones hadn't been on the scene when the body was discovered. I explained to Valley who they were. Was their absence suspicious?

"Did they interact with Chloe DeVore at any time? Talk to her, or whatever?"

"No. But they seemed very angry that she was here." Remembering their faces at the reception, I wondered if *anger* was the right word. They seemed more disgusted or aggrieved.

It was after midnight, but Valley nodded and asked for the two Wharton organization presidents to be brought in.

They entered with all the bonhomie of two escaped chain gang prisoners still manacled to each other's legs. Gallup and Jones both seemed to be pretending the other didn't exist, and they sat down with a seat between them.

Valley gaped a little at Gallup. She was such a knockout that I half expected him to ask her what she was doing in a dump like this.

Valley did ask where they'd been when Chloe's body was discovered.

Jones sniffily glanced at Gallup, clearly waiting for her to go first. But she was silent, as if hoping to mortify Jones in his attempt to be polite. I suppose she wanted to show up the bankruptcy of such a gesture when they were not even remotely interested in treating each other with civility.

"I don't recall," Jones said sharply.

"I don't either," Gallup said with exaggerated calm, smoothing the inch-long hair above her ears with both hands. The gesture made her large breasts bobble, and Valley's eyes widened. Verity abruptly pulled her jacket closed. She kept her own eyes forward, as did Jones. Watching them, I thought they were like petulant little kids who'd been separated after fighting in the sandbox. It was so undignified I wanted to laugh, but I couldn't.

Valley moved on. "I hear neither of you liked the deceased."

"Never met her," Jones shot. Then he jerked a thumb at Verity. "She probably loved the woman."

Gallup rounded on him, eyes flashing. "What?"

"Chloe DeVore," he said as spitefully as if the name were a curse, "was the kind of dreary, overrated writer you feminists love to make outrageous claims for, wasn't she? You're desperate to create this myth of unacknowledged talent. Now that she's dead you can launch a damned revival." It was so brutal and cold even Valley looked shocked. I know I was.

Jones was also completely off-base about Chloe. She had never been unrecognized in her lifetime.

"I hated her!" Verity shrieked. She looked around at our startled faces, deeply embarrassed. "Not *her*. I hated the kind of writing she did. It was empty and pretentious. She had no real style, no sense of irony, no vision."

All of which Edith Wharton had, I thought, and in spades.

Van Deegan Jones frowned, as if he couldn't believe his rival was telling the truth. But what amazed me was that the two of them even had opinions of Chloe DeVore's work. Most academics are stuck in their own specialties and don't read widely. Yet Jones and Gallup knew Chloe's work—another sign of how she had established herself as a literary writer.

"It kills me to see writers like her get so much support from the publishing world," Gallup went on. "It's just tokenism."

Valley looked a bit out of his depth. "Hey," he said, "can we keep to the subject? There's a dead woman out there. Now, what do you know about her?"

They both professed to having never met Chloe before tonight.

"Then why were you so pissed off she was here?"

Jones looked down at his lap. Gallup raised her chin a little defiantly.

"If either one of you is hiding anything, and this turns into a murder case—" Valley left the sentence unfinished.

Jones snorted, unimpressed by the threat. Verity Gallup surveyed Valley quite coolly, equally self-possessed.

Then they both suddenly looked at me, as if daring me to explain Chloe's presence at the conference.

I quailed. "I didn't invite Chloe! She just registered."

"Forget Chloe," Jones said. "What about that Grace-Dawn Vaughn? Whose idea was that?"

"How could you permit such a performance?" Verity snapped.

Jones nodded agreement, then caught himself.

Verity lashed out at me. "Grace-Dawn Vaughn was pathetic. The kind of sentimental, mawkish writer who tranquilizes women and blinds them to the brutal realities of their lives. Opium to keep them mindless, powerless slaves."

"She *was* lively," I said.

"Oh, cut the pseudo-Marxist bull," Jones snapped at Verity, and for a moment I thought she was going to lunge at him from her chair, but Valley interrupted.

"That's it for tonight." He impatiently dismissed Gallup and Jones, and when they'd left, he told me he might need my advice and information about all these "fruitcakes" as the case unfolded. "If there *is* a case. But stay out of the investigation! I'm assigning two other detectives to help me out. I don't want *any* interference."

Of course, I said I would mind my own business.

As we headed out of the room, Valley added, "I'm curious about something. Do you think it's a good idea for someone like you to be heading up this kind of conference?"

"That," I said, "is the smartest question you've asked all night."

# 6

OUTSIDE THE SEMINAR room, I was chilled by the yellow police tape stretched across the entrance to the corridor, even though Chloe's body had been removed. Almost everyone had gone now and the brightly lit building seemed ghostly.

I breathed in and out a few times, wondering what was next.

"Dr. Hoffman! Hi!"

It was Angie Sandoval, looking as cheerful and relaxed as always. "I was visiting a friend in a dorm across the street," she chirped. "Then I saw the Campus Police cars outside and I just knew I had to come over. Is it true there's been a possible murder? Wow!"

Angie was a Criminal Justice major, and last year she had explained to me the role of the Campus Police, as well as putting me in touch with the county Medical Examiner when I had some questions about the death of my office mate.

"So can I help?"

"Help with what?"

"The investigation! God, you have such an exciting life!"

"Angie, I'm really tired tonight. Why don't we talk about this some other time?"

"Cool! I'll look for you tomorrow," she said, bounding off.

When I got home, I was almost too tired to feel a sense of relief. The whole evening seemed like a nightmare fever that was creeping over me, blurring my thoughts, weighing down my arms and legs. Yet I was still able to take some dim pleasure from our tree-lined street and our lovely house.

Letting myself in, I found lights on everywhere. Stefan had fallen asleep on the blue and gold living room couch with the radio tuned to a local jazz station. Ella was singing "They Can't Take That Away from Me." With her crystal-clear voice gently filling the room, it moved me that Stefan had waited up. Stefan has the craggy good looks of Ben Cross, the actor who played the Jewish runner in *Chariots of Fire*. I studied his face now, marveling at my fortune in having found not just a lover or partner twelve years ago, but a soul mate.

I sat on the edge of the couch and Stefan shifted a bit, muttering "Wha—"

I took his hand and then dropped it, remembering how I'd checked for Chloe DeVore's pulse. Would I ever forget the feel of her wrist?

"Stefan."

He opened his eyes and smiled as warmly as if I'd been gone a very long time.

"There's been a death at the conference," I said.

Stefan pulled himself up, alarmed. "Who?"

"Chloe DeVore."

"Are you kidding? Nick, don't joke about something like that."

I shook my head. "It's true. Detective Valley was there, with a bunch of campus cops, and he questioned me, and—"

"You're serious. Are you okay?"

"This conference is a disaster."

I recounted everything that had happened from the reception onwards, including all the odd reactions to Chloe's entrance after her argument with Vivianne, and ending with the bizarre keynote speeches. It all seemed so sinister now, the prelude to ineluctable death.

"And I can't believe I had to be around Valley. He's so creepy. I don't think I noticed it before, but he looks like an alien."

Stefan frowned. "What are you talking about?"

"It's his eyes. I mean, his skin is milky white, even with the freckles, and that makes his eyes just look too dark, like they're not really eyes but something dead or inhuman. Don't tell me you haven't noticed."

"You have to stop watching *The X-Files.*"

"You think I'm being silly."

"Nick, you're beyond silly. There's no word to describe what you are."

I smiled. There was something oddly comforting in his assessment. But the smile didn't last, because Stefan asked me to explain how I knew so much about what Valley asked Vivianne and everyone else.

"I sat in on the questioning."

"Isn't that unusual?"

It suddenly struck me that he was right. "Valley said he wanted me there because I was cochair of the conference. No, that wasn't it—it was because of the bibliography, and my knowing all about Wharton scholarship."

"Nick. Priscilla hasn't written about Wharton. Neither has Serena, or the Gillians . . ."

"I'm a moron! He wanted to keep his eyes on me." I moaned. "I bet he thinks *I* did it! Why didn't I see that! Of course he suspects me!"

Stefan shook his head, either at my having been fooled or at my wild speculations. "I suppose you could ask him," he suggested mildly. "Ask him what he was up to." Then, almost to himself, he added, "Valley probably wouldn't tell you."

"I'm such a shmuck! I was like a little kid riding on a fire engine! I was flattered and excited that I got to watch him do his Perry Mason thing, but it was just a setup."

"Maybe," Stefan pointed out. "Maybe not." He went off to the dining room to pour us both some Mandarin Napoleon, which we'd brought back from our last trip to Paris. Mixed with tonic water, the tangy orange-flavored liqueur perked us both up, and we sat side-by-side, considering Chloe's death long into the night.

"What was the argument about?" Stefan asked, frowning. "Between Chloe and Vivianne?"

I reminded him that the brawl was in French, which I couldn't follow at high speed or at high volume. This was a sore point for me, since I had grown up hearing French but had resisted speaking it. Stefan, with his perfect accent in French, consistently charmed my parents, and while the three of them made their elegant twists and turns on the conversational dance floor, I was the perpetual wallflower.

"But why would anyone want to kill Chloe?" I asked. "What's she got to do with the rivalry between the two Wharton societies?"

"You think that's what's going on?"

"Stefan, they hate each other, they're on the same campus together, and someone's dead. Of *course* that has to be what's going on."

Stefan shook his head. "Academics are cowards, for the most part."

"And cowards have never killed anyone?"

"If Chloe was murdered," Stefan said firmly, "Vivianne did it. She must have been the one to decide they'd come to the conference. What other reason would there be? They don't write about Wharton, you said so yourself."

"So she brought Chloe to SUM to kill her, and then what?"

"She's planning to blame Priscilla, because all that mess with Priscilla, Chloe, and Vivianne is bound to leak out."

I disagreed. "That's much too tortured an explanation. Vivianne's no dummy. She could have figured out a way to kill Chloe in France, couldn't she? And besides, I told you, it was almost like Vivianne was *protecting* Priscilla! I was there—I heard it."

"Why would Vivianne be concerned about Priscilla? That doesn't make any sense."

He had a good point.

Stefan asked me who *I* suspected.

I didn't like saying it, but this was Stefan I was talking to, so I didn't hold back. "I think Priscilla probably did it. Look at how freaked out she was when the body was discovered. And you know how much she's felt that Chloe's this kind of curse she can't shake. I can't even count all the times that Priscilla's complained about how famous Chloe was, and how she didn't deserve it. I just wonder—"

"What?"

"Well, what am I going to do when Valley starts probing deeper into how Priscilla felt about Chloe, and why? What do I do if he really pushes me?"

"You'll tell the truth," Stefan warned.


I WOKE BEFORE the alarm, and before Stefan. I took my coffee out onto the sunroom, which is a very hopefully named room since Michiganapolis is the second cloudiest city in the country. It's got something to do with where we're situated in relation to Lake Michigan and Lake Huron, I think. But whatever the case, flying into the Michiganapolis airport, you invariably descend through thickening layers of clouds. This morning was typical, though it looked as if the sun might possibly burn through enough to make the day just *partly* cloudy.

Stretching along the back of the house, the large, long sunroom had become my favorite place at home. When we moved in, it was just a ratty screen porch, but with a beautiful floor of gray slate tiles. We had the porch enclosed, painted, and replaced the screens with large picture windows and two sliding doors, connecting the room to the heat and the central air-conditioning so we could use it comfortably year-round. Now it was hung with baskets of grape ivy and dotted with ferns on English-style plant stands. The couch, chairs, and glass-topped tables were solid and comfortable wicker, and the colors of the area rug, blinds, and cushions here were the same blue and gold as in the adjoining living room.

What I most enjoyed was the view of our large backyard with its lovely garden bisected by brick walks leading to and from the little gazebo, and the herb garden edged with miniature roses. I can't take credit for the garden—that was planted and designed by the previous owners, and a wonderful bonus when we bought the house. It was too cool yet this morning to open the sliding doors and let in the spring air, but even with them closed, I could hear the peaceful cooing of the mourning doves.

The first time my parents had seen the house, they'd been impressed by its size, but found the whole prized faculty neighborhood north of campus too quiet. "So many trees," my mother had whispered to my father, clearly longing to be back in New York, where trees apparently knew their place and kept themselves more inconspicuous.

Stefan and I had driven my parents around Michiganapolis, pointing out the gold-domed capitol and anything else that could pass for a landmark, unsuccessfully trying to get them to appreciate our unpretentious but beautiful little college town with its attractive homes on clean and pleasant streets.

I didn't win any points either by trying to demonstrate that Michiganapolis was in its own way as easy to figure out as Manhattan's grid. Michigan Avenue ran east from the capitol into the suburbs, with the university spreading south of it and faculty, professionals, and students living north. West, north, and south of the capitol and what passed for downtown were factories, middle- and working-class neighborhoods, with strip malls lining the major north-south roads and the gigantic Capital City Mall sitting athwart Michiganapolis's western border like a brooding medieval fortress. The Michigan River ran roughly south of

Michigan Avenue, parallel to it, and from the air, it all seemed well laid out.

My parents kept saying yes and nodding at our tour guide comments, but it was as if we were speaking a language they didn't know and they were merely being agreeable. Their distance was even greater when we drove them across SUM's verdant huge campus. We hit them with what I thought were impressive statistics: the campus's nearly six thousand acres were traversed by fifty miles of road and 150 miles of walkway.

But they just listened to that. From the turreted sandstone buildings dating back to the 1850s to the enormous fields of experimental crops stretching from the campus's southern edge back into SUM's entirely agricultural past, none of it registered with my parents. Their polite murmurs seemed almost a way of keeping themselves from saying, "Surely there's more?"

My parents clearly considered my life and my home in Michiganapolis pretty but dull, just as they thought my teaching career wasn't very stimulating to even think about. When I told my mother years ago that I wanted to teach composition, she crinkled her nose. "Why teach the masses to write better? What will they write after college? Shopping lists? Birthday cards?"

Becoming a bibliographer hadn't added any luster to my image for them. They clearly considered doing a bibliography as little more than intellectual accounting. I know both of them would have preferred me to have branched into something flashier. How on earth was a bibliographer going to ignite any sparks, or be amusing?

I did have in my favor the fact that Edith Wharton had lived in France and had three homes there, and so was a suitably sophisticated writer to work on, but that was counterbalanced by the bibliography itself. I'll never forget the way my mother leafed through its earnest dull pages bristling with numbers and cross-references, thoughtfully stroking the brown library binding. "No photographs," she observed.

"It's not a biography," I said.

She nodded. "No, of course not."

My mother had helped me with the French accents and some difficult translations, but she didn't seem at all pleased when I pointed out her name on the acknowledgments page. She held the book out as if she were a diva wanly fingering a lover's bouquet that had faded before she'd had a chance to enjoy it.

My father was the director and part-owner of a very old, very fine, small New York publishing house and so I suppose my mother took for granted the gorgeously designed and produced art books that graced his catalogue. In comparison, my bibliography looked like some improving text printed by missionaries. I don't even think that hearing that their boring son was hosting a conference which had started with a suspicious death would make much of a difference in how they thought of me. When I'd recounted the chaos I'd been involved in on campus the previous year, my father had said a bit disdainfully, "It sounds like that idiotic TV program, *Rescue Seven-eleven.*"

"That's '*Rescue Nine-one-one,*'" my mother corrected, amused.

"Why are you smiling?" Stefan asked now from the doorway.

"How long have you been standing there?"

"A minute or two."

I smiled even more broadly, enjoying the warmth in his eyes. I often found him looking at me, drinking me in. Stefan's gaze had a touch of rueful surprise, as if he couldn't believe he had risked ruining our relationship. It was gratifying to feel admired and wanted again, but sometimes his appreciation had the opposite effect, reminding me of how much he had hurt me. Luckily that wasn't the case this morning.

Stefan was wearing the black silk robe I'd bought him for his birthday, and he looked very tousled and sexy. I told him I'd made some coffee, and he nodded. "I'll get some after I shower."

He came to sit by me.

"You don't need a shower—you smell fine," I said. And he did. His natural odor was fresh and vernal, like grass cuttings. He crossed his bare legs at the ankle, his high-arched feet as beautiful as an angel's in a Renaissance fresco.

"Couldn't sleep?" Stefan asked sympathetically.

"I can't remember anything specific from my dreams, but they were epic. Crammed with people and full of disaster. Kind of a mix of *War and Peace* and *Towering Inferno.*"

Stefan smiled gently.

"No symbols to analyze," I said. "It was all right there in front of me."

Stefan nodded. "Remember what your cousin Sharon said once? That the things you dread never happen—it's always something different, and most of the time, it's something worse."

"I wish she were here." Sharon's practically my sister, and always supportive in a crisis. I couldn't even call her now, since she was traveling up the Yangtze River on a two-week holiday. "She's so sensible."

"And I'm not?"

I met Stefan's eyes, and he looked away, embarrassed at the unspoken reference to his crazy behavior last year. For years I'd thought of him as stable and calm, and so when I suddenly learned that he was attracted to an ex-lover, and had helped that ex get a job at SUM, I was betrayed not just by him but by my own faith in his steadiness. After it was all over, I'd shouted, "It doesn't matter how old you and Perry were. You were just like some fucking paunchy fifty-year-old straight guy chasing after a bimbo because he's getting old. Well, you can lust after anyone you want to, but you're still gonna die."

And then I got *really* nasty.

I broke the silence now. "This is unbelievable. I was worried about the conference turning into the Montagues and the Capulets, and what happens? Someone ends up dead without any pitched battles—"

"Nick, Chloe was murdered," Stefan said quietly. "I heard on the radio a few minutes ago that they're saying it was definitely murder." He brought that out tentatively, and then added, "Chloe DeVore," as if somehow I could have forgotten who had died last night. "They said something about blunt force and head wounds."

From the moment I'd seen her body and the bloody granite tile nearby, I'd been sure that it was no accident. Despite myself, I had imagined someone bringing the granite tile down on her head. Once, twice. It wasn't a very heavy tile, but it was stone, and deadly.

THAT FRIDAY MORNING, I returned to the Campus Center feeling as apprehensive as a substitute high school teacher facing a class full of malcontents, bullies, and thugs.

What the hell was I supposed to do? Was I supposed to cancel the conference? I couldn't do that by myself, could I? I'd have to talk to Serena, and more importantly, to Coral Greathouse. What *were* you supposed to do when a conferee was murdered? I felt dizzy at the blizzard of complications that would engulf me and Serena if the conference was canceled: the Campus Center hotel reservations, trying to change flights, arranging for registration refunds.

And there would be a storm front of complaints moving in.

I wasn't up to all that, and I wondered if even Serena had the skills to handle such a profound mess.

When I got to the private paneled dining room reserved for all our conference meals, I was surprised by the pleasant buzz of conversation that carried out into the hallway.

It was actually more than pleasant. I could see that when I stepped inside. There was a strangely festive air at the ten round tables draped with generic-looking white tablecloths. Young, pimply student waiters and waitresses weaved among the tables with standard white coffee carafes, murmuring, "Decaf or regular?" About half of the conferees were here, and everyone seemed to be reading the *Michiganapolis Tribune* with its vile headline, LESBIAN KILLED AT SUM.

Serena saw me and waved me over as familiarly as if we were old friends breakfasting on her terrace. She was alone, swathed in purple.

"It's amazing," she whispered as I sat down, nodding in all directions to be polite. "Look at them!"

I did. Instead of casting a pall on the conference, Chloe's death had jazzed everyone up.

"They love the bad news," Serena said.

A waiter set orange juice in front of me and pointed out the breakfast buffet table at one end of the room.

"But what should we do?" I asked. "How can we keep the conference going now?"

"You mean should we pull the plug? Not a chance! Not unless Coral or someone higher up says so. We soldier on. This is going to be a real success. Can't you feel it? I do."

I studied the tables and understood Serena's assessment: there was some tentative mixing of the two Wharton groups, as if last night's face-off at the reception hadn't happened, as if Chloe's death was a reason to build bridges.

Going over to the buffet table to help myself to some fragrant waffles, I wondered if the buoyant mood in the room wasn't simply due to people realizing how lucky they were to be alive. But as more and more conferees entered for breakfast, the energy built. They were like a tour group in Hawaii unexpectedly getting to see an active volcano from a safe distance—and at no extra charge. Serena was right. The murder was spicing up their weekend.

"These waffles are terrific," I said, amazed at how hungry I was.

Serena nodded graciously as if she'd made them herself. "Buckwheat," she said. Then I remembered that she had tried all the food in advance and assured me it would be more than acceptable.

I devoured the waffles and went back for more. While I worked on my second stack, Serena showed me the SUM student newspaper. Someone in that coven of funky illiterates had managed to throw together a short article on Chloe's death, spelling both her names wrong. But I was appalled to read that our president, Webb Littleterry, had issued a statement condemning "the climate of violence at SUM."

I started to choke and Serena slapped my back.

"This is ridiculous! Why the hell is he blaming gays and lesbians for Chloe's death? You know that's what he's trying to do, connect this to the protest at the Board of Trustees meeting. This sucks! It's Joanne Gillian's work, because she was doing the same damn thing when she talked to Valley."

"Of course," Serena said calmly. "Littleterry doesn't have a brain in his head. He has no idea how to run a school. But what can you expect? Look at his lousy playbook when he was coach. We were just lucky Ohio State and Michigan were weak that year, with all those players sidelined by injuries. Otherwise we'd never have gone to the Rose Bowl—not that we won." Serena went on to rave about Littleterry's weaknesses as a coach.

This was a side of Serena I'd never seen: the football fanatic. I'm sure she had season tickets, wore the school colors to each game, and screamed abuse as much as encouragement at our team. SUM had devoted—and, some say, demented—fans. They kept coming back for punishment year after year, since SUM's football team was notorious for starting a season well and then losing it on the road, or at a crucial home game. I knew enough about our team to know why people groaned whenever SUM's Tribunes got inside the ten-yard line: they always blew it. And you could almost always expect the Tribunes not to convert an interception into points—not even a field goal.

I tuned out, but ignoring Serena, I picked up on what was passing between Grace-Dawn Vaughan and Devon Davenport, who had sat down at the table right behind me.

They were whispering about Chloe. Vaughan was saying, "She was just stringing you along, Dee-dee."

Dee-dee! What a bizarrely cute nickname for that dragon.

Curious, I moved my chair back a little, but they must have caught me trying to eavesdrop, because Vaughan abruptly changed the subject.

Serena wound up her football jeremiad with a shake of her head and I nodded vigorously in support. Go, team, go.

"At least that bitch isn't here," Serena said, looking around. "Joanne Gillian," she added, reading my confusion.

Serena was right. Neither Joanne nor Bob Gillian was there today.

"Maybe they're superstitious," I said. And in a hushed movie preview voice, I went on, "Maybe they think that Death is stalking the conference."

"That would be lovely," Serena said.

I looked around some more. Verity Gallup at her table, and Van Deegan Jones at his, both seemed strangely subdued, even though their table mates were engaged in animated discussion. I couldn't help cynically wondering if they each thought that Chloe's death was taking attention away from their societies and their agendas. But maybe there was something more going on?

Why had they both been so angry about Chloe's presence at the conference? I wondered if their argument about Grace-Dawn Vaughn wasn't an attempt to divert Valley's attention, and even mine.

I was almost done with my third cup of coffee when silence spread across the room and I had that eerie sense that people were staring at someone—maybe me. I turned and saw Detective Valley heading right for my table, quiet, implacable. I felt like a swimmer in *Jaws*.

Serena patted my hand as if she expected I was about to face some ordeal. She was right. Valley asked me to step outside.

I rose and followed him, smiling benignly at each table I passed. Some conferees looked away as if embarrassed; others appeared to be eagerly awaiting my arrest. Obviously there were hard feelings after last night's offensive keynoters.

Out in the hallway, Valley drew a small Penguin paperback from his jacket pocket. It looked like a brand-new copy of Edith Wharton's novel *The House of Mirth.*

"We found this at the crime scene." Then he corrected himself. "Murder scene. Next to the body."

"How did it happen?"

Valley looked away, clearly unwilling to tell me any more than he wanted to.

"But I didn't see that book there."

Valley glared at me as if I were Johnnie Cochran and he was Mark Fuhrman.

"Sorry. I wasn't suggesting that you—"

Valley cut me off. "Whatever."

I reached for the book, then stopped. "Is it okay for me to touch this?"

If he had been a student, he would have said *"Duh."* But since he was a detective, he explained with some annoyance that of course the book had already been checked for fingerprints, and yes, I could touch it. I looked it over.

"What did you find?" He didn't answer, so I asked, "Was this Chloe's?"

"We don't know. Her name's not in it."

"If it wasn't hers, then—"

Now he shrugged. "It could have been the murderer's, or someone else's. Maybe Mrs. Gillian. She did find the body. Maybe she dropped it."

"Oh, I don't think Joanne Gillian reads Wharton. Hell, I don't think she reads anything much—remember, her husband said she's dyslexic. Even if that's not true, this isn't her kind of book." I turned the shiny paperback over and over in my hands as if it were the key to some door.

"It could have been planted," Valley said, eyeing me carefully for my response.

"Planted? Like some kind of deliberate clue? Jesus, that's what serial killers do to taunt the police!"

He shushed me and drew me further from the dining room door. People passing in the wide hallway glanced at us curiously.

"That could be what's going on here."

How could Detective Valley talk so calmly about the possibility of a maniac at the conference? I lowered my voice but couldn't keep the panic out of it. "You mean there's some kind of Edith Wharton Zodiac Killer loose at this conference? That's crazy. There's only one person dead."

"So far," he said ominously. "Yesterday was only the first day of the conference."

I made my way to a nearby seating area and sank into a high-backed deep chair, sorry that I had ever read a single Patricia Cornwell novel. Valley sat down opposite me, leaning forward, drilling me with his eyes as if commanding me not to freak out. I think I was very close to it.

"Can you explain how this book might be significant?"

I buried my face in my hands. "How am I supposed to know?"

"You're the expert."

Well, that got through, since I prided myself on having read more about Wharton than anyone in the galaxy. I put my hands down, sat up straighter, crossed my legs, breathed in deeply a few times. "Okay. *The House of Mirth,* it's set in turn-of-the-century New York, and it's about a society woman who's really beautiful, but even though she doesn't have any money of her own and she's growing older and needs to get married to be financially secure, she keeps screwing up her chances to nab eligible men." I took a breath.

"She probably loves somebody who's poor like she is, huh?"

I laughed. "How'd you figure that out?"

Valley shrugged. "Sounds like the kind of book my wife reads—those Silhouette things. She's always telling me the plots, and they all sound the same."

"This one doesn't have a happy ending."

"No?"

"Not at all. Lily Bart—that's the woman—keeps moving down the social ladder, falling, really, until—"

"Until she's a hooker?"

"Jesus, no! This was published in 1905. She commits suicide."

Valley frowned. "Suicide? Chloe DeVore didn't commit suicide."

"Right."

"How's she do it in the book?"

"Chloral. It's something people used to mix with water to help themselves sleep. She takes an overdose—and actually, it might be accidental."

"Chloral," Valley repeated. "Chloral."

"Is it a revenge killing? Was the murderer saying that Chloe was responsible for someone's suicide? That's too weird."

Valley scratched an ear.

"Wait!" I said. "I know this is bizarre, but listen: Chloe—chloral. It sort of sounds the same. Maybe it's some kind of pun."

Swayed by my eagerness, Valley stared at me as if waiting for the solution to the puzzle, but I admitted I didn't have one. If the killer had been making a sick pun, its deeper significance was too subtle for me to get.

After a moment, Valley said he needed a registration list from me so that the Campus Police could start fingerprinting all the conferees to compare them.

Then there *were* fingerprints on the book, I thought, keeping that to myself.

I had a copy of the final registration list in my jacket pocket and handed it over. Just then, Priscilla Davidoff arrived for the morning session of panels, looking dazed. Valley slipped off and I waved to Priscilla to join me.

"Let me get some coffee first," she said glumly, and in a few minutes she was back, slumped over where Valley had been sitting. She was a wreck.

"Nick, Nick, I swear to you that I did not kill Chloe DeVore."

I studied her face. I didn't know Priscilla well enough to be able to tell if she was lying or not. All I could see was the probable ravages of a sleepless night. Even under her makeup, it was clear that she was pale, and that her eyes were red and bleary.

"But I do feel guilty." She hung her head. "Incredibly guilty."

"What are you talking about?"

"Don't you see what's happened here? It's all my hatred for Chloe! It's crystallized. I spent years hating her, and it's backfired on me."

She looked so woeful and distressed that I was torn between trying to ease her out of her guilt, and suspicion that she was attempting to snow me.

"You have no idea what I've done," she said. "It's terrible. There are times I've been in bookstores and when I saw her books face out, I turned them so that only the spine was visible. And that's not all. I've slipped her books behind others on a shelf so no one could see them unless they were looking for them."

"That's not so bad," I said, unsure if I believed what I was saying.

"Once," she said, breathing in as if to fuel the fire of confession, "once, right after Chloe got a rave review in the *New York Times Book Review,* I bought a copy of her book, tore the title page out, ripped it up, and flushed it down the toilet. I was trying to curse her, and her book."

Just then, Vivianne Fresnel sauntered past into the dining room, dressed in a stylish black pants suit. She nodded good morning to me, but she didn't see Priscilla, who was hidden by the high-backed chair.

Priscilla saw Vivianne. "She's the one who did it!" Priscilla moaned. "But it's still my fault."

"Listen," I said. "Vivianne covered for you last night when she was being questioned. I don't know why—or what she suspects, but she wasn't out to get you."

Priscilla finished her coffee without looking at me.

"And why would she kill Chloe? They were back together. Their book's a best-seller. Why now?"

"It doesn't have to make sense to you. And I'm sure you misinterpreted what was going on. She's French, remember? It's easy to misread people if you don't know their culture."

"Bullshit," I said. "She was saving your ass."

"I don't believe that." Priscilla set her mug on the floor.

"Okay, maybe I'm wrong. Maybe I did misunderstand what she was saying, though it's unlikely since my parents are Belgian. But why didn't Vivianne say anything about you? About your letting her know where to find Chloe after they broke up? About staging a public brawl, practically, because you knew Vivianne and Chloe had argued about that stupid Byzantine Empire book and if they were in the same room it would happen again in stereo."

Priscilla flinched and I was sure I'd gotten that piece right. Bringing them together at my party hadn't been a scientific exercise in mixing incompatible elements to see how they interacted. No, she must have had inside information through her network of Chloe DeVore spies that the two women had argued about plagiarism.

I pushed. "Explain that to me, okay? Why would she keep it all to herself?"

In a faint voice, Priscilla said, "Because she's going to torpedo me when she can get the most out of it. She's biding her time, Nick. She's French, she's a Latin—she'll get revenge, but only when she's ready."

Priscilla seemed on the point of tears.

Suddenly I remembered something that Chloe had said to Priscilla at the reception, something that had stunned her.

"Last night you looked miserable when Chloe attacked you. What did she mean when she said your 'plan' wasn't original, that it was right out of one of your books?"

With a pained smile, Priscilla said, "I don't know what you're talking about." She got up and strode off to the women's room down the hall.

Why didn't I believe her?

BEFORE THE MORNING sessions got under way, two Campus Policemen armed with copies of the registration list arrived at the dining room to announce that they were there to take fingerprints. Some conferees objected, but others were delighted and practically waved their hands like eager-beaver students hoping to get called with the right answer on their lips.

After that was accomplished, I sat in for part of each session and all three that morning went very well. The comments and questions were surprisingly polite and uncontentious, given that the audience was heterogeneous. I mean, in each room there were members of the Wharton Association and the Wharton Collective, though Serena and I had segregated the panels themselves as best we could to avoid conflict. It was as if everyone was trying to be on their best behavior after the murder. But then I knew from my own department that academics were skilled at being nice to someone, and shafting him without hesitation when they got the chance.

One session was called "Is Wharton Dead?" and the aim there was to deconstruct Wharton criticism itself. At least that's what I think was the aim, because surely we all knew that Wharton was indeed dead.

I wanted to smile when I listened to the paper given by Gustaf

Carmichael. He ignored Wharton entirely to discuss an unknown Swiss woman novelist, Greta Inderbitzen, who was Wharton's contemporary and might even have met her in Paris. Around the small room I could sense how baffled and jealous the audience was. Carmichael was doing the ultimate act of academic one-upmanship by championing a writer no one had heard of or read.

He could make whatever claims for Inderbitzen's novels (all thirty-eight of them!) he wanted and no one could challenge him. It wasn't any more sophisticated, really, than a little kid sticking his tongue out and mocking his peers with a singsong "Nanny, nanny poo-poo!"

He was such a weasel in his leather pants and Vatican City T-shirt.

But I suppose his paper could have been much worse. After all, that well-known and unreadable academic writer Eve Kosofsky Sedgwick had practically said that one of Henry James's novels was really about fisting, so ever since I'd read that nonsense, I'd been expecting someone to claim that *The Age of Innocence* was about piercing. Or tattoos.

I found myself idly wishing that Joanne Gillian *were* attending this morning. I would have delighted in her frustration, because I was sure that she wouldn't understand a word of the critical jargon being slung around, especially in the more recondite papers, while she would assume it was probably pornography—or satanism.

I slipped off at one point to get myself another cup of coffee, hearing Stefan's voice in my head as I poured, telling me I'd had enough that morning. I drank it anyway, enjoying every sip. And it brought me some clarity. I headed down the hall to the small bank of phone booths and slipped into one to call the county Medical Examiner, Dr. Margaret Case.

I couldn't get past her brisk, cheerful secretary, so I left a message, and the secretary's very careful repetition of my name convinced me I wouldn't get a return call soon. After reading about Chloe and the conference in today's *Tribune,* where my name was mentioned as conference coordinator, I bet Dr. Case had warned her secretary to put me off if I called.

I checked my watch. It wasn't quite 11:15, and lunch started at noon after half an hour of free time for the conferees. It'd be okay for me to skip out, and I decided to see if I could find out which one of Priscilla's mystery novels Chloe had been making fun of last night, and why.

But it was more than just mockery, I thought: something in one of Priscilla's books was connected to her involvement with Vivianne and Chloe. Otherwise, why would Priscilla have looked so upset when Chloe brought it up, and then, when I asked, pretended that she didn't follow what I was saying?

It was a relief to get outside the Campus Center, to get away from SUM even though I only crossed Michigan Avenue. I was hitting "The Mile," as students called it. Nothing magnificent like the one in Chicago, just a stretch of mostly student-oriented stores and restaurants running for almost twenty blocks across the northern edge of SUM's mammoth campus. It was a commercial wall behind which the faculty and student residential area swelled northward.

A second, more substantial and upscale business area clustered around the state capitol to the west, along with a handful of small office towers. Malls and minimalls sailed on seas of concrete to our east and south amid the suburbs that eventually gave way to rural towns and farmland.

I strolled down The Mile a few blocks. Actually, I wasn't as far away as I might have liked. The antique-looking lampposts down the main street are SUM crimson and gray, and the ornamental brickwork on every street corner spells out the school's initials. Some days it strikes me as charming boosterism. Today wasn't one of them.

But at least the sun was making an effort to come out.

The mile has a proliferating set of T-shirt and sweatshirt shops, all teeming with SUM-related articles in the school colors, but it has the only locally owned bookstore in town (in addition to the small-scale Border's). And that's where I was headed.

Priscilla had told me once that Ferguson's, which sold new and used books, had copies of all her mysteries because the owner was a fan; but that was balanced by her lament that Border's almost never had more than one of her titles in stock.

Ferguson's was a showy, large, theatrical-looking store with thick carpeting and looming dark bookcases. The owner had gone for an antiquarian feel (though he didn't do much business in rare or first editions), so there were miles of antique prints adorning the flocked wallpaper, and the store bristled with busts, bronzes, statuettes, decrepit musical instruments, old advertising posters. It was just this side of parody—

like one of those train stations that's been turned into a restaurant and the decorator corralled every moose head he could find.

Ferguson's was empty today except for Cal, who was reading *Details* behind the counter.

"My mom says she hasn't seen you at the gym lately," Cal said.

"Nobody has, hardly. I've been swamped. How'd you do last night? Make any money for the store?"

Cal shook his head. "Not much. They sure liked to browse. How's Stefan?"

"Glad he didn't go to the reception. They can be deadly."

From Cal's expression, I could tell he was dismayed by my choice of words. Obviously, he hadn't intended to mention Chloe's death, and my gaffe didn't seem to change his mind. He just smiled, gently letting me off the hook.

I plunged into the depths of Ferguson's. The mystery section there was reasonably large and well stocked, but badly lit, and in a far corner. I suppose that was intentional, to set a creepy mood.

I found five of Priscilla's books there right between Amanda Cross and Peter Dickinson, looking faded. Was that all of them? I hadn't kept track of her writing, so I plucked the lot from their shelf, sat down on a stool, and scanned the "Also By" pages in each one. Yes, it seemed I had all of her mysteries there.

What had Chloe said? Something about Priscilla plotting against her, and being unoriginal. Was that all? No, there was something more. Something about death.

I looked at each title, and the last one hit me: *Dancing with Death.* Chloe had said something like "dabbling with death" last night, and I'd had no idea what she meant. Maybe it was a mistake for this title— unless it was a deliberate insult.

But could it be that obvious? I skimmed the plot description on the back, and started to feel flushed. Shaken, I put the other books away.

"Doing research?" a voice asked from behind me, and I jumped up, but held on to the paperback.

It was Detective Valley.

"Are you following me?" I said, knowing that if I were a stutterer, I'd be trapped in my own shuddering syllables right now. I kept the book down at my side, cover facing in so he couldn't see Priscilla's name on it.

"Should I be following you? What are you up to?"

I mumbled something about needing a break from the conference.

"And you come here?" Valley shook his head, glancing around as if he'd found an alcoholic at a bar. "I guess you can't escape books in your business."

"That's true." I headed for the counter near the door. Then I stopped and turned. "What are *you* doing here?"

Valley smiled but didn't respond, like a therapist making sure the focus stayed on his client. He followed me to the counter, and waited for me to make my purchase. I kept the book cover down on the counter, and luckily Cal had good eyes, because he didn't bring it up to read the price tag stuck to the back. Valley would have seen the cover that way.

When I left, Valley nodded good-bye, and once outside, I saw him lean on the counter and talk to Cal. Was he asking about me?

Lunchtime traffic—cars and pedestrians—was pretty bad, so I had plenty of time to think about what had brought Valley to Ferguson's as I made my way back to the Campus Center.

Crossing evergreen-lined Michigan Avenue, I decided that Valley must be checking on who had bought copies of Wharton's *The House of Mirth* at the reception. Maybe that's all it would take to discover the murderer—that, and fingerprints. Maybe they'd catch the murderer today, even this afternoon, and the rest of the conference could go on without trouble.

But what if the murderer was Priscilla? The idea made me sick. It's not that I cared for her deeply; we were only beginning to be friends. But she seemed too normal. Surely she was just a frustrated author, not a killer.

Then I remembered Stefan in one of his darkest moods this winter during the envy months suddenly launching into a quiet tirade one night in front of the fire. We'd been listening to Shura Cherkassky play Chopin polonaises. I was reading a hypnotically plangent novel of Anita Brookner's; Stefan was just brooding.

"Why," he said, "why is it always postal workers who go crazy and shoot a crowd of people? What's so bad about their lives? What do they have to complain about? I keep waiting for a writer to go berserk. I can see him barging into a publishing house, one that hasn't published Salman Rushdie so the security isn't very good, nobody stops him, and he blasts his editor right through the wall, machine-guns the entire publicity department, firebombs marketing, and then takes out the publisher himself. Like a movie with drug lords or terrorists seizing a building. And they drop hostages out a window, one by one . . ."

Stefan had a rapt look on his face that scared me. He could have been a channel into the collective unconscious of all abused writers. He went on.

"Remember that Stephen King movie, *Misery?* King got it all wrong. No fan's going to kidnap a writer and break his legs. It should have been a writer kidnapping an editor, or a reviewer. Now that's a movie to love. That's a movie to *own.*"

All that from a writer who was fairly successful compared to Priscilla.

Back at the Campus Center, I shuddered thinking about how hatred could lurk in the most unexpected places. And I wondered where I could hide out to go through Priscilla's book. I didn't see any conferees loitering in the hallway outside the dining room, so I ducked into the nearest men's room, and chose a stall at the end when I saw there was no one around.

Damn. The light wasn't very good in there. It was much brighter over by the sinks, but I couldn't examine her mystery out in the open. Before I could even sit down on the closed toilet seat, I heard laughter and familiar voices, and something about Edith Wharton.

I recognized both voices. It was Gustaf Carmichael and Crane Taylor, which was proof that the two Wharton groups were mixing, since they were such completely different people. Carmichael pretentiously pseudohip, Taylor arrogant and old-fashioned.

They were at the sinks washing their hands, from the sound of it. I was hoping to hear some praise or approval of the conference arrangements, and dreading even mild criticism.

What I did hear shocked me.

Gustaf Carmichael joked, "Most conferences don't include murder as entertainment."

He was disgusting.

But Crane was worse. He said, "I'm glad Chloe DeVore's dead."

Gustaf Carmichael chuckled. "You, too?" They both laughed heartily, as if at a private joke, and I heard the door close.

How the hell did they know Chloe DeVore—and why had they disliked her enough to enjoy her death? What had she ever done to *them?*

# 7

I SAT THERE in the toilet stall for a moment or two. It was as if Crane Taylor's and Gustaf Carmichael's mocking voices were echoing around me. I'd been wrong to think they were so different, since they both hated Chloe DeVore. But why?

Startled and confused, I slid Priscilla's unread book into my jacket pocket, but I almost felt as if my hand were moving on its own. What the hell was going on at this conference?

I checked my watch and hurriedly unbolted the stall door, yanked it open, and stepped outside. The door hit the partition wall and swung back into place with a thunk. The cool, clean rest room was empty except for the sounds drifting in from the hallway and the whisper of water shifting in tanks and pipes. Remodeling had added recessed lighting, marble tiles near the sinks, and the kind of improbable, annoying chartreuse and violet color scheme you find in doctors' offices.

I had to get to the dining room for lunch, and there wasn't time to waste. Serena had warned me over and over that the worst part of a conference was the inevitable creeping lateness that would start in the morning and then gradually overwhelm each day, slopping over to the next, causing crankiness and fatigue. She made it sound fairly dire, and did not smile when I'd quipped, "So that's why the Roman Empire collapsed! Tardiness. I should have known."

As official conference chair, I had to set a good example by being as prompt as possible. She had impressed upon me the image of myself as a dike holding back the sea of chaos. It was not an image (or a word!) I found very appropriate. And maybe it was too late for order to be restored at this conference. I didn't see how we were going to end up with harmony, peace, and merriment like at the end of a Shakespearean comedy.

Outside the men's room, in the now-crowded hallway, I was flagged down by Angie Sandoval.

"Professor Hoffman. Wait!"

There was something so refreshingly normal about Angie, I found myself beaming hello and giving her my full attention. I didn't care now if I was late. It wasn't just her youth, it was the kind of youth she represented: eager, enthusiastic, helpful. She wasn't sullen or cynical, and I could talk to her easily, unlike lots of her peers at SUM, because her face wasn't marred by ugly and painful-looking piercings in her tongue, her eyebrows, her lips. With those students, I kept forcing myself not to stare or squirm—or ask why they didn't go whole hog and put plates in their lips like that African tribe I'd seen on the Discovery channel.

So I welcomed Angie's interruption as a dose of normality at that moment.

"Guess what? I've registered for the conference!"

That's when I noticed she was wearing a plastic Wharton badge. "What? Why?"

She lowered her voice and moved a step closer while the crowd eddied around us.

"I'm going to observe everyone. And take notes! I got my Criminal Justice professors to let me out of my classes for the day so I can do real-life crime work after I told them I was assisting you in the investigation."

Great—I hoped Valley wouldn't hear about this.

"Isn't that cool?"

I smiled and said that yes, it was cool. And then I lowered *my* voice. "Are you serious about snooping around?"

Angie cocked her head as if she was about to do a dumb blond imitation complete with "Fer sure," but she just said, "Totally."

"Okay. Then can you keep an eye on Priscilla Davidoff? She's tall, dark hair—"

"The one who looks like Geena Davis?"

"Yes, that's her. If I do it, it'll be too obvious."

"Right! I can be inconspicuous, I'm just a student. Hey, is she a suspect?"

I mumbled something vague about Priscilla being "possibly involved."

I felt awful about setting someone to spy on Priscilla, especially since Valley had told me to stay out of the investigation. But he hadn't said anything about encouraging anyone else, had he?

"Wow! This is like an independent study!"

I warned Angie to be careful. "Listen, we're dealing with a real murder. It's not a game show."

"Oh, totally," Angie agreed. And she set off for the dining room, as intrepid as Sherlock Holmes and Dr. Watson rolled into one.

I followed at a discreet distance, suddenly reminded of all the high school students who toured the campus in the spring on their college visits, led around by snappy, hectoring guides who made fun of the University of Michigan down in Ann Arbor at every opportunity. Those kids on tour not only looked painfully shy and overwhelmed, since many of them came from Michigan towns smaller than SUM, they also looked amazingly fresh and unspoiled. That was because you'd see them standing next to their often haggard-looking parents, and you'd know how ruined and fallen those unlined faces and vigorous bodies would be a mere two decades later.

Inside the crowded dining room, I saw Vivianne heading for a table, and I hurried up to her.

"Can I talk to you?"

She turned and spoke as graciously as a medieval lady granting her suitor a boon. "Of course. Shall we find seats?"

"It won't take long."

"Ah, bon." She nodded, and stepped out of the way of some conferees, guiding me over to a window that looked out on a very wooded part of campus. It seemed a lovely spot for a tête-à-tête, but I had only one thing I wanted to know.

"Why were you so reticent about Priscilla when the detective questioned you yesterday?"

Vivianne shrugged as if the answer was obvious. "Why make more trouble?" And her broad, gentle smile seemed to ask if I was done.

"I don't understand."

She sighed. "Priscilla is a very troubled woman. Her life displeases her." Vivianne shrugged again. "Does she need another burden?"

"So you think she—?"

Vivianne reached over to put two fingers against my lips. "It doesn't matter what I think." She slipped off to find a seat.

I saw Angie Sandoval taking a seat at a table where Priscilla sat with her arms crossed, looking very glum. Serena waved me over, pointing dramatically at the empty seat next to her as if she were waving a semaphore flag. Joining Serena, I was even more convinced now that Vivianne could not have killed Chloe. Wouldn't a real killer want to cast suspicion on someone else?

I nodded and smiled at everyone seated at my table. Another sign of progress at the conference: the table was equally divided between the Wharton Association and the Wharton Collective. There were three "suits" and three pseudopunks, the pinstripes balanced by the earrings (on men). Gustaf Carmichael and Crane Taylor were unfortunately not among them. I would have liked studying those two to see what they betrayed about Chloe when other people were around.

As I said hello and exchanged a few words of greeting with each scholar, I mentally recalled their varied contributions to the field. That was easy, since everyone wore a conference name tag and Serena had insisted that we make the print on them very large. "I hate people breathing all over my breasts while they try to read the damned things."

This was a fairly undistinguished group whose work was derivative—the kind of people who like to talk about Wharton's social satire (that was the suits), or dress up banal observations about her fiction in modish critical jargon (the punks).

I'll never forget reading a vaporous, baffling essay by one of the guys at the table, Pete Levinsky, about *The House of Mirth* and midpoint practically howling, "I got it! He's saying Wharton's heroines are in conflict with their male-dominated society! Amazing!"

That was the kind of outburst Stefan had to put up with for five years as I worked on the Wharton bibliography, wading through file cards and fits. The explosion would usually be followed by an overly detailed explanation of what I was reading, then a philippic of one form or another. No wonder he was sick of everything Wharton.

Sitting there at lunch, I sensed what I often did when I was with a group of Wharton scholars. They were recalling the brief paragraphs in my bibliography in which I'd described their articles or books, and if

I'd been sparing and overly judicious, they probably wondered what I really thought. Or they were pissed off that I hadn't—as when I judged work to be truly significant—used any adjectives like "major," "unique," "important," since each of them thought they'd written the definitive work about Wharton.

Right now, everyone rushed to praise the conference, and I tried to seem grateful. The awkwardness passed as real conversations broke out and people started on the salads that had been waiting for us. They were small but attractive, with what tasted like a lime vinaigrette.

Serena whispered, "They weren't bullshitting you. Everything's going very well. I've been catching pieces of what people say, and it's all positive."

I nodded, unable to feel happy.

While one waiter took away our salad plates, another set down our cream of broccoli soup, which was peppery and delicious. I ate it with surprising gusto while around me the discussion whirled from one paper topic that morning to another. There was some delicate sparring, but it didn't seem any more serious than the early stages of conflict at a family reunion.

As the lunchtime din rose around me, sealing me off, all I could think of was Chloe's murder. With so many people milling around last night, but apparently not one witness, how could the killer be found? And what if Valley had been right, and Joanne Gillian was the intended target? Wouldn't the killer try again?

I glanced around me, wondering who would want to kill Joanne. I saw her glowering a few tables off at something her husband was saying. Jeez—why not Bob Gillian? Why couldn't he have wanted to kill Joanne? She was certainly hateful enough in public—maybe she was even more of a monster at home. Maybe when he married her, she hadn't been a narrow-minded harridan, and he was actually appalled at the woman she'd become. Perhaps he'd seized his one chance to break free.

But wait, wouldn't he have known what his own wife looked like, even in a darkened hallway? Admittedly, the corridor had been quite dark, and he might have been rushed, but still—

This was crazy.

Serena said, "What? What's crazy?"

Everyone at the table was staring at me. I blushed, realizing I must have spoken aloud. I had to calm myself down.

"I mean, like the beatniks used to say it. You know: Crazy, man."

If I weren't the Wharton bibliographer and so essential to Wharton studies, I don't think the scholars sitting at that table would have smiled and nodded.

But they kept looking at me, and as if to shoo them off, Serena addressed the table at large. "Have any of you noticed that Wharton's lover was always photographed sitting down with his legs crossed, or behind a desk?"

There were blank and puzzled looks around the table, and then they were replaced with recognition. Serena was right. I had never seen a picture of dapper, mustachioed Morton Fullerton—the lover Wharton took in her forties—standing up.

"Why do you think that is?" Serena asked, a strange glint in her eyes. She seemed to know the answer, and she let the silence draw itself out.

A few puzzled scholars bit and said, "Why?"

"He was so enormously hung it would have been embarrassing. It may even have been a Parisian *law.*" She pronounced it "low," like Peter Sellers as Inspector Clouseau, but I don't think anyone sitting with us got the reference or could tell she was being salacious just to cause trouble. I was the only one who laughed.

But Serena wasn't done. "I've been thinking of doing an essay," she announced. "About the way that Fullerton's sexuality affected Wharton after their affair. I'm calling it 'The Penis as Protagonist in Wharton's Later Fiction.' "

What was this? Wharton stand-up?

Serena laughed gaily. "Just kidding," she said, but one or two scholars at the table seemed to be considering the possibilities of the subject.

"Pleased?" Serena asked me, as everyone turned to other topics.

I shook my head. I'd drifted off to thinking about Chloe's murder again. "About what?"

"The chicken." She pointed.

I looked down at my plate. I had been eating chicken breast stuffed with spinach and fontina and only at that moment did I realize it was very good. It was as if my taste buds had gone completely off-line while I mused about Joanne and Chloe.

I took another forkful, but before I even got it to my mouth, I was struck by a question that Valley hadn't really asked anyone last night. What was Chloe doing in that dark corridor? If Joanne Gillian often got confused because of her dyslexia, that was one thing, but Chloe would have known where she was going, wouldn't she? Even if she was lost, which was easy to do in the Campus Center, that corridor was dark and there was a heap of tiles at one end. Why would anyone think that was the right way to go?

Someone must have lured her there—but how? With a note? A phone call?

When the coffee came, Serena leaned closer and said, "I love this, you know."

"What?" I turned to her.

"Oh, being an éminence grise. Nobody really knows what I'm doing here, or that I've been as involved as you are in the conference."

"More," I said.

Serena waved that off. "And when they ask what my area is and I say Canadian Studies, it throws them. I like confusing my peers—they're so used to thinking they know everything."

"Have you been reading about Wharton?" She must have, to be familiar with photographs of Morton Fullerton.

"A biography or two, and I looked through your book, as well." Her tone made my bibliography sound arduous and punishing. I couldn't blame her. Bibliographies are pretty scary if that's not the kind of work you do or enjoy. "Say, Nick. Remember *Laugh-In*?" she asked. "Remember the joke wall, and Goldie Hawn? Well, since Edith Wharton was so bossy, if she had married Morton Fullerton, would he have been Morton Wharton?"

Despite myself, I chuckled. It might have been an idiotic joke, but I was in need of some laughs, even cheap ones. And Serena seemed to sense that.

"Maybe we should have scheduled a talent show for tonight," I said. "First prize to the best Wharton look-alike."

Serena pursed her lips. "Too tame. What about a prize for juggling the most numbers of flaming copies of *The Age of Innocence?*"

Before I could answer, she tapped my wrist, pointing at my watch, and I realized it was time to get going with the lunchtime speaker, Van

Deegan Jones. I've always hated listening to people at the end of a conference meal; I'd rather just digest in quiet. I wonder if it's really respectful anyway for people to be chewing and slurping while someone tries to weave an argument or build a theory. But now that I'd been on the other side as an organizer, I understood the pressure to cram in as much as you can in a few days.

I headed for the oak lectern that had been set up near the window where I'd talked to Vivianne. I didn't embarrass myself or anyone in the room by tapping the lectern or making any kind of teacherlike announcement. I just started right in on my introduction.

And it worked. Everyone shut up, turned or yanked around their chairs. It was easy to introduce Van Deegan Jones since he was a pillar of Wharton studies. I even called him that. He nodded gravely from his seat, acknowledging the justice of my praise, looking very professorial in his dark blue suit, blue shirt with white collar and cuffs, and sober red and blue print tie. Applause was hearty, though louder from his cohorts than from Verity Gallup's minions.

Jones sauntered up from his table with suitable gravitas as I thanked him and headed back to my seat.

"Don't you mean pill, not pillar?" Serena asked out of the side of her mouth like a scrappy gun moll.

"Ladies and gentlemen," Jones said magisterially, waving a small sheaf of paper that was evidently his talk. "We've experienced a tragedy here. A terrible tragedy, even though to most of us the victim was a stranger. Be that as it may, in all good conscience, I think this conference should be disbanded. I ask you, how else can we show respect for the dead?" He surveyed the audience as if daring someone to prove their rudeness and disagree. "I'm sure this is what Mrs. Wharton would have wanted."

There was a confused silence as people registered the implications of what Jones was saying, and then came a general outcry.

Verity Gallup roared from her seat at a table near the door: "Patriarchal bullshit! How the hell would someone like you know what Wharton would think—unless it's because you're *both* dead!" She leapt to her feet, looking, with her blond hair and leather jacket, like a funky Amazon. "How dare you talk about what Edith Wharton would want? You've never cared about that when it comes to her fiction! All you want to do is subvert her voice. You're not suggesting we leave because of the murder. It's because you're desperate to flee the unmistakable evidence of your intellectual sterility. Now that you're face-to-face with *really* original scholarship, you want to bolt."

Looking like he was ready to throttle Gallup, Van Deegan Jones shouted back, "You're a fraud, an imposter, a charlatan. You jumped on the Wharton bandwagon because she was trendy. And ever since, you've been covering up your lack of knowledge about Wharton with abstruse critical language. You're the last person in the world to talk about original scholarship! You have nothing to say so you hide behind Derrida and Lacan. Derrida is caca, and Lacan is a con!"

I was stunned by this mean-spirited display, even while the bibliographer in me noted some inaccuracies. Actually, Verity Gallup's book had used the boring theorist Bakhtin, not Derrida or Lucan, to mask the triviality of her analysis of Wharton's short stories. But it was unfair to say that she had come to Wharton late; she'd been writing on Wharton for years. I was the bibliographer. I knew.

"You want to cover up everything negative about Wharton!" Verity Gallup yelled at Jones. "You want her to be a fucking saint!"

"You're bottom feeders! You thrive on garbage—innuendo—rumor—gossip—fantasy! That's not literary criticism, that's literary terrorism!"

So now the hostility between the two groups was completely out in the open, and the bloody line drawn deep in the sand of the bull ring. Around me, people looked either stunned or excited, and I half expected a circle to form around Jones and Gallup, with chants of "Fight! Fight!"

At her table, Joanne Gillian sat there with eyes aglow, eagerly taking in the melee like a pyromaniac enjoying someone else's fire. Bob Gillian looked perplexed, but then he wasn't a Wharton scholar, so he probably didn't know what the argument was about. I thought he was despicable, coming here with Joanne to help her gather evidence of SUM's moral collapse.

I'm not sure what possessed me, but I felt fired by some strange elation. Before Gallup or Jones could say another word, or call on their supporters for help, I rose from my seat and shouted, "Wharton studies are alive!"

I don't think it's an exaggeration to say that all eyes were on me at that moment. "They're vital! They're exciting! They go to the heart of the academy, challenging us all—"

Well, you get the picture. I was an academic version of a preacher, except my gospel was more mealy-mouthed, I guess. I wasn't challenging people to change their ways, I was piling on the flattery and bombast, improbably claiming that the intensity in the room was a sign of intellectual vigor.

No one gagged. In fact, they applauded.

I know Stefan would have been appalled by my outrageousness—at least at first—but he wasn't there to pull me back into my seat, so I went over the top. Like President Clinton with Yasir Arafat and Yitzhak Rabin, I held out my arms, waving both Jones and Gallup over to my table.

Reluctantly, they were drawn to my display of fellowship, and they shook hands. The crowd was ecstatic. They gave us a standing ovation. Some even cheered, which made me think they were definitely lacking for real drama in their lives.

Priscilla, however, did not rise. I could see her sitting with her head bent and hands clasped on the table as if in silent prayer.

Verity Gallup and Van Deegan Jones muttered what might have been thank-yous to me, and broke away, heading for their acolytes. As people filed out to the afternoon sessions somewhat early, I sank into my chair. I was grateful that Serena was the only person still at my table.

From over by the door, I heard someone say rather loudly, "I came all the way from San Diego to give my paper and I'll give it even if there's a car bombing!"

Serena Fisch grinned at me. "Can we arrange that?" She shook her head. "What dedication."

"Him? Me?"

"You. I couldn't have managed that Elmer Gantry jazz. I guess every conference needs some kind of holy roller." And then while I grabbed my napkin to wipe my sweaty face, she changed subjects without warning. "Do you think Jones did it? Killed Chloe? Why else would he want to decamp? Look how he made Chloe sound like someone who wandered in off the street. And haven't you noticed how odd he's seemed since Chloe's body was found?"

I reached for my water goblet and drank greedily from it, though I'd have enjoyed pouring it over my head to cool off. I set it down and pulled open my tie and unbuttoned the top of my shirt. If Jones had killed Chloe, what was the connection with the Wharton societies?

"Serena, what are you talking about?"

"It's simple. Chloe has such an evil reputation for blighting people's careers, right? Then it's possible she might have done something once that earned her Jones's hatred."

But what about Verity Gallup? I wondered.

"Are you speaking from experience?" I asked her. "Did something happen between you and Chloe? What you told Detective Valley last night didn't sound like the whole story to me."

Serena grimaced. "That's because it wasn't." She patted at her hair as if she'd just come off a ferry ride. "Years ago, when the Rhetoric Department was axed and I lost my chairmanship, I went job hunting, but quietly."

"Last year you told me you didn't want to leave Michigan back then."

Serena rolled her eyes. "I was *dying* to get out. I was mortified to go from being in charge to being one of the crowd. It's not easy for me to talk about it. The job search was a disaster. Only one interview, at Emory," she said bitterly. "That was a success, but Chloe was writer-in-residence there that year and threw her weight. I know for a fact from someone on the hiring committee that Chloe blackballed me. It was my best chance to get out of Michigan, to leave behind the cold, and to forget having my department ripped out from under me."

"And Chloe ruined it."

"Yes. Chloe ruined it."

"Why?"

Serena frowned. "Does it matter? She didn't like me, or my work, or my nail polish. Maybe she just wanted to veto some candidates to show off. People like Chloe don't need a reason to inflict cruelty on others, to shaft them. She's like Tom and Daisy Buchanan, breaking people and things, but she doesn't retreat into her money, she scuttles back into her ego." After a second or two she said, "Scuttled."

"But are you sure Chloe was the one who spoiled your chance?"

"Sure enough. And whoever killed her should get a medal," Serena hissed.

I was shocked by the hatred in her face and voice, and Serena hurried off as if she felt the same. So that's why she hadn't come to our reception for Chloe . . .

I was alone in the littered dining room, except for the waiters cleaning up, so I gathered myself together, picked up a nearby program, and headed outside.

I didn't get far.

"You're Dr. Hoffman?"

The question came from a slim, pasty-faced young woman in a brick-red suit. Her blond hair was a squashed beehive, and she looked like one of the B-52s gone to seed. I didn't recognize her, and felt at a sharp disadvantage.

"I'm Brenda Bolinski, with the *Michiganapolis Tribune*. Hi." We shook hands. "I'd love to interview you about the conference."

"And the murder?"

She simpered. "I'm sure that would come up."

I sighed and she must have taken that for assent, because she flipped open a notepad and started right in, without even suggesting we go have a cup of coffee or sit down. "Now, who exactly is this Edith Wharton and who else besides Chloe DeVore was going to be in the movie?"

"The movie. What movie?"

"The movie about Edith Wharton. Isn't there a movie being made here?" Puzzled, she glanced down at her notepad, leafed through a few pages.

I couldn't imagine where she'd gotten the misinformation, unless she was confused about the film we were showing that evening, but it didn't matter. I was about to make up something about Denzel Washington and Demi Moore, when the reporter whirled around, her face suddenly ablaze. She pointed wildly down the hall at Grace-Dawn Vaughan, sheathed in a green and red scarf dress. Vaughan was headed for the ladies' room.

"I know her! She's famous! I saw her on *Oprah!*" Grace-Dawn disappeared into the ladies' room and Brenda Bolinski abandoned me for bigger game.

I was relieved to be left alone. For one wild moment I thought of jumping in my car, picking up Stefan, and driving north to our cabin, but just as I was picturing the glories of Lake Michigan, Serena came bustling down the hall.

"Nick, I was looking for you. There's a local news crew here and they want to do an interview for tonight's six o'clock show. Joanne Gillian's been calling the media and claiming that what's happened at the conference is a sign of SUM's—" Serena closed her eyes in an effort to remember the exact phrase. They flashed open. "A sign of 'rampant immorality and decay.' Can you believe it?"

I couldn't answer, and Serena asked if I was okay, and wasn't I planning to come to any of the afternoon sessions.

Her question decided me. I grabbed one of her hands. "Please," I said, "please take over for me for the rest of the afternoon. I have to go home and relax a little or I will explode."

Wide-eyed, Serena nodded her assent, and withdrew her hand, which I must have been squeezing too tightly.

"Sure," she said. "No problem. I'll do the interview, okay?"

"Anything."

I turned and walked to the Campus Center garage, amazed that I was actually going to escape this hothouse environment of murder, newshounds, and scholarship.


WHEN I GOT home, I almost burst into tears. Stefan had filled several vases with clematis and set them around the house; I felt I was entering a sanctuary. Well, wasn't I?

"You're early," he said with delight, giving me a big long hug.

"I escaped. If Tommy Lee Jones lands a chopper in the backyard, tell him you didn't see me."

Still holding on, Stefan squeezed his arms together and cracked my back, the tension flying out of it at light speed.

"You're strong."

Stefan gave a Tarzan grunt and led me into the kitchen, slipping my jacket off for me and draping it over the back of one of the low-backed kitchen stools.

"This has been a shitty day. I need a vacation. I need detox. I need Mace!"

"How about this?" Stefan opened the fridge and brought out a platter. "Behold," he said proudly, setting it at the center of the table. He'd made one of my favorite appetizers, crabmeat mousse, and decorated it with sprigs of fresh dill. Then he whisked something else out of the fridge: a bottle of the Kendall Jackson Reserve chardonnay we'd been enjoying more and more.

I was too overwhelmed to say thanks, but my face must have shown my gratitude.

Stefan smiled warmly. "With all those Whartonites, I figured you'd probably be a basket case by the time you got back."

"You think Whartonites are bad? We've got Wharton wannabees. Profs who haven't really written about Wharton except to include her in books or articles about other writers. They're cashing in, getting a free trip."

"To glamorous Michiganapolis," Stefan said wryly.

"Listen. You and I both know that there are towns and universities in this country that make Michiganapolis and SUM seem like Paris and the Sorbonne."

He nodded gravely. We'd both interviewed for jobs at such places, schools that had new libraries but hardly any books, or grim campuses that looked like a truck stop—without the ambience.

"Wait till I tell you what happened today. I mean, it's not like there's been an arrest, or another murder, but still—"

Stefan shushed me, poured the wine and served us each a slice of the mousse, and then led me out onto the sunroom, where the conference, and the world, seemed very far away.

Feeling protected and loved, I told Stefan all about the breakfast and Valley snagging me and mentioning the possibility of a serial killer; about the copy of Wharton's *The House of Mirth* found at the murder scene; about Priscilla blaming herself but seeming evasive when I talked to her; about Serena's confession; about how I thought Valley had followed me to Ferguson's.

"Jeez, Priscilla's book! I still haven't looked at it." I was about to race into the kitchen for the paperback in my jacket, but Stefan ordered me to stay put and finish filling him in. I did. And when it was all done, he looked almost as exhausted as I felt.

"All that happened in one day?"

"Not even one day—a morning and just part of the afternoon. This isn't a conference," I said. "It's a marathon."

"And Verity Gallup and Van Deegan Jones really yelled at each other at lunch? You're not being dramatic?"

"Stefan, even the Dalai Lama couldn't describe what happened today and make it sound peaceful." I felt battered and dazed. "Was there any mail for me? Did I get any faxes or phone calls?"

"Forget about all that. You need a nap," Stefan said, looking ready to admonish me if I argued.

I simply nodded, finished the glass of crisp wine and my slice of creamy mousse, and headed upstairs for our bedroom. Being taken care of felt wonderful, and I was glad that Stefan could put aside his hard feelings about the conference and my Wharton mania.

As I slipped off my shoes and climbed onto the bed, I was too tired to even pull back the quilt. Falling asleep, I imagined fleeing the conference and Michiganapolis with Stefan, driving north to Boyne City, and having dinner at its historic Wolverine-Dilworth Inn, a beautiful relic of the town's roistering lumber days. Hanging from the lobby's beamed ceiling were big brass chandeliers lighting up an unusual white tile floor spotted with tile flowers in orange, gray, yellow, black, and green. We'd have a drink inside first, since it'd be too cool to sit out on the porch, and then a simple dinner in the dark dining room: cherry-wine-soaked chicken breast with Michigan cherries. It was only four or so hours away . . .

I WOKE UP feeling released, as if a fever had burned off. My head was clear, my body felt lighter, and if I didn't burst into song and gambol down the stairs, I certainly wasn't feeling like the walking dead anymore.

Stefan had brewed a pot of Sumatra, and I thought, well, being addicted does have its advantages, like the rush I felt that very moment as the heavenly strong aroma grabbed me like a forklift.

"You're in a good mood," I noted, as Stefan poured me a mug of coffee and stirred in the warmed milk.

He shrugged. "That's because the *New Yorker* came and it didn't bug me that I'll probably never be in there again."

"But you were, once, and how can you take that rag seriously anyway? It's so overrated. The Williams-Sonoma catalogue is much more fun, and the writing's better any day."

He grinned and shook his head. "I love you."

"Of course you do. I'm pretty lovable." And then my mood shifted instantly as I remembered what I had to do. "I think I should read

Priscilla's novel now," I said, sipping from my mug and reveling in the jolt. "I'll take it out to the sunroom."

"How about some music?"

"Sure. You pick."

He chose a Liszt piano concerto, which was appropriate, given the drama of what I discovered in Priscilla's *Dancing with Death.*

I didn't read it so much as skim to follow the plot. What I found was devastating. As I had feared or guessed, there was a situation in this mystery alarmingly close to the real-life one of Chloe, Vivianne, and Priscilla winding up at my party. The plot revolved around a triangle of three women in which one arranges for the other two to meet publicly when they're very hostile. They argue and one of the two is murdered by the other that same night. The dead woman is wildly unpopular, so there are lots of suspects. Well, that wasn't quite the case here.

None of the women were writers, two were dancers with small companies, one a choreographer. But that didn't really matter because the general resemblance was clear.

Stefan emerged onto the sunroom after an hour had passed, with the strains of something quieter behind him. The Trout Quintet?

"So what do you think?" he asked.

"This is terrible." I explained why. "If Valley finds out about the book, he'll be convinced that Priscilla killed Chloe, unconsciously imitating her own mystery."

"It's too obvious. I still think Vivianne set it up to look that way."

"But shouldn't I tell Valley about the book? If I don't, doesn't that mean I'm withholding evidence?"

"If he's been talking to people about the reception, Valley may already know."

The idea of Valley working behind the scenes—though nothing out of the ordinary—chilled me.

"Let's shower," Stefan said. "For Shabbat."

While I was asleep, Stefan had set the dining room table for Shabbat dinner, and it was time to start getting ready to enter that peaceful place. Late each Friday afternoon, we showered together to wash the week's trouble away, and to relax. Then we set the table with a lace tablecloth my mother had brought from Belgium and our good dishes, while the stereo played soothing Jewish songs or chants.

We lit the candles, said kiddush (the blessing over the wine), washed our hands, and blessed the challah as slowly and mindfully as possible, trying at each stage to leave the world further behind us, to draw closer to one another.

Once he had seen that observing Shabbat even minimally wasn't a burden, but like going off on a retreat every week and emerging refreshed, Stefan had embraced it wholeheartedly.

Tonight, though, I found it difficult to unwind because I knew we weren't staying home after dinner, but returning to the Campus Center, and eating another dinner—with a murderer.

I made the best of it, tried to drink the kiddush wine slowly, to let the sweetness spread through my body and sway my mind. Stefan had made something light since we'd be eating again soon, and the pasta primavera with grilled salmon was just right. I was lolling in my chair after we'd said a short version of the postmeal prayers, thinking how lucky I was, when the phone rang.

"Should I just let whoever it is leave a message?" I wanted Stefan to decide, but he shook his head and told me I should do what I wanted to.

The mood seemed broken and I headed into my study, where I heard the clipped tones of Webb Littleterry's secretary saying, "I have the president on the line, Dr. Hoffman."

I snatched up the phone and said I was there.

And of course, I got the ritual, "Hold for President Littleterry, please."

I marveled at the president's secretary being in on a Friday afternoon after five. Stefan had wandered into the room and I told him it was Littleterry calling.

He slumped a bit, and I waved him to a chair.

Checking my desk clock, I counted a full minute of waiting, and then Littleterry's gruff, nasal voice exploded in my ear: "What the hell's going on with that conference of yours!"

"Excuse me?"

"That's how you show this university cares about women? You kill one?"

"I didn't kill anyone, sir."

"It sounds like criminal negligence to me. But don't quote me!"

"The Campus Police are investigating—"

"Fuck your excuses! You're making this university look like Bosnia! We're overexposed!"

Seething, I asked Littleterry what I was supposed to do about it.

"You should apologize! It's your fucking conference and your fault!" The president slammed down his phone before I could think of anything to say. It was a rare moment, and Stefan watched me cope with my own speechlessness.

Finally, I found my voice. "Littleterry wants me to apologize. Because Chloe's dead."

"Apologize? To whom?"

I shrugged. "The Board of Trustees? The alumni? Who the hell knows?"

"But what for?"

"This is bad PR for SUM. It won't look good in an annual report."

Stefan sighed. "That man is a menace. He's like what Winston Churchill said about Clement Atlee: 'Every time he speaks, he subtracts from the sum total of human knowledge.' "

I nodded, unable to savor the quotation. "We should probably clean up and change for tonight."

"Fine."

I followed Stefan back out to the dining room, feeling certain that I would never get tenure at SUM now that the head of the Board of Trustees thought I was a pervert and the president thought I was responsible for a death that was tarnishing the university's image.

# Part Three

"*. . . each evening had brought its new problem
and its renewed distress . . .*"

—EDITH WHARTON, *The Reef*

# 8

DRIVING TO THE Campus Center with Stefan, I felt a growing sense of despair. If I didn't get tenure, I could go up for it a second time, but that wasn't usually how things played out. Being denied tenure was as much a warning as the grade of B was to a graduate student. Or more to the point, bloody footsteps in a haunted house: Get Out.

But I was sure as shit not going to stay in Michiganapolis without a teaching position at SUM. I couldn't imagine the ordeal of looking for another job and hoping that Stefan would be able to land something at a school within commuting distance (since our finding jobs at the same university again was unlikely).

As we drove into the Campus Center's banal concrete parking structure and began circling up its ramps in the hunt for a space, Stefan seemed to have picked up on my thoughts. He said, "We might be able to make it without your salary."

"Yeah—for how long? We'd eventually have to sell the house and live in an apartment. And why would I want to stay here unemployed, anyway? For the rich cultural life? Please."

Michiganapolis might have had scenery on its side, clean air and water, a low crime rate, and friendly people, but it was culturally dead— the kind of town where deluded provincial directors offered up stale theater as if it were daring. When was the last time anyone was shocked by *Mrs. Warren's Profession?*

"And what would I do if I wasn't teaching? Become your houseboy?"

Stefan grinned. "You look good in thongs."

"Sorry—you're the one with the great feet."

Pulling into a space between two hulking Jeep Cherokees that made

Stefan's Volvo look like a VW bug, I didn't ask Stefan to confirm the obvious: he, too was worried about my chances for tenure.

Well. My academic career might be about to implode through no fault of my own, but at least I had Stefan. And when he got out of the car, I couldn't help feeling a slight lift, knowing (or at least hoping) that we would get through this new crisis together. After all, we'd managed to hang on through the terrible years he couldn't get published, so surely there was hope for *us*, if not my job.

AT THE COCKTAIL hour, or half hour, before dinner, I found myself studying Vivianne Fresnel, maybe because she reminded me a little of my mother. They shared a European confidence, though my mother wasn't quite as pretty.

As we all mingled around the set tables sporting yellow and purple Peruvian lilies, Vivianne seemed to be having a wonderful time, chatting amiably, posed with the haughty elegance of a ballerina. She was wearing a midcalf clinging black dress and high-heeled black boots.

"Mikimoto pearls," I said to Stefan, motioning to the unusual three-stranded necklace she wore. "Three thousand dollars." The strands weren't rounded at the bottom but formed a large *V.*

"How do you know?"

"I saw the identical necklace in a *New York Times* ad last week. And Jeez, look at the minaudière!"

"The what?"

"Her purse." It was a glittering little *objet* like the kind you'd see in a shop on the Rue du Faubourg St.-Honoré in Paris, pedestaled and lit like an icon, with an unbelievable price in script on a tiny, discreet tag.

Stefan wasn't thinking about Vivianne's jewels or her minaudière. "She's not very upset for someone who's lost her lover," he observed quietly. "Even if they did argue a lot."

It struck me that maybe Stefan was imagining what his life would be like without me. I felt warm, but a little on edge. Had he dreaded my walking out on him over Perry Cross, or afterwards? It was certainly possible for a while, and that had been the surprise. For weeks after the drama was over, I felt relief, but that ended abruptly the day I woke up so angry I wanted to kick Stefan right out of bed. For over a month, I called my cousin Sharon every day, sometimes twice a day, to complain about Stefan.

Each time, at some point in the torrent, Sharon had very sensibly, but very kindly, said, "Well, that's over. So what do you want to do?"

It didn't take long for me to decide that I wanted to stay, and try to heal.

"What are you thinking about?" Stefan asked now.

I didn't lie. "Last year."

He looked pained, but if he didn't feel that, he wouldn't feel anything.

Before he could comment, Serena sailed over, trailing chiffon and Chanel No. 5, which she once told me was the only perfume suitable for a woman "her age."

"Haven't seen you lately," Serena purred at Stefan. "You look appetizing." She held up her cheek to him for a kiss.

"Jeez, Serena, I forgot about the interview! How did it go? We didn't catch the news."

She grimaced. "Okay, but I got bumped. There was a big fire they covered instead. It was at a bowling alley—burned it to the ground—much more interesting. You were talking about Vivianne," she said knowingly, eyeing the two of us.

"You read lips?" I asked.

Serena went on unperturbed. "She's remarkably composed, don't you think? You can't even count her wearing black as a sign of mourning. They all wear black in Paris, even the infants."

"So why isn't she more distraught?" I wondered.

Serena had a quick answer. "Maybe she knows she's inheriting Chloe's money. Or is she the murderer and trying to act innocent?"

We all looked at each other, intrigued and a little embarrassed, I think. Here we were, making cocktail chat about a woman's death. It was obscene, wasn't it? But somehow very natural, and maybe even part of what made us human. I'm sure people stood around just like this in Nebuchadnezzar's day, taking odds on who'd poisoned the vizier.

"You were wrong," I said to Serena. "You told me all the wrong things to be prepared for. Flight delays. Lost luggage. Room reservations getting screwed up. Not enough coffee or iced water in the seminar rooms. Microphones not working. None of that's happened."

Serena considered my outburst. "Nick, Nick, Nick. If I'd somehow known there was going to be a murder last night, and an intellectual food fight at lunch, what would you have done?"

She stumped me there.

"Are you blaming me, Nick?"

I crumpled a little, and Stefan told her that President Littleterry was blaming *me*.

Serena drew herself up like an operatic heroine about to denounce her oppressor. "That's absurd. The man's just a mouthpiece for Joanne Gillian. Now *there's* a real candidate for murder . . . Say, maybe she was the intended victim. Joanne and Chloe look a bit alike, don't they? And weren't they wearing similar, rather unflattering suits last night?"

"I don't remember," I said, hoping Serena would drop the subject. But if she had put this together, perhaps other conferees had come to the same conclusion. That meant Joanne Gillian would, too, or at least she'd hear about it, and make another assault on the media.

Serena backed off by herself. "No, it couldn't have been a mistake. Chloe's even more unpopular than that wench Joanne."

Stefan and I exchanged a glance I don't think Serena caught.

It was almost seven and time to sit down for dinner, so we moved to a table. Van Deegan Jones, red-faced and looking distracted, sidled into the room just then, trying to be inconspicuous. It didn't work because he was greeted by several colleagues. What was *he* up to?

Crane Taylor was sitting opposite me, but I couldn't talk to him about Chloe because Serena and Stefan dominated dinner debating the merits of some Michael Cunningham novel. Serena thought it was moving and beautifully written, while Stefan called it pretentious pseudopoetry, and quoted many lines as evidence. The one that struck me most was something about a white bedspread teaching a woman "the patience of whiteness." Inveighing against the idiocy of that image, Stefan sounded like me on one of my high horses, and that was certainly diverting, since he's usually so serene.

It was also amusing to note that hardly anyone else at the table had even heard of Cunningham, who'd been reviewed in the *New York Times*. Wharton scholars, like most academic specialists, tend to know only their field, and even there, just a small part of it. I'm not sure that

I would read as widely as I do if not for Stefan making constant rec-ommendations of fiction and nonfiction that I couldn't ignore.

*Couldn't* ignore, because Stefan read aloud from these books before he was finished, and then left them in my study after he was done. With Post-it notes attached, explaining what was so good about each!

While Serena and Stefan did their literary point-counterpoint, I en-joyed the fish stew and mused about Priscilla. Maybe I'd assumed too quickly that she was guilty. And maybe life was more like art than I'd been willing to imagine—that is, like her mystery, I mean, with a lot of suspects. Wasn't that true here? Look at what had happened at the re-ception the previous evening. Weren't all those people as suspicious as Priscilla? I glanced around for her, wishing she were there to buttress my growing belief in her innocence.

After all, what was Devon Davenport so angry about at the recep-tion and even afterwards? And wasn't it possible that Grace-Dawn Vaughan hated Chloe more than anyone else did? Chloe had satirized her pretty devastatingly. And when Vaughan admitted that she had never gotten over it, that could just have been a canny way of diverting Valley's attention.

Davenport and Vaughan had been whispering about Chloe at lunch today, but stopped when I tried to catch what they were saying—so didn't that mean they both had something to hide? And why did Gustaf Carmichael and Crane Taylor hate Chloe, too? What were their links to her?

I noticed Devon Davenport get up from his table and go over to Vi-vianne's to say something to her. She airily waved her hand, dismissing him. What was *that* all about, I wondered.

Then, for a moment, I felt overwhelmed by my own suspiciousness. Hell, maybe everyone in the room had a reason to kill Chloe. Like *Mur-der on the Orient Express,* where they'd all done it. All except me and Stefan, of course.

I came out of my fog when I heard Chloe's name.

One woman at the table, whose conference tag said "Billy Se-faris/Cornell," asked if anyone had heard more about the investigation. In her late sixties, Billy had a shivery-sounding voice and very large eyes, and looked trim, like an avid golfer.

There were various comments from others, all of which added up to zilch. Stefan and Serena kept out of it, forking up their mocha cake, which was surprisingly tasty.

"It's so sad," this Sefaris woman went on, "when an artist dies young. All those unwritten books."

"Thank God there won't be any more," Crane Taylor said, nodding vigorously as if agreeing with some unseen commentator. "She was a lousy writer, not any better than that Cunnilingus guy you were talking about."

"Cunningham," Serena corrected modestly.

"Ham, sham, who cares. Chloe was a shitty writer and a real bitch from day one."

The silence at our table rippled outward.

"How did you know her?" I asked.

Taylor seemed to snap out of his reverie. He fixed me with his beady, contemptuous eyes and said bitterly, "None of your fucking business." He shoved his chair back and exited.

I got lots of sympathetic looks and apologies, though why people apologize for someone else's crudity, I don't know. How can it make a difference?

Stefan tapped my foot under the table, and I made a mental note to ask Angie Sandoval if she could find out anything about Taylor's connection to Chloe. Or Gustaf Carmichael's. And I had to try getting in touch with the Medical Examiner again to see if she'd tell me anything specific about the way Chloe died.

I stood up and announced that we had another half hour after dinner before our screening of Martin Scorsese's *The Age of Innocence* in the auditorium, and invited the conferees to enjoy more coffee or take a short walk south of the Campus Center to the Michigan River, which curves through SUM. There was a lovely bridge down the road, with benches, and there were also benches on either bank under enormous weeping willows. The ducks would be idling in the current and it would be very restful.

Serena rose wearily. "I think I'll go find my drug connection," she drawled, and sauntered off.

I didn't feel like going far at all, so Stefan and I took cups of coffee out into the hall and then wandered down near the entrance to the parking structure, where there was a lounge far enough away for us to have privacy. It wasn't entirely private, of course, more like a place where the architect had decided for some reason that the hallway should be double in width, so he'd done that and created a visual divider with several ugly, wide pillars.

Windows looked out onto a barren courtyard that you couldn't see at night. The designers had stuffed the lounge with boxy armchairs that were comfortable enough for university furniture, though they were a strange shade of blue that somehow looked curdled or boiled.

We were alone, and we sat in chairs side-by-side and talked about the murder. Even though people walked by—mostly students, and none of them associated with the conference—it felt as if we had achieved real isolation.

"You know," Stefan said, "I think you're right about Priscilla."

"Do you?"

"What's wrong?"

"I just feel depressed. I like her. What about Crane Taylor freaking out just now at dinner? Maybe he did it—though God knows why."

"He kills her," Stefan said carefully, "and then bitches her out in public."

"I know it's not sensible. But murder isn't sensible either."

"Nick, it's what you told me about Priscilla's book that convinced me. She wrote out the fantasy, and then she lived it. I'm not saying she planned everything exactly, but having to be around Chloe at the conference made her snap. I can see it happening."

"Good for you." I didn't know why I felt so sullen.

"Nick, you have to tell Detective Valley."

"I don't want to."

"I can't believe you'd keep it to yourself. That could be a crime."

"But he'll find out by himself," I argued. "*Somebody* must have heard Chloe mentioning Priscilla's book at the reception, even if she got the title wrong, and they're going to put it all together without me."

"Are you stalling so that Priscilla can get away?"

I glared at him, ready to call him an asshole, but the anger instantly drained out of me. He was right, dead right. I realized that unconsciously, that's exactly what I'd hoped to do. I'd keep quiet about Priscilla and not tip off Valley to what was in her book, and maybe she'd get herself away, somewhere, I don't know where.

Jeez, I wasn't any better than President Littleterry; I wanted the whole thing to just disappear.

Stefan was angry, his voice low, eyes dark. "Nick, you have to tell Detective Valley everything you know or suspect."

"Tell me what?" Valley asked, stepping out from behind one of the nearby pillars.

He looked so damned pleased with himself that I leapt to my feet and started shouting, "Quit spying on me!"

Stefan tried to grab my arm and drag me back into my seat, but I fended him off.

"You turn up everywhere I go, and don't tell me it's an accident!"

Now, I should explain about loud voices on campus, and in town. As a rule, Michiganders do not freely burst into raving abuse the way New Yorkers do, except at football games, where they can be as vicious as any old-time Big Apple cabbie. So my outrage had brought a few passersby to a complete standstill. They stared at me, at Valley, and at Stefan, trying to figure out this peculiar and noisy tableau.

Valley turned to them and said, "Police business," and they moved off without a word. He turned back, unfazed, and asked with the same intonation, "Tell me what?"

Defeated, hopeless, I sank into my chair. Valley didn't sit in a facing chair but on one of its wide arms. I guess that was so he could look down at me, which he couldn't do if we were face-to-face. Valley didn't have to drag out any confession. I told him all about Priscilla's novel and the way Chloe had mocked it at the reception. I felt Stefan's quiet approval and relief as I spoke.

Standing up, Valley said, "If Priscilla is the murderer and she's fled town, you could be charged as an accessory."

I was too miserable to care at this point. Valley nodded a warning at me, and walked off, I assume to locate Priscilla. After a few depressed moments in which neither one of us spoke, Stefan and I headed to the other side of the Campus Center for the screening.

The auditorium was full of animated discussion and even laughter. This was what I'd hoped for. I saw Priscilla looking quite haggard, sitting in the center of a row, far from the aisle, so I couldn't conveniently reach her to talk. Well, at least she hadn't left town, so there wasn't any way I'd be charged with helping her escape.

Where was Angie Sandoval? I wondered. I hadn't seen her at dinner either. I guessed that she must have gotten bored playing sleuth. Who could blame her?

My introduction was quick. All I had to do was praise Laurie Scherby, the Wharton scholar who'd studied Wharton on film. With my brain on autopilot, I made some general comments about her contributions to the field and fled back to my seat.

Scherby, from San Diego State University, was a warm, unpretentious woman full of Hollywood and Wharton anecdotes. She was very entertaining for her fifteen minutes, at least if the audience's laughter and applause were any indication. Stefan kept asking me if I was all right, and I'd just nod or say, "I'm tired."

Yes, I was dead tired. I'm not ashamed to say it.

But once *The Age of Innocence* began, for two hours I was blissfully free of my fatigue and any thoughts about Chloe DeVore, Priscilla, murder, and my own jeopardy. That lavish, stupid film was as comforting as a fat summer read that makes you feel like a hippo blissfully wallowing in a swollen river at high noon.

When it was over, and Scherby returned to the stage to lead the discussion, I saw I'd been right to pick this film. It had done exactly what I'd hoped for: brought the conference closer together, with almost everyone united in contempt and superiority.

There weren't questions, except those fake academic conference questions that are thinly disguised speeches, and everyone who stood up to talk had the same spirited distaste for Scorcese's work. There was little or no dispute about any point as the criticism rose and crested.

Van Deegan Jones derided Scorcese. "He's been seduced by surfaces. He's gotten the book all wrong and made a showy, vulgar movie out of a witty and subtle novel."

Lusty applause. Even I joined in, since Jones was right.

The casting was the next target, for being so out of synch with the book. Slight and mousy Winona Ryder wasn't remotely like the statuesque blond May Welland, whom Wharton describes as an athletic Diana. And Michelle Pfeiffer wasn't remotely lustrous, dark, or exotic enough to play Ellen Olenska.

"And don't forget boobs!" Verity Gallup bellowed. She reminded us that Ellen Olenska's low-cut dress is a scandal at the opening of the novel, but this couldn't happen in the movie with Michelle Pfeiffer since she's flat-chested. Everyone laughed, but would they have booed if a man had made the same remark? Then it occurred to me that I hadn't seen Verity at dinner, had I?

Stefan said to me, "I haven't read the book, so I can't compare them. I just thought the movie was slow."

The academic slash and burn drew itself out for another ten minutes, and then I stood up and thanked Scherby "for leading the massacre—I mean, discussion."

More laughter, and people started stretching and wandering into the aisles.

So many conferees came down the aisle to congratulate my choice of entertainment for the evening I felt overwhelmed. But academics enjoy nothing so much as a golden opportunity to feel superior, and in this case, impecunious and bedraggled professors could sail off having felt that they had bested wealth, beauty, stardom, and Hollywood itself.

Just when I was feeling relaxed and about to suggest to Stefan we go out for a drink, Valley strode down the aisle looking very stern, but it wasn't me he headed for, it was Priscilla, who froze when she saw him and looked around as if she were planning an escape. The only other way out would be up across the stage and through a fire exit, but she still wouldn't make it far.

Valley spoke to her in the thinning crowd, rounded her up, and led her down to where I was chatting with Stefan.

"I want both of you to wait until everyone's out of here."

He eyed Stefan, who got the message and said to me, "I'll be outside."

When it was just the three of us, Valley sat us down in the center of the front row. He stood leaning back against the lip of the stage, not ten feet away, as if he were a principal reprimanding two students for cutting up during assembly.

"I want you to tell me everything about your relationship with Chloe DeVore, and what happened at this guy's party"—here he pointed at me—"in February."

I couldn't look at Priscilla, since I'd given him a general idea of the confrontation between Vivianne and Chloe, and that Priscilla helped set it up. Priscilla didn't know I'd squealed on her, but I still felt low.

"I didn't have a relationship with Chloe DeVore," she said weakly.

"Bullshit. You hated her. You said it. How can you hate a stranger?"

Priscilla shrugged helplessly, clearly so strung out she could barely marshal the resources to defend herself. "Am I going to be arrested?"

Valley shook his head. "Not yet."

I asked him, "Are her fingerprints on the Wharton paperback you found by Chloe's body?"

"Are you her lawyer?"

Now it was my turn to meet his comment with silence. Reluctantly, Valley said no. "The prints don't match hers, or anyone else's at the conference, except the clerk who sold her the book, and he has an alibi. He was picked up by the store manager right after the reception and they went back to tally receipts, replace some stock, and package returns. They weren't finished until after the body was found." He was clearly disappointed.

"What paperback?" Priscilla said, and I explained that a copy of *The House of Mirth* had been found by Chloe's body.

"But I checked the credit card receipts at Ferguson's," Valley continued, stopping right there.

"And?" I asked.

Valley smiled and turned to Priscilla. "Why did you buy a brand new copy of *The House of Mirth* last night? And where is it?"

Priscilla frowned. "Why shouldn't I buy any book I want to? My only copy was torn, so I wanted a new one. What's wrong with that?" She reached into the side pocket of her enormous brown canvas shoulder bag, then started scrabbling around in the other pockets, and then the center, tossing aside keys, tissues, sunglasses.

Valley watched her intently, and my heart sank when she looked up, pale. "It's not there."

Valley nodded. "There were only two copies of *The House of Mirth* sold at the bookstore table during the reception. One was paid for with cash, and the clerk can't remember who bought it. The other was a credit card purchase. Yours, Professor Davidoff."

Priscilla hung her head briefly, then sat up straighter, suddenly looking much less beaten down. "Vivianne must have seen me buy it," she said defiantly. "And she stole it from me to leave by the body!"

I asked, "But what about the other person who bought the same book?"

Valley ignored me and told Priscilla not to leave Michiganapolis.

She protested, "I didn't do anything—why would I leave?" But after a policeman has warned you like that, how can anything you say not sound like a lie?

Priscilla sank her head and started to cry. Valley walked off, and I wondered why he'd wanted me there. To watch how I reacted, like the night before? What did he hope to find?

As soon as Valley was gone, Stefan hurried down to the front row. We both tried comforting Priscilla, but even Stefan's reassuring, warm voice and manner didn't have any effect. Sobbing now, hands over her face, she just begged us to leave her alone.

We did, and I felt horrible for suspecting her, for telling Valley about her mystery, and for having let myself be bullied into the whole damned conference to begin with. Stefan had said I was too accommodating, but cowardly was more accurate. I had never been good at standing up to authority figures, even when I was right. Behind them always loomed the slim, slight, but powerful figures of my parents, whose approval I'd never quite been able to snag (showing them my bibliography wasn't any different from bringing a poster paint scrawl back from kindergarten).

We walked out, and I started replaying for Stefan what Valley had asked Priscilla, when Angie Sandoval cornered me outside the auditorium.

"I know it's late and you must be zonked, Professor Hoffman, but I have to talk to you about our case. It's urgent." She was brimming over with excitement that left me cold.

"Unless you know without a doubt who killed Chloe DeVore, it has to wait," I said, brushing her off.

I walked away, and Stefan followed, whispering at me, "How can you be so rude to a student? You *like* her."

I didn't answer for a while, but when we got to the car, I exploded. "I'm sick of this whole business. I wish I'd never come to SUM. I wish I'd never heard of Chloe DeVore! It's not enough that I was trapped into doing the conference, and yes, I know I helped set that up because I was too much of a wuss to say no! But it's been spoiled, ruined. And Littleterry's on my back," I moaned. "And Joanne Gillian thinks I'm Satan, and Coral Greathouse is going to be next because this conference is a fiasco."

Driving away into the cool crisp night, Stefan said very calmly, "It's not a fiasco. You said everything's going well. Littleterry's a pompous idiot, and Joanne Gillian's a religious thug. If they try to stop you from getting tenure, we'll threaten an ACLU suit, and you know they'll probably back down to avoid the bad publicity."

"That's true," I muttered, not quite ready to be talked down from my ledge.

"And whatever Chloe's faults, Nick, she didn't deserve to die. That's the real tragedy, not what happens to your conference. Or even your job."

"I know. I'm sorry. I didn't mean to make it sound like her death is just an inconvenience. I guess it's easier to bitch and groan about everything else, because it hides what's really going on."

Driving through the calm, bright, tree-lined, and almost picture-perfect streets north of campus where breaking the law generally amounted to illegal parking or a frat house hosting a noisy party, the idea that our lives had been touched by murder yet again seemed preposterous.

When we got home, my answering machine read only one message. Stefan waited there while I played it.

"Nick?" It was Priscilla, voice quavering. "I didn't kill Chloe. I did not kill her. You have to believe me."

Perhaps because I'd been rude to Angie, I decided I had to return Priscilla's call. I looked up her number in my faculty directory while Stefan was off in the kitchen pouring us glasses of Perrier. There was no answer at Priscilla's, and her machine wasn't on. Maybe she hadn't been home when she called. I could picture her drunk in some bar. Hey, that's where I'd be after a threat from a policeman when I was the chief suspect in a murder.

Falling asleep that night, I felt sorry again that I'd just ignored Angie, but I was too tired to try calling her (I knew she'd be up late—all my students were). In a sudden flowering of clarity just before I drifted off, it occurred to me that Angie's enthusiasm might have been based on something real. I had asked her to check out Priscilla, hadn't I? So maybe she'd seen or heard something I needed to know.

But right now, sleep was more important.

THE NEXT MORNING, Saturday, my first thought was, "It's almost over." The conference was half done, and I would never have another burden like this again.

"How about coffee in bed?" Stefan asked.

"How about breakfast in bed? Hell, how about the weekend in bed, maybe my whole life. I'll become a wisecracking invalid and make sardonic observations about politics and my health, like Alice James."

Stefan was pulling on his black silk robe and turned from his closet.

"Alice James? Why not aim a little higher?"

"Okay. Alice Kramden? No, Alice in Chains."

"Don't show off. You've never heard a single one of their songs."

"Maybe not. But my students play them in class on their Sony Discmen—that is, when they're not getting calls on their cell phones or using their laptops to do a paper for another class."

Stefan left the room before I got started on my "O tempora, O mores!" aria. I lolled under the covers, glad that we'd had the bedroom redone over the summer. The fresh wallpaper and paint made the room seem lighter and more open.

I fell back asleep, but Stefan's gentle hand on my shoulder woke me up. He'd put a small tray on my night table with two fragrant mugs of coffee. Vanilla hazelnut—not a bad choice for a Saturday morning. Stefan sat on the edge of the bed near me, blowing on his coffee to cool it.

"Maybe I won't bother going up for tenure," I brought out. "I could just quit and hang out here. Shop, cook, read."

"Like your mother," Stefan said.

"Exactly!"

For as long as I could remember, my mother had lived what Stefan recently dubbed the Countess Tolstoy life. Even when she was taking care of me as a child, she still managed to have long lunches with her friends, take walks in Riverside Park, read important long books like *The Magic Mountain, The Brothers Karamazov, A Dance to the Music of Time, The Alexandria Quartet,* and of course *Remembrance of Things Past* (once each in French and English). She even dabbled in contemporary criticism, delighting in Foucault. "Oh, he's delicious. Just like science fiction!" she had announced with glee.

Because Stefan knew my mother's literary tastes, I said, "I won't read anything heavy, just beach trash."

"Will you have time while you're packing because we have to move to an apartment?"

With cinematic wistfulness, I batted my eyelashes and said, "A girl can dream, can't she?"

Stefan wasn't the only one to remind me of reality that morning. When we were dressed and having breakfast, the doorbell rang, and I was sure it had to be bad news.

I approached the front door as carefully as if it might come flying open under the assault of commandos.

Detective Valley stood there, looking as bilious as his green suit. He barged into the front hall. "Have you seen Priscilla Davidoff? She's wanted for questioning and can't be located."

I closed the door behind him. "You think she's here?" I asked sweetly. "Do you want to search the house? Where should we start?"

Valley cooled off a little.

Stefan asked Valley if he wanted to sit down and we all headed for the kitchen. Valley passed on coffee, tea, or even water.

"We obtained a search warrant for Priscilla Davidoff's house late last night, but no one was home. And her car wasn't there. But that's not the best part. The lady, she had hundreds of books about murder and crime and such."

"Of course she did," I said. "She was a mystery writer. It was part of her research."

"Research, huh? Is it research when there's a whole wall of her study that's covered with news clippings and magazine articles about Chloe DeVore? *And* a dartboard with DeVore's photo in the center?"

I hesitated, and looked at Stefan, who mouthed, "I told you so." I cringed at the thought of someone getting a search warrant to go through *my* study. Who knows what they'd find and what they'd think.

"You want more?" Valley said. "On her desk, the last page in her diary that she wrote on, it talks all about how crazy she felt to be around Chloe DeVore."

"But she told you she hated Chloe. That's nothing new."

"How about this?" Valley pulled a slip of paper from his shirt pocket where he'd evidently copied something down from Priscilla's diary. He read it slowly: " 'I feel like an animal with its leg caught in a trap, only I can't figure out how to chew it off to get free.' "

Stefan and I both shuddered.

"It's all there," Valley said.

I had no idea where Priscilla was, but Valley's certainty infuriated me.

"So what if she hated Chloe DeVore? So what if she was even obsessed with Chloe, and wished she was dead? That doesn't automatically make her a murderer, does it? Lots of writers hate other writers and hope they die or disappear or somehow get stopped from writing. But how often does that translate into murder?"

I looked to Stefan for confirmation, but he wouldn't meet my eyes.

Valley was not impressed by my defense. "You tell me this. How often is the jealous writer a mystery writer, and she's playing out one of her own plots?"

"You're being too literal. Only an idiot would kill someone just like they'd killed a person in their own book."

Valley smiled as if I'd just placed a bet on a losing hand. "Remember last year, when you told me that at SUM, people hate each other so much it's deadly? And I know for a fact that professors can be stupid, real stupid. So, yeah, Priscilla Davidoff killed someone and wasn't too bright about it. That's hard to believe?"

I kept at it. "What about the two Wharton societies and how much they hate each other?"

Valley shrugged. "None of that seems connected to Chloe DeVore."

I poured myself more coffee, unable to back down. I was as stubborn now as one of my overconfident students arguing for a higher grade. "Okay, then look at all the people who acted strangely at the reception when Chloe and Vivianne walked in. They could be guilty. Crane Taylor, Devon Davenport, Gustaf Carmichael, Grace-Dawn Vaughan, even Van Deegan Jones and Verity Gallup."

Valley smirked. "Maybe they just don't like lesbians."

I closed my eyes, fighting the very foolish temptation to say that Gustaf Carmichael was probably a lesbian.

"She called me last night to tell me she didn't do it. Why would she call *me* if it wasn't the truth?"

Valley dismissed that. "Maybe she thinks you have some pull. Who cares? It doesn't mean anything."

Valley asked me who Priscilla's friends were in the EAR department, but I couldn't really answer that. And I had to admit I didn't know that much about her personal life, hadn't ever been to her home or gone out to dinner with her.

"Then you're not in any position to judge if she's a killer, are you?"

Bested, I gave up.

As he left, Valley warned me (and Stefan), that if I heard from Priscilla, I had to tell her to contact him immediately—or else—and I had to call him as soon as I heard from Priscilla. "I'm heading to my office," he said.

I trailed back to the kitchen, and Stefan set his empty mug down noisily on the counter. "What the hell where you doing, grandstanding like that? Why are you suddenly defending Priscilla? It made you look like an accomplice."

I hadn't yelled at Valley, so Stefan got the blast instead. "Because I killed Chloe DeVore, okay!"

Before Stefan could shout back at me, the doorbell rang again. We looked at each other and, yes, he said the clichéd "Who could that be?"

"It's probably Joanne Gillian and she wants to do an exorcism. Are we busy?"

# 9

When I opened the front door gingerly, Angie Sandoval was there, smiling and waving at me as if she were a game show contestant greeting "the folks at home."

"Can I come in, Professor Hoffman? I know you're probably thinking, like, ohmigod!, who does she think she is? But I have to talk to you because my news can't wait, so please, please, please can I come in? It'll just take a few minutes!"

"Of course," I said, deeply mortified to have stomped on her enthusiasm last night. Jeez, was I going to turn into a bitter old man like so many of the other professors at SUM? Was that my future?

I let Angie in and started apologizing about my rudeness last night, but she shrugged it off, clearly still so excited by her news that last night didn't matter.

"No prob! It was pretty late."

I suppose that meant late for someone my age . . .

"Can I have some coffee?" Angie barreled down to the kitchen, where Stefan was already pouring her coffee, since her bright cheery voice carried quite well. He asked if she'd had breakfast, and she nodded.

"This coffee is kickin'. Thanks." Angie parked herself in the same chair Detective Valley had loomed in just a few minutes before, and the contrast almost made me laugh. He was a gargoyle, she was a teddy bear.

She dumped a small shoulder bag at her feet.

"Okay," she said as authoritatively as a judge banging his gavel. "This is all the stuff I've been checking out. I've been into SUM's periodical holdings on computer and surfing through the libraries at other schools. Like, is there a link between Chloe DeVore and other people attending the conference? Anything that would be a reason for murder?"

I looked at Stefan, who seemed just as impressed by Angie's doing what was obvious to her, but we hadn't even thought of. That was the age difference. The Internet wasn't second nature to us, though it was to a college student.

"That's great!" I said.

Angie smiled and went on. "They're literary scholars, right? So I figured maybe something to do with books or articles or something academic. And I found a shitload of stuff."

"What did you find?" Stefan asked.

Angie bounced a little in her seat. "This is so cool! I found a book review in the *New York Times* years ago." She reached down into her shoulder bag and pulled out a small fuschia ring binder with three-by-five file cards in it, and flipped open to the first one. I was tempted to ask if she'd ever considered bibliographies as a career.

"This review? Chloe DeVore totaled some novel by that Gustaf Carmichael." Angie added that it was the last reference she could find anywhere to any book of his.

"I didn't know he wrote a novel," I said. "Boy. What a nightmare that must have been to have someone as big as Chloe DeVore trash your first book—and in the *Times*. It's the kiss of death." I was imagining what that might have done to Stefan, and from the stricken look on his face, I think he was having the same dark fantasy. "So unless Carmichael wrote under a pseudonym after that, Chloe killed his career."

Angie nodded vigorously. "And then he killed her, when he got the chance."

"Maybe," Stefan said.

Angie and I exchanged an indulgent smile that said, Yeah, right! Of course he did it. Well, probably.

"It gets better." Angie flipped to another file card. "Did you know that Chloe DeVore was once married to Crane Taylor?"

"No way!"

Angie nodded. "Way."

It was Stefan's turn to smile.

"I found a reference to an essay or paper they did together and Chloe's name on it was DeVore-Taylor. Which means they were married, right?"

Stefan told Angie then that Crane Taylor had fled the reception room when he saw Chloe, so this could explain his behavior, and why he was upset about her memoir. "Either the marriage ended badly, or he's jealous of her success, or—"

"Or he's just a miserable human being," I said. "We don't know if whoever got Chloe intended to *kill* her, do we? Maybe it was an argument that got out of control."

Angie shook her head. "There wasn't any argument. No one heard any voices down the corridor. I haven't overheard anyone at the conference talking about it. But wait, there's lots more." She turned a few cards over. "Devon Davenport? He was almost Chloe's first editor."

Stefan frowned. "Almost—what does that mean?"

Angie explained. "He was working on her first book, but they had a fight about something and she refused to stay with him after that. She ended up at a different publisher, and she's the only writer he ever lost like that. She was a big success, right? So that would piss him off mega big-time, I bet."

"It sure would," I said.

"Where'd you find that out?" Stefan asked her. "I don't remember it at all." In a lower voice he added, almost to himself, "Well, it's not like I've studied her career."

Angie consulted her file cards. "I read it in *Publishers Weekly*. Something really small."

I grinned. "What a blow to that bastard's pride!"

"I've got all the photocopies and stuff if you need them as evidence or anything," Angie said, reaching for her bag. But I assured her we had enough for the moment.

"Wow," I said, thinking of the strange confluence that had brought these Chloe-haters together. All because of the move at SUM to prove it was friendly to women!

Stefan sat down at the table with us. "I have a question. We didn't know about Davenport and Chloe, but Priscilla had to. So why didn't she mention it?"

Well, I was stumped on that one, and so was Angie.

"Whatever the case," I said, "Davenport must have been trying to get Chloe back as one of his authors by buying her memoir. It looked like she said no, and humiliated him at the reception for a second time."

Stefan shook his head. "This is all interesting, but it doesn't amount to much, does it? Is any of it a reason to kill a woman?"

Fumbling at her index cards, Angie looked hurt and baffled by Stefan's skepticism.

"It's plenty," I shot back. "Hatred, jealousy, vindictiveness. Those are the reasons why Priscilla looks like a murderer, right? Plus some very circumstantial evidence? So why are Devon Davenport, Crane Taylor, and Gustaf Carmichael any less likely as murderers? And don't forget Grace-Dawn Vaughan either. Just because she was so open about hating Chloe for dumping on her in a novel didn't mean she ever forgave Chloe. Talking about it openly is a perfect cover."

Angie muttered, "Grace-Dawn Vaughan," and made some notes. Evidently she hadn't tracked down that piece of scandal.

"Did you find anything about Jones or Gallup?"

"No." Angie made more notes.

"How about Chloe's connection to Edith Wharton?" Stefan asked. "And the two societies?"

Angie seemed puzzled. "There isn't anything, I don't think."

Stefan gave me an annoying "Told you so" look.

I asked him to hand me the cordless phone from the counter by the refrigerator and pulled out my wallet for Valley's card. Stefan and Angie watched intently, as if I was doing something dramatic, and both of them drooped a little when I said, "He's out? No, no message."

I hung up, drooping myself. "We'll just have to tell him later. Listen, there's still time to make breakfast at the Campus Center. Is your car here, Angie?"

"No, it's on campus. I walked."

So WE DROVE over together, completely unprepared for the mob scene in the dining room. The noise was so loud out in the hallway I was sure that another dispute had broken out between the rival societies. Inside, the room was electric with tension. Conferees were walking around, gesticulating, waving pieces of toast to emphasize their points, guzzling coffee. Their faces were alive. Well, as alive as they'd ever get.

It was as if they were at NASA headquarters dealing with a space shuttle in trouble.

Serena spotted me and beetled over. "Priscilla Davidoff was just mentioned on SUM radio. She's dead."

Around me, I heard other people saying Priscilla's name. I fell into the nearest chair and Serena filled me in. "A student found her this morning, in her car."

Serena explained that Priscilla's car had been parked in one of the vast commuter lots at the edge of campus, and she'd apparently shot herself. The student who found her was in shock after the discovery, and currently being treated at SUM's Health Center. Serena repeated everything as if unsure I'd comprehended it all. Maybe I hadn't. Behind me, I heard Angie say "Wow" over and over. Stefan stood with his hands on my shoulders as if to steady me.

It was my fault. Priscilla had killed herself because I'd told Valley too much. I should have just kept it all to myself.

"What a story," Devon Davenport was crowing to Grace-Dawn Vaughan. " 'Jealous Lesbo Writer Kills Famous Author and Offs Herself.' It's an instant book and a fucking movie of the week. This conference is a gold mine!"

Most of the conferees were silenced by his little harangue. But Grace-Dawn Vaughan slapped his face. "Beast! Two women have died and all you can think about is publicity!"

There was scattered applause in the room for her rebuke, but even in my dazed state, I could see that a scattering of the conferees looked guilty, as if they'd been planning to write about the conference themselves. Hoping to cash in on true-crime publishing bucks, I guess. To do him justice, Davenport looked abashed by his author's denunciation, and he simmered right down.

Serena told me she had a call to make, and Stefan, Angie, and I sat together, huddled in chairs at the edge of the room like refugees.

"I don't believe it," I said more than once, and Stefan just nodded and agreed.

Van Deegan Jones and Verity Gallup were talking quietly in a corner and I thought with relief that this news would probably convince her that the conference had to be canceled, no matter how inconvenient that might be. Good. There was nothing I wanted more than to get out of town. It wouldn't be so bad, would it? After all, we just had today and Sunday morning left. So it was only half a conference—wasn't that better than none at all?

Jones and Gallup got up and walked over.

"I'm very sorry for the terrible trouble you've had," Van Deegan Jones began. Verity Gallup nodded at his side. "It's not at all what one expects at this kind of meeting."

He made Chloe's and Priscilla's deaths sound like a lapse of manners at a garden party.

"It's awful," Verity said. "The conference has been very well run so far."

"Yes," Jones added. "And quite enjoyable."

I waited for their announcement that they wanted to end the conference despite how well Serena and I had managed things, but they were clearly waiting for a response from *me*, and when I said "Thanks," they just nodded.

This had to be some kind of bizarre joke. Jones and Gallup were so relaxed around each other you'd never have believed they'd been shrill and enraged at lunch yesterday. Was it simply that death had brought these enemies together? Or were they in cahoots?

"Nick," Jones said genially, "why don't you and your companions have your breakfast with us?" We all trooped over to their table. Everyone else had settled down by now and was back to the main business of gorging themselves, and gossip.

I introduced Stefan to Jones and Gallup as SUM's writer-in-residence, but both of them knew who he was (Stefan grinned his pleasure). I told them that Angie was a former student and Criminal Justice major.

Languidly, buttering a roll, Jones asked Angie, "What do you think about the two murders?" Jones could have been trying to get a dog to do a trick, and I saw Verity bristle at his attitude. "I say two, because suicide is murder, in a way. Murdering oneself, that is." He chuckled indulgently at Angie.

Angie either didn't pick up on his air of superiority or she ignored it. Matter-of-factly, she said, "It sure sounds like Priscilla killed Chloe and then killed herself, probably because she was afraid of being arrested. Women over forty do tend to hang themselves, but overall, guns *are* the primary weapon in suicide."

Jones nodded.

"One thing's kind of weird, though," Angie continued, her eyes off to one side as if she were picturing the scene. "Why did she kill herself on campus, even all the way down there on the south end? Why not at home? Or someplace more secluded?"

Yes, I thought, why not?

"Are you suggesting that someone else murdered both women, or that there might even be two separate murderers?" Van Deegan Jones spoke so sharply that many conferees at other tables stopped talking.

Angie didn't back down. "It depends—"

She didn't get to finish what she was going to say, because Detective Valley walked into the dining room and stood where we all could see him. Instant attention.

He spoke. "I assume you've all heard by now that Professor Priscilla Davidoff is dead. I'm asking that no one leave the conference ahead of schedule, because the investigation of her death, and Chloe DeVore's, is ongoing."

"You're not trapping me in this dump!" Devon Davenport swore.

Grace-Dawn Vaughan shushed him. "He said not to leave before the conference is *over.*"

"No one's telling me what to do," Davenport rumbled, but he must've known it was pointless.

There weren't any questions for Valley, and I'm sure at that moment you would've had to pay most of the conferees to leave before they'd planned. Two deaths—maybe two murders! It *was* turning into an Agatha Christie movie.

I caught Valley's eye as he turned to go, and he nodded, so I left with him. In the hallway—where I felt I'd spent most of my recent life—I asked, "Was it suicide?"

"Too soon to tell. No note, but it looks like suicide. Like she shot herself." Valley paused, and I asked him if they'd found a Wharton book in her car. He grunted out a yes.

Then maybe we did have some kind of serial killer here. Someone obsessed with Edith Wharton. I could understand Jodi Foster as the object of a fixation, but Edith Wharton? Why? How? And who ever heard of a maniac being fixated on a *dead* writer? It didn't bear thinking about.

I swallowed, and asked what the book was.

"A paperback of *Ethan Frome.* It's got Professor Davidoff's name written in it. We need to check her handwriting to make sure it's her book. Does it have any significance?"

"Oh, jeez. Absolutely. Near the end of *Ethan Frome,* the main character tries to commit suicide—and he fails."

"Looks like maybe Professor Davidoff did better than her inspiration." Valley walked off without giving me any other details.

What next? Were there other Wharton books with suicide in them? And if so, were there going to be more deaths? How many more—and all before the end of the conference?

I closed my eyes as if I could visualize my entire Wharton bibliography, page by page, but I couldn't recall any other suicide in her novels. Which left the short stories to consider, and there were over eighty of those.

Before I made any discoveries, Stefan and Angie emerged from the dining room to find me. I told them what little information Valley had shared, feeling pissed off. "We don't even know how exactly Chloe was killed!"

Angie blurted out, "It was one of those granite tiles. She was struck once at the back of the head with the center of the tile, once with the edge. But there weren't any fingerprints on it."

Stefan and I rounded on her. "How do you know that?" we asked together. But she clammed up. In fact, she basically fled, and Serena appeared at the door before I could even consider anything as crazy as chasing Angie down the hallway.

I looked at Stefan, who said, "Those tiles are heavy, aren't they? Which means the killer had to be pretty strong."

"No. They're only a foot square, and half an inch thick. I picked one up when I was in the hallway a few weeks ago. I was checking on how much progress they were making with the remodeling."

"People," Serena called out, "it's time to move on to the panels. Well past time. We can't let this news keep us from our work."

Well, it wasn't as inspiring as De Gaulle rallying the French under German occupation, but it was enough.

Stefan said he'd wait for me in the hallway. Inside, I made the appropriate announcements. This was the last full set of panels. We had other events scheduled for the afternoon and evening, and Sunday morning.

As the crowd began to scatter, Verity Gallup and Van Deegan Jones passed me. Her voice low, she was griping at Jones. "I can't believe how sexist and condescending you are. You talked to that young woman as if she were a child."

"She is a child," Jones groused. "And you, you're a menopausal bitch."

I didn't catch the rest of their edifying exchange.

Out in the hallway, Stefan took me aside, looking very concerned. "There's no way Priscilla killed herself."

"How do you know?"

Stefan grabbed my arm as if he were a union boss and I was a strike breaker. "Didn't you tell me a while back that she had a new book coming out in the summer? How could she miss the excitement of that?"

Around us, conferees were taking their notebooks, notes, programs, briefcases to various seminar rooms. Order seemed restored.

And then I was ambushed by the EAR chair, Coral Greathouse.

Wearing a drab, square-cut brown suit that made her look like a stewardess on a 1950s Iron Curtain airline, she held herself very stiffly today, as if determined not to be emotional.

"Nick, I heard about Priscilla and I am very concerned. The conference wasn't supposed to be like this."

With false sympathy, I said, "I know. Two deaths here make the department look bad. And now you have to find someone to take Priscilla's classes. It's very inconvenient."

Coral nodded, looking aggrieved but pleased that I understood her problems as an administrator. Then she scowled, and her eyes narrowed behind those enormous red-framed glasses.

"Nick, I came here to urge you to get this conference under control."

"By doing what?" I snapped. "Frisking everybody? Renting a metal detector?"

She seemed to be counting to ten, silently, as if to show off how patient she could be. "I think your attitude is all wrong." She stalked off after a curt, angry nod at Stefan.

"Well, add her to the list," I said to Stefan. "Everyone hates me. My department chair, the president of the university, and the head of the Board of Trustees. One more day and I'll have the secretaries and the maintenance staff out on picket lines. Maybe they'll even burn me in effigy on the steps of the Administration Building."

"Not on the weekend," Stefan said. "You'll have to wait until Monday."

I laughed. What else could I do?

THOUGH I SAT in on a session with Stefan at my side, I couldn't concentrate at all. Coral was right. The conference was out of control, but only the Campus Police could end the chaos, and they didn't seem anywhere near making progress.

Chloe's death had seemed so bizarre to me, and Chloe herself so much more a figure than a real person, that I'd been able to feel a little distance. It helped me keep my balance. But I'd been getting to know Priscilla better, and I'd imagined we might have become friends down the road. I still couldn't believe she was dead.

Sitting there in the crowded meeting room, I felt guilty about my assessment of her mystery novels. Maybe I was too harsh in privately dismissing them as second-rate. And I felt even guiltier remembering her despairing phone message the night before. Priscilla had called me, and all I did was phone her back. She'd obviously been desperate. Why didn't I go over to her house? Priscilla might have answered the door even if she wasn't answering the phone.

Unless she was already dead.

Then I recalled something chilling: how I'd tried to joke her out of dreading Chloe and Vivianne's presence at the conference by making references to *Fatal Attraction.*

When I came out of my fog and glanced around the room, the panel was over. People were standing around and chatting. Stefan gave me a sympathetic smile as if to say that taking a mental nap was okay.

Vivianne sat near the back of the room, looking dazed herself. In fact, she looked worse now after Priscilla's death than she had after Chloe's.

Some people were heading off, to take advantage, I guess, of their free half hour before lunch. I asked Stefan to wait for me outside, and I moved to the back to sit by Vivianne.

She greeted me by shaking her head. *"Je suis malheureuse comme les pierres, moi."*

I'd never heard that phrase before for expressing sorrow. She was as unhappy as a stone, and using more French with me because of it, I supposed.

"You know, I thought she did it for me," Vivianne said so softly that I could barely hear her.

I wasn't sure what she meant, but I prompted her with a quiet "You did?" No one could overhear us from the front of the room.

Vivianne nodded. "Priscilla and I, we had what you call a fling. Many summers ago back in Aix. We were both teaching. Chloe found out, and demanded we desist from all future contact. We have been out of touch, you see, for years. *Donc,* when she wrote me about Chloe's engagement to speak at your university in February, I assumed she wanted an excuse to contact me."

I was bowled over by these revelations, unsure now what was true and what was false. "Then Priscilla *didn't* write anonymously to you about the President's Lecture, and Chloe replacing Cynthia Ozick?"

Vivianne smiled wanly. "Yes, it was 'anonymous.' But I knew her handwriting, and the letter bore a Michigan postmark. *C'est pas sorcier.* It's not magic—one doesn't have to be Hercule Poirot." She shrugged, and I almost told her my parents were Belgian like Poirot.

Vivianne went on. "It rekindled something for me, you know? I was quite eager to see Priscilla again, but the drama of confronting Chloe, this eclipsed everything else."

"Did she love you?"

"Who can say? I think I probably felt more for Priscilla than she ever cared about me, and it was the same with Chloe."

"You mean Chloe and Priscilla—?"

"Oh, no. I mean that I loved Chloe more. There is always one who loves more, and one who loves less." Looking bereft, Vivianne said, "Now they are both dead. *J'ai la main malheureuse, moi.* I am unlucky."

Face to face with Vivianne's grief, I felt utterly helpless.

LUNCH WAS A very subdued affair. If the conferees were excited after Chloe's death, and buzzing with reactions, opinions, and gossip, now they were deflated. I think the typical conference fatigue was overlaid with exhaustion in the wake of the shouting match between Van Deegan Jones and Verity Gallup. As far as I could tell, their anger had sent their myrmidons back into opposing camps, waiting for the signal to launch total war. But the leaders were strangely absent. Had they retired to their battle tents and summoned their counselors to plan strategy?

Maybe I was tired.

Joanne and Bob Gillian were back. They were vultures, probably attracted by the trouble, like reporters sensing a politician's downfall.

What made people like that tick? Where did Joanne's hatred come from, and how could Bob, who had seemed so reasonable at times in our office, not only be married to her, but believe the same things she did?

Sitting with Stefan, Serena, and some Wharton Collective folks, I picked at my spinach quiche while others at the table made listless conversation. There were no complaints about the morning session, but also not much enthusiasm.

I could hear Joanne Gillian two tables away declaiming about "the wages of sin." Her voice and her very being grated on me more than ever before. I was about to go over and upbraid her, but Stefan stopped me.

"What's the point?" he asked wearily, and I had to agree.

But a moment later, Devon Davenport, sitting at Joanne and Bob's table, said, "Why don't you shut the fuck up? You're just like those lunatics on the subway in New York. Can't you let people eat in peace without shoving Jesus down our throats?"

Once again, the room was silent.

Glowering, Bob Gillian said, "I should punch you in the nose."

"You should tell your wife to put a sock in it."

Before Gillian and Davenport could start throttling each other, Grace-Dawn Vaughan burst into tears. "This whole conference," she lamented. "It's been too much for my tormented nerves."

"Amen," I muttered, as Devon Davenport and Bob Gillian offered her handkerchiefs. She graciously accepted them both.

As lunch wound to a close and people started drifting from their tables, Bob Gillian strolled over.

"Joanne wanted me to tell you that if you'd like to come pray at our church tomorrow morning, we'd be happy to have you."

Stefan and I gaped at him. "We're Jewish," I said. "You know that."

"And you're practicing homosexuals," Bob added, his face blank. Then he smiled. "But it's never too late to find Jesus."

He sauntered off, leaving me unsure whether to laugh or cry.

I WAS COMPLETELY off the hook for the afternoon because there weren't any sessions. The main event was an extended horticultural tour of SUM: of the greenhouses, the vast and gloriously landscaped campus, and the many spectacular gardens. Of course it was a little early in the season, but luckily the day was sunny and warm. Since Wharton herself was a devoted gardener, most conferees had signed up for the tour. When lunch ended, people filed off to prepare for the tour, which was being led by one of the Horticulture Department professors. I heard other conferees talk about napping or reading.

With the conference lurching to its finish, I felt even more adrift. Stefan suggested we play hooky because the weather was so inviting.

"Why not drive to Holland even if it means getting back late for dinner?"

I was tempted by the image of Lake Michigan two hours west, but I saw Angie down the hall, talking on a public phone. I was about to call out that I wanted to speak with her when she started waving frantically at me and Stefan.

We walked over as she hung up, and she said, "We have to talk!"

"Why did you disappear before?" I asked.

"I had to make a phone call. I'll explain everything, I promise. But right now we have to plan our strategy."

"Strategy," I repeated dully. I couldn't imagine finding the energy to do something so exacting. "What for?"

"Because," she said, drawing the word out. "Because there's just as much chance Priscilla was murdered as that her death was a suicide."

Stefan suggested we get away from campus to someplace quiet.

"I'm hungry," Angie said, and I realized that I was, too. I'd barely been able to eat lunch. Stefan suggested the delightful small Vietnamese restaurant right across from campus on Michigan Avenue, about half a mile down from the Campus Center. Angie said she'd meet us there since her car was parked in a nearby pay lot and she was out of quarters; she'd drive to the restaurant.

Strolling over, enjoying the seventy-degree weather and the sunshine (which you never take for granted in Michiganapolis), I told Stefan that I agreed with him. I believed Priscilla must have been murdered, that she didn't seem suicidal or even deeply depressed, just distraught over Chloe's murder.

Ever careful, Stefan reminded me that Angie had only said there was a chance it was murder. "Why don't we wait to hear what she has to tell us?"

Because it was after noon, Le Village was almost empty. The French name was as close as Michiganapolis got to a French restaurant, that and the interior, which was in country French colors of rose and apple green. All very restful, from the frilly café curtains to the delicately floral wallpaper. The menu was broad (Vietnamese, Chinese, Korean, Thai), the food tasty and relatively inexpensive. One of the waiters, Nguyen, seemed to dote on me and Stefan in his shy way, smiling whenever we were affectionate with each other.

He was there today, and waved us to our favorite corner table. I prayed that he wouldn't mention the conference deaths. He didn't.

"There'll be three of us," Stefan said, and Nguyen moved over another chair. His black pants and white shirt made me think of waiters in Paris.

Angie bounced in right after we were seated, and plopped into her seat, looking like a breathless, delighted Claudette Colbert.

"I haven't been completely honest with you," she announced.

Nguyen brought us tea and Stefan poured for all three of us. It was strong and hot.

"I've been talking to the Medical Examiner."

"Margaret Case?" I asked. So that explained the phone calls.

"Right. That's how I knew details about the way Chloe died." She shrugged. "I dated her son Neil two years ago. We broke up, but it wasn't nasty or anything, and since then, his mom's been really nice to me. Hey, maybe she wanted him to date someone else!"

I didn't tell Angie that Dr. Case had refused to talk to me about Chloe, or at least hadn't returned my phone call. But maybe that was just because she was busy. Stefan was often reminding me not to take things like that personally, to remember that other people had lives, too, and crises, and family trouble, and illnesses, and crowded schedules.

I was jealous of Angie's access and also felt stupid, because I'd forgotten to try getting in touch with Dr. Case again. But I was glad that someone knew more about what was going on.

We ordered, and Stefan said to Angie, "How could you find things out at all? Isn't the information confidential?"

"It should be, I guess, but then people don't always go by the book. It'll be in the paper tomorrow, anyway. Most of it."

I halted Stefan's interrogation. "Listen, I don't care about the ethics right now. What I want to know is why Priscilla's death is suspicious."

"Okay," Angie began. "There were anomalies on the scene."

"Anomalies," I repeated, pouring myself more tea.

"Yeah. It's definitely her gun—"

"I still can't believe Priscilla owned a gun."

Angie shrugged. "That's no big deal. Lots of women do." She picked up the thread: "And there was the gunpowder you'd expect to find on Priscilla's hand, and for sure her finger was on the trigger."

"But?" I asked.

"But the bullet's angle of entry was off."

Stefan asked what that meant.

Angie warmed to her theme, face beginning to flush. "See, suicides generally shoot themselves in the temple, or put the gun in their mouths. Shooting yourself in the heart is much less common, and the bullet didn't seem aimed right. It came up towards her chest"—Angie demonstrated—"and not straight in."

Our food arrived. We were sharing shrimp in a tangy sesame seed and orange sauce and shredded lamb sauteed with scallions. For a few minutes, we piled our plates with rice and vegetables, shrimp and lamb.

Then Angie continued, wielding a mean set of chopsticks while she spoke. "There weren't any signs of a struggle, but the most compelling piece of evidence was the position of Priscilla's body. She was in the passenger's seat, not the driver's seat. That only makes sense if someone else drove her to the parking lot."

"I don't follow," I said, relishing my shrimp.

"Okay. Picture this. Why would Priscilla drive into the parking lot, park, then move over to the other side to shoot herself?"

Stefan had an answer. "Maybe Priscilla didn't want to call attention to herself by slumping over onto the wheel after she shot herself, and getting the horn stuck. She wrote mysteries. That's the kind of thing she would have figured out."

Angie shook her head. "They tested that already. Even if you lay right on top of it, that's not enough. You have to press down with your hand. Hard. So if a body fell on it, it wouldn't have got stuck and stayed that way."

We were talking about death and a body—the body of a friend—but I ate as if I hadn't eaten all week.

Stefan sat back in his chair just as Nguyen came by to ask if everything was all right. I smiled at him and said, "Perfect." He thanked me and went back to the kitchen. We were all alone in Le Village, and it felt good not having to worry about being overheard.

"But what about the paperback of *The House of Mirth?*" Stefan threw out to both of us. "If it was Priscilla's book, whether there were fingerprints or not, maybe she left it at Chloe's body so people would know that she was going to kill herself."

Angie frowned. "That's kind of twisted, isn't it?"

"Not really. The second Wharton book, *Ethan Frome,* which was in Priscilla's car, points to suicide, doesn't it?" Stefan was looking to me for confirmation.

I wasn't sure. "The main character in *Ethan Frome* unsuccessfully tries to kill himself, so how does that make sense? Unless the book was there accidentally. I think Priscilla must have known something about Chloe's death, or seen something that made her dangerous. The murderer assumed she'd be arrested—didn't we all?—and would reveal what she knew. But who drove Priscilla to the parking lot, and why, and why would she let someone who was going to kill her drive her anywhere?"

"We haven't gotten very far," Stefan brought out gloomily, pushing some shrimp around his plate with his fork. "There weren't any eyewitnesses either time, and checking people's whereabouts hasn't helped the Campus Police, has it? What can the three of us possibly accomplish?"

Even though I felt wasted, the food had changed my mood, and I wasn't ready to give up.

To Angie, I explained that I'd tried making mental lists of the suspects before, but it was obviously time to start over.

Munching on some lamb, Angie said, "Professor Fisch."

Both Stefan and I came out with a surprised "What?"

Angie held her hands out as if it were obvious. "I've been wondering what her thing is with the conference. What's she doing there?"

"She offered to help me, since she's good at the detail work. There's nothing suspicious about that." But even as I said it, I thought about Serena's growing involvement with the conference. She'd had a strong distaste for Chloe, which I explained now to Angie. It certainly looked odd, didn't it?

"Wait a minute, Angie! Serena may have hated Chloe, too, but how did she know that Chloe was coming to the conference?"

Stefan disagreed. "She could have found out the same way Priscilla did, and sooner—through gossip, through a colleague, who knows. And the point is, could Serena Fisch kill someone, kill a colleague?"

"Definitely," I said, remembering her quote from *Conan.* Then I told them about Joanne Gillian's recent tirade.

Stefan said, "I forgot about her. You think she's really nuts, not just rabidly conservative, and she has some kind of kink about lesbians."

I glanced at Angie to see if she knew that Priscilla was gay; she seemed up to speed on that. I nodded at Stefan. "It's possible. She killed them both, and maybe Bob helped psych her up to it. He gets more creepy each time I see him. By himself, he seems decent enough, but he's just a shadow around her."

"But she's on the Board of Trustees," Angie said.

"She's the chair, to be precise. Does that make her a good person?" I asked.

"No. It just means she has a lot to lose. She's so visible."

Stefan pointed out that a murderer might feel visibility was a protection.

The three of us had no trouble agreeing that egotistical and rageful Devon Davenport, whose pride had been hurt twice by Chloe, was as likely a candidate as Grace-Dawn Vaughan. It was Angie, though, who suggested that perhaps they did it together, since they seemed chummier than you'd expect from an editor and his author.

Having overheard Crane Taylor and Gustaf Carmichael reveal that they both hated Chloe, I assumed that only one of them could have killed her—but both could have been involved in Priscilla's murder. Then there was Vivianne, Angie said. Hadn't she been a little too cool about it all until Priscilla's death?

I recounted my sad conversation with Vivianne at the back of the meeting room this morning at the Campus Center, repeating the last thing she'd said in French.

Stefan said it perfectly. *"La main malheureuse?"*

Angie wanted to know what it meant.

"Unlucky," Stefan said. "It's an idiom. Literally, an unfortunate hand."

"An unfortunate hand," I repeated, not having seen when Vivianne said it how the phrase might have been more revealing than she intended. We all seemed to consider that, picturing the hand or hands that had struck down Chloe and possibly Priscilla as well.

Then I sighed. "Maybe Priscilla was killed because she knew who killed Chloe, but if she spotted the murderer, how did that happen, and where?"

Stefan asked me about Van Deegan Jones and Verity Gallup. "Didn't you say that both of them have been looking uncomfortable or strange since Chloe's death?"

"Furtive is more accurate."

"Okay, furtive. Maybe they had some connection with Chloe— after all, Chloe's been at lots of conferences and universities, I assume. Who knew how they might have run afoul of her?"

"The first night, Valley suggested that Chloe might not have been the real target, that maybe it was Joanne Gillian because of her homophobia, and Chloe was killed by mistake."

Angie said, "You mean there's some Queer Crusader at SUM? As *if*!"

We all laughed, but it didn't last long, because we were faced with our lack of real evidence. All we had were suspicions.

"We must be missing something," Angie said. "But what? Where do the Edith Wharton books fit in? They have to be clues."

Stefan eyed me challengingly, as if to say: Five years working on a Wharton bibliography, reading every word ever written about Wharton in all quadrants of the galaxy, and you can't figure this out?

Cringing, I said, "There's no real connection between the two books, except suicide, but it doesn't work in *Ethan Frome,* and it may be accidental death in *The House of Mirth.* If someone's trying to make a point about failure or missed chances, it's pretty severe, don't you think?"

"Fingerprints?" Angie asked. "What about fingerprints?"

"Valley told me that the fingerprints on the first book didn't match anyone's at the conference."

Angie frowned. "They cross-checked with the registration list?"

I nodded, and Angie asked to see it.

"I gave my only copy to Valley."

Angie frowned, tormenting a blob of rice on her plate with her chopsticks. "Is everyone at the conference registered?"

"They're supposed to be, but I can't remember. Serena's the one who handled the registrations and made up the final list."

Stefan said it before I could. "So the fingerprints on the paperback of *The House of Mirth* might belong to the murderer. We just have to find out who's been attending the conference and didn't get fingerprinted. Maybe there's someone who doesn't have a conference badge."

I raised my hand. "I don't. Does that make me a suspect? I didn't register, and neither did Serena. I've never bothered even thinking about checking badges. Who's going to crash a Wharton conference?"

Stefan said, "Who's going to run amok at a Wharton conference and kill two people? Wharton has nothing to do with it."

"Okay. Serena will know who else doesn't have a badge. But will she tell the truth, or try to cast suspicion on someone else? We have to find Serena, or get the final list back from Valley. How about this: one of us heads back to campus to tag along with the garden tour and try to pick up anything we can about the suspects. Someone else should go check out the commuter lot and the Campus Center and examine the murder scenes again to see if something pops up—I don't know, an idea, a possibility we haven't figured out. And the third person should try to find Serena."

"Where is she?" Stefan asked.

"I don't know if she's on the tour or not, but it's doubtful she'd take it." Stefan was looking kind of dubious, so I asked him what was wrong.

"Is any of this going to make a difference?"

"Well, maybe it's all a wild-goose chase, but what else can we try? I've got to do something. This is my conference, and if I don't help figure out why Chloe and Priscilla died, it'll haunt me forever. Personally *and* professionally. You know what academics are like, Stefan. They'll call it the Killer's Conference or some shit like that!"

"I'll do the tour," Angie volunteered. "After I try contacting Detective Valley like we tried before."

I said it made sense for me to look for Serena, and that left Stefan heading for the Campus Center. We agreed to rendezvous in a few hours back there.

We paid up, and Nguyen said with concern, "You look sad."

I nodded. "I am sad."

Outside in the small parking lot, Angie said, "There's one more thing to tell you. I've been wondering if I might have seen the killer."

# IO

STEFAN AND I were both speechless, but Angie wasn't paying attention. Her eyes were turned inward, remembering. Traffic buzzed along Michigan Avenue behind us, and students filed in and out of the giant, gleaming Kinko's next door. The day had turned even more beautiful, highlighted now by a light breeze.

"See," Angie said, "I live in the neighborhood where Priscilla Davidoff did, near Blanchard High School."

I knew that neighborhood: a mixed one of faculty and students, not as quiet or as pleasant as ours.

"And I share this house with three other girls, and we're kind of across the street from Professor Davidoff's house and just a few houses down. Two nights ago, the night Chloe was murdered, I was up late studying after I got back from the Campus Center. I got up from my desk to stretch, and I looked out the window. This car was pulling out of Priscilla's driveway. It was pretty late, like three or four."

"How do you know that wasn't Priscilla?"

Angie shook her head, looking very definite. "It wasn't her car. She had a VW Bug—I've seen her driving that. This was something much bigger, and expensive-looking."

"But why do you think that might have been the killer?" I asked, starting to feel confused. "And *which* killer?"

"Whoever killed Professor Davidoff, if it was murder, was probably someone she knows well, since it's doubtful she went to the parking lot at SUM with a stranger, right? And someone leaving her house that late probably also knew her pretty well."

I was agog now because it made sense. "Did you see the driver?!"

"I wish." Angie frowned.

"Priscilla may have been having an affair," Stefan concluded. "An affair with someone who didn't want to be recognized, or even risk being seen. Why else leave so late at night?"

"That's kind of what I thought," Angie said. "And maybe her being dead doesn't have anything to do with Chloe DeVore. Maybe that's, like, a separate thing."

"You're right, Angie. It really could have been the killer you saw," I said, as chilled as if the car had driven right past me. "But it could be anyone on the list—or at least any of the women on our list of suspects, I suppose." Then a terrible possibility occurred to me. "No—it could have been any of the women at the conference! What if Priscilla was having a quiet long-distance relationship with some woman who showed up at the conference? Shit, this is impossible."

Stefan threw in another monkey wrench. "Nick, how do we know that Priscilla wasn't bisexual and trying to hide it? Look at all the lesbians abandoning ship and sleeping with men these days. The person driving away from her house late at night might have been a man."

"You're both jumping to conclusions," Angie said confidently. "Why does it have to be an affair? Whoever was at Professor Davidoff's house late at night could have been a friend." She added a little vaguely, "A friend who had some reason to kill her."

Having delivered herself of that analysis, Angie smiled at both of us, unlocked the door to her battered Honda, got in wishing us luck, and drove off.

Stefan and I walked back to the Campus Center along Michigan Avenue, which was bursting with students in shorts and T-shirts.

"Listen, Nick. Whatever Angie saw the other night, it's tantalizing, but it doesn't get us any further."

"Why not? How about canvassing Priscilla's next-door neighbors to find out if they saw who it was driving away that night? Even if the Michiganapolis police already asked, it can't hurt to follow up." I didn't let Stefan object. "I'll do it! I'll say I'm a bereaved friend who's desperate to know more about Priscilla's death."

Stefan stopped and looked me right in the eye. "That is a stupid idea."

Feeling a surge of bravado, I said, "I'll try it anyway, and if it doesn't work, I'll come up with something else. You know I can."

Stefan nodded glumly.

I TOOK STEFAN'S car when we got back to the Campus Center, but as soon as I drove off campus, I felt my energy vanish like water into sand. I found the nearest cappuccino place—they'd been springing up all over town this year—parked, and dragged myself inside.

The caffeine in the air and the sweet aromas wafting from the gleaming ranks of sugary desserts in glass counters enveloped me. I took a double mocha and a white chocolate cheesecake brownie to a quiet corner as if I was about to do something illicit. Given the load of sugar and fat grams in that brownie, I suppose I was.

The café was filled with intense and nervous-looking students, some of whom I recognized from last year's Gay Pride parade. They were what I thought of as theme-park queers: slim and shiny and up-to-date in their goatees, beads, oversized baggy thin sweaters, and high-top sneakers or Birkenstocks. A few of them nodded at me, and I tried to smile. I'm sure they were wondering where Stefan was.

He was the star, he was the one students looked up to, and I always heard "Is Stefan with you?" when I was out by myself.

But I was very glad now to be just that: by myself. The tangled talk at Le Village about Chloe's murder and Priscilla's death (which was probably a murder) had covered up what I was really feeling: a terrible, numbing fatigue that made my very bones ache.

All those months worrying about the conference, and now I was in the middle of two deaths. How had the conference come to this? How had it become the scene of some kind of visitation, a curse?

I knew that Stefan would have snorted at my attempt to understand the past few days' events, to find some meaning in them. After the Oklahoma City bombing, the news media had been full of sententious references to the survivors making sense of the tragedy. Stefan had roared at the TV one night, "It doesn't *make* any fucking sense! Why don't they shut up?"

I was afraid he'd throw a book at the screen or even kick it in, but the outburst seemed to have untwisted something inside of him, at least momentarily, and he didn't say anything more. He didn't have to. I could fill in the rest.

At seventeen, Stefan had found out that he was Jewish, and that his parents and his uncle Sasha were Holocaust survivors. They had tried to escape and obliterate their past by raising him vaguely Catholic and ethnically Polish. He'd told me that for years after finding out he was really a Jew, he had felt like Frankenstein's monster wheeled down from the lightning: grotesque, cobbled together, anxiously, crazily studied to see if he would scream or go berserk.

Instead, he'd withdrawn, favoring the cruelty of silence, until he eventually poured his pain into his writing. And that was an almost unforgivable act to them: revealing family secrets.

Did any of it make sense? To them, maybe. To Stefan, never.

Sitting hunched over my coffee, I thought, My dad looks like this when business isn't going well. As he would say at such a time, I had *le cafard*. And you didn't need to pronounce it perfectly to feel its effects. Vivianne's pain and sadness had rekindled my own about last year, not that it was ever very far from the surface.

I looked out onto the ordinary Michiganapolis street and wished for one of those consuming summer rains where the sky is almost white and the lightning hits the ground like a stalking beast. A storm I could lose myself in. A storm that would remind me my life didn't mean very much, that it was all a very small thing.

But I had to smile. Wouldn't my cousin Sharon cock her beautiful head at me right now and say, "So one murder and one possible murder, that's not enough of a storm for you? You want sound effects, too? And better lighting?"

My coffee was done, and though the brownie was terrific, it was so rich that another would have turned me as mindlessly chipper as Kathie Lee Gifford. It was time to get to work.

I DIDN'T HAVE much luck with the first two of Priscilla's neighbors, those on either side of her house.

The first house looked like something out of a kid's storybook: The Goblin's Lair. Faced completely with undressed stone, it had a low brooding roofline, tiny casement windows like beady eyes, and a crooked paved path to a front door rounded like an arch. Overgrown arbor vitae trees ringed the entire house, and I wondered how anyone could live there without light penetrating through the trees. Michiganapolis was cloudy enough as it was, and its people heavily afflicted by seasonal affective disorder.

Whoever lived in this house was a candidate for light therapy on an industrial scale.

The owner was in the foul mood that I would have expected.

When she yanked open the front door, she glowered at me. Behind her, I saw two little boys bouncing around in a playpen in the chaotic living room, which looked as if a tidal wave of toys and kiddie stuff had broken across it and receded unevenly. The kids were fairly quiet, but the room's disorder screamed at you. And the room stank.

But she didn't. She was drenched in some floral perfume as harsh as Lysol (maybe it *was* Lysol). Fortyish, she surveyed me contemptuously, holding her left hand in her right, and squeezing her ring finger, which was bare.

Divorced, I figured.

The name on the mailbox was Jorgenson, so I said, "Hello, Mrs. Jorgenson."

"What the hell do you want? You can't be selling anything, you're not dressed well enough for that."

Mrs. Jorgenson was wearing unattractive purple sweats, and she made me think of a skunk because her roots needed retouching badly: there was a band two inches wide along the top of her blond head at the part. Maybe she was letting her hair stay like that as a protest.

"You know about Priscilla Davidoff, your neighbor?" I motioned to Priscilla's house.

"That she's a dead dyke. Yeah, I know about that. So what? You can't be a reporter, you don't look that smart."

"Actually, I teach at SUM—"

"Figures! So does that moron, my ex-husband. Well, he *says* he teaches there. Mostly he's tolling for babes. That's probably what he's doing right now. If he isn't actually screwing one in his office. That's how I found out—"

I tried to stem the tide a little. "Priscilla was a friend of mine." I smiled, hoping to ingratiate myself a little.

"It must be nice," she snapped.

"Excuse me?"

"It must be nice to have friends. I don't have any. Not now. They all dumped me just like Gary did."

Gamely, I forged ahead. "You see, I've been trying to figure out what happened to Priscilla, and one of the things I'm looking into is whether she had a late-night visitor this week, and if you noticed."

"You're not some kind of militia nut, are you? This isn't about one-world government or anything, is it?"

"No!"

"Then why are you poking around like you're the police? Listen, I've got two little kids, and I don't have time to pay attention to other people's business. If you were doing your job and earning the money us tax-payers paid you, you wouldn't have the time to be so nosy!"

She didn't slam the door. She didn't have to. I gave up and wished her a nice day.

The next neighbor was a shy and befuddled elderly man with poor eyesight who seemed almost frightened of me, and wouldn't talk at all. I walked away from his front door thinking, I hope I never get like that, but knowing I probably would. Didn't everyone?

My luck changed, though, when I tried the house directly across the street from Priscilla's. The woman answering the door, Mrs. Lorraine, in her seventies, had a great wide smile that was so bright it practically threw the rest of her face into shadow.

I introduced myself, told her that I was a friend of Priscilla's and that I was distraught about her death. Mrs. Lorraine seemed quite willing to chat, and she instantly invited me into her pleasant little ranch house, which was so filled with pink it could have been a set for *Funny Face*. Mrs. Lorraine was quite pink herself, round, friendly, and she wore the current American uniform of the elderly: a thin track suit. Pink, of course.

Two white bichon frises came snuffling up to me when I sat on the well-padded sofa. The dogs were apparently prepared to be quite sociable in a calm sort of way, and while Mrs. Lorraine made some coffee and chatted from the kitchen, I admired their cute gorillalike faces and talked baby talk to them.

Stefan was not convinced we could live with a dog, so whenever I was around dogs, I felt like I was auditioning—them, and myself.

"They look like those fuzzy little warriors in the third *Star Wars* movie, don't they?" Mrs. Lorraine asked, bringing in a tray with coffee and homemade shortbread.

As she poured and served the shortbread, we chatted. That is, Mrs. Lorraine talked about herself. She was a retired high school English teacher, had lived her whole life in Michiganapolis, and right now, she was working on a book.

"My daughter's an agent in New York. She's promised me that if it's halfway decent, she'll be able to find me a publisher. It'll be marketable largely because of my age," she laughed. "But that's okay with me. My daughter says I might be like the author of . . . *And Ladies of the Club,* or that *Stones for Ibarra* woman. You know. An isn't-it-amazing-this-old-lady-wrote-a-book kind of deal."

I was glad Stefan wasn't there, since he'd dread being asked to read the manuscript. Because he'd been profiled several times in the *Michiganapolis Tribune,* people recognized him, and were often stopping him at malls, in the post office, even the gym, to ask if he'd read their books and help get them sold.

Sitting there with Mrs. Lorraine and her adorable dogs was so much nicer than being sniped at by Priscilla's other neighbor that I just relaxed into the couch. And even though I was full, I savored the shortbread.

Mrs. Lorraine talked about how nice Priscilla had been to her, helping her in with groceries sometimes, and even mowing the lawn for her when Mrs. Lorraine was out of town. She even helped Mrs. Lorraine with some remodeling, "because she was so good with her hands."

"You might be interested to know, young man, that the police asked me a good many questions, but they didn't get at the most interesting point, to my mind."

"What was that?" Her coffee was a little weak, but the shortbread was superb, and I helped myself to more.

"Well, I'll tell you. The same night every week, Priscilla had a car in her driveway. There was one a few days ago, the night that Chloe De-Vore woman was killed on campus. This went on for months."

"Why didn't you tell the police?"

"They didn't ask. More coffee?"

I passed.

"I should say that they asked if I'd seen anything or anyone unusual, and this looked to be the same person who'd been arriving after midnight and leaving around three or four A.M. for months, so it wasn't really unusual. But whoever it was probably knows something important about Priscilla. And I've been working the details into my own book. Guess what I'm writing."

"A mystery?"

"Heavens, no! Who reads that junk? I'm writing a *memoir.*" She said the word with an amused shiver. "That's because my daughter told me that memoirs are very popular these days."

Wasn't that the truth! I couldn't believe how many unknown writers were getting enormous advances for memoirs—some of them not even thirty years old! What could *they* have to remember?

"Of course," Mrs. Lorraine was saying, "I know it helps to be schizophrenic, or deformed, or a criminal, or a politician—but I've led an interesting life all the same."

"Do you know who Priscilla's visitor was? Could you recognize them?"

"You mean him or her, not them. Them is plural, young man." She waited for my acquiescence and when I nodded and dutifully repeated, "Him or her," she continued. "All I can tell you is that it was someone of average height, and the car was definitely a BMW. The driver was wearing a hat and a raincoat with the collar up. It might have been a man, but it might have been a woman trying to look like a man. It was definitely somebody who didn't want to be seen. This person turned off the headlights before pulling into the driveway, which was always dark, and didn't put the headlights on until way down the street. Being quite careful. I never made out the license plate, because the car lights were off and the street was pretty dark. Also, my eyes—" She smiled ruefully.

A BMW, I thought, wasn't unusual enough a car in our college town. It could be anyone. Was the weekly visitor a lover or just a friend Priscilla counseled in some way? And was there any connection to Chloe's and Priscilla's deaths, or was this new piece of information just tangential?

I thanked Mrs. Lorraine for the coffee and shortbread, feeling full but pretty frustrated.

We headed for the door, the bichon frises following at a respectful distance.

"May I say something personal?" she asked.

Hesitating, I said, "Sure."

"You're not a very good liar, young man. I could see right off you weren't that old a friend of Priscilla's."

Blushing, I asked her how she could tell.

"You didn't seem truly shaken by her being dead. I've lost a lot of folks over the years, so I know. And it wasn't as if you were trying to be brave or anything. You were just curious. No offense! Also, when I said Priscilla was good with her hands and she mowed my lawn, you didn't object. That girl was a total klutz! She paid to have her own yard mowed. Besides, weren't you involved in a murder at SUM last year? I'm sure I can remember reading about it and seeing your photograph in the *Tribune*."

"That was me."

But far from being upset, Mrs. Lorraine was delighted at her own cleverness. "I have to warn you. If you're going to investigate things, you should have worked a little harder at being believable."

I held up my hands. "You win."

"So," she said a little breathlessly. "You don't think Priscilla Davidoff's death was a suicide?"

"Not really. She didn't seem depressed enough, and—Well, I'm just not convinced, and I understand that some evidence at the crime scene is ambiguous."

"How exciting! Perhaps I *should* write a mystery instead of a memoir!" She frowned, puzzling it out: "A retired old lady sees lots of mysterious doings in her town. No, isn't that a bit too much like that Jessica Fletcher show? I wonder what the market is for mysteries. I'll have to ask my daughter."

"Good idea," I said.

"I suppose you must be right about Priscilla not being depressed, if you worked with her at SUM. That part is true, isn't it? Good. I only knew her well enough to have an extra key and take UPS deliveries for her—"

"You have a key to Priscilla's house? Do the police know?"

"Don't raise your voice—it upsets the dogs."

I looked at their friendly white faces; they seemed unperturbed.

"The answer's no, since they didn't ask. Can you use the key?"

I wanted to hug her. Of course I could use the key. There might be something I could find that the police had missed, some clue that would reveal who was visiting Priscilla regularly, and if that had any connection with her death.

Mrs. Lorraine took my hands in hers. "Yes. You can borrow the key. As long as you bring it right back. Only you have to tell me everything you dig up over there so I can decide if I want to get any of it into my book."

Mrs. Lorraine's dogs eyed me steadily, and I imagined they were thinking, Sucker.

I agreed, reluctantly, to give Mrs. Lorraine what she wanted.

ANXIOUS AND GRATEFUL, I slipped across the street to Priscilla's house with the spare key.

Like many others in that neighborhood, Priscilla's house was a fifties-era ranch house with white siding, mildly decorative shutters, and ordinary foundation plants. A generic house except for the beautiful roof of clay tiles, which added an incongruous touch of the Southwest, I thought.

I let myself into a tiny hallway quickly, unsure how I would explain my presence if I was discovered trespassing. But was it trespassing, exactly, if I had a key? And I hadn't *stolen* the key; I'd borrowed it from someone who had the right to have one. But did Mrs. Lorraine have the right to lend the key? And was talking about rights foolish anyway in this context?

That roof didn't seem so incongruous when I looked around inside. The cheerful house was decorated in the bright Southwest colors and geometrics that can sometimes seem oppressive and even bizarre in the Midwest. Here, though, it was all done with a light touch, not making the white walls seem too stark, and thankfully, there was not one Georgia O'Keefe poster, so I didn't feel that I was stepping into the page of a catalogue or a cliché.

I stood in the little hall, orienting myself. Straight ahead was the kitchen, the living room-dining room (a "great room" in real estate parlance) lay to my left, and two small rooms were to my right. I assumed one was Priscilla's bedroom, the other her study.

I'd expected to feel a little creeped out in the house of someone recently dead, maybe murdered, but I didn't. There wasn't anything immediately weird or mysterious about Priscilla's comfortable home, and of course it hadn't been abandoned long enough for there to be any signs of neglect or decay.

There were no plants that I could see from where I stood, but lots of books. The hallway was lined with books on gleaming, lacquered white shelves, and from the titles I guessed they were mostly mysteries, hardcover and paperback. I moved into the living room, with its oranges, blues, and greens, glancing around for—well, for what? I didn't really know what I was looking for, what I expected to find, or what I hoped would leap out at me, shouting "Clue! Clue!"

Stefan, of course, would be horrified that I was doing this at all. He'd probably call it breaking and entering. Or, at the very least, ill-advised.

Orange and green countertop tiles brightened the kitchen. Here, too, there wasn't anything that drew me closer. No heavily marked calendar or revealing memo pad by the phone. No hastily abandoned meal or broken dishes. All I was learning was that Priscilla had been very neat.

The bedroom revealed much more, and that's the first room I was truly uncomfortable in. It wasn't the intimacy of her futon or dresser top, or the pot of Claire Burke potpourri near the door, her favorite, I knew, from being in her SUM office.

The wall space not taken up with bookshelves was crammed with her book covers in frames, framed reviews of her books (including a starred *PW*, which I knew from Stefan meant a lot); pictures of Priscilla with other authors like Anne Rice and Patricia Cornwell. I couldn't tell from the poses if they were good friends or if the photos had been taken at writers' conferences. But I suspected they were the latter, because Priscilla looked somewhat needy in each one, pinched around the eyes.

There was so much of it that the whole room reeked of desperation despite the potpourri, as if Priscilla had to prove to herself her career was alive, and that she was connected.

But the heart of the house was definitely her small study next door, which was just as Detective Valley had described it. There were hundreds of true crime and other research books for her mysteries, and over her desk, the corkboard-covered wall was filled with clippings and photos of Chloe DeVore.

Here was Chloe getting inducted into the American Academy of Arts and Letters. And accepting her Pulitzer. Chloe getting some kind of French award. Chloe with Saul Bellow. Chloe with Salman Rushdie. Chloe with Steven Spielberg, for God's sake! Profiles and interviews cut out of newspapers and magazines from around the world. Had Priscilla actually hired a clippings service to track Chloe DeVore's career? Or had this all been sent to her by that informal network of Chloe-watchers she had talked about?

In some spots, the articles were two and even three deep.

The dartboard with a much-pierced photo of Chloe was right in the middle, and underneath, Priscilla had pinned an index card with a typed quotation from *Emma:* "One half of the world does not understand the pleasures of the other half."

What could that mean? And how could Priscilla have worked here with the roiling evidence of Chloe's success staring her in the face? Or was that very pain what she needed to keep going? The power of Priscilla's obsession alarmed me. Even the sunshine coming through the venetian blinds seemed tainted and somehow malign. This wasn't a place to work, it was a sepulchre. She had been digging her own grave.

For a few moments, overwhelmed by the evidence of her single-minded focus on Chloe, I thought that maybe she *had* killed herself, despite the anomalies Angie had reported to us. But it wasn't because she was afraid of being arrested and tried for murder. It was the loss. If her emotional life and her career had revolved around Chloe for so many years, without Chloe life was meaningless.

Which led to the conclusion that Chloe was killed by someone else. How could Priscilla knowingly deprive herself of the touchstone in her life?

I sat down at her desk, feeling burdened by the sadness of her life, of every writer's life (including Stefan) who hadn't made it into the upper echelons of publishing where your books simply became products and served as wallpaper in the chain stores.

Thankfully, I was just a bibliographer, with no hope of ever becoming even moderately famous or making much money on my writing. The Wharton scholars all knew me, and so did other bibliographers, librarians, and people like that. I had my certain small fame, my share of dusty immortality.

I shook myself, trying to focus on why I was there. Okay, how should I start?

Remembering Angie's computer search, I turned on Priscilla's computer, glad that it was an IBM just like mine. I was pretty sure that she used the same Word Perfect word processing program I did, because we'd talked about installing a new virus protection program some months earlier after a departmental memo.

Yes. She hadn't updated her word processing program since then. We'd joked about being Neanderthals because we didn't have Windows and didn't use a mouse and it shocked some people as much as if we'd said we had outdoor toilets. I suppose it was a small protest against the speed at which computer technology was advancing—and it really didn't do us any harm.

Her screen was the same size as mine and I felt oddly comfortable. When the directories came up, I chose LETTERS. I skimmed the hundreds of file names, looking for anything familiar, anyone from the conference, but I drew a complete blank.

Since I had the time, I decided to scan the letters more carefully, running the cursor rather than going down screen by screen. One file name was unusual: a series of exclamation points.

With a tinge of excitement, I pulled up the letter, but it was just a letter to a magazine, complaining about its review of one of her novels. Embarrassed, I turned away from the screen.

This was exactly the kind of thing that made me cringe when I read the *New York Times Book Review.* Was there anything as undignified and demeaning as an author writing in to rebuke a reviewer for having missed the point of a book, or misquoting it, or something? Why couldn't authors just let it go? Why couldn't they turn their anger and humiliation back into their writing, instead of trying to defend themselves in print? It was almost always a waste of time, because the reviewer got a chance to reply and demolish the author once again—coolly and diplomatically, of course.

I turned back, wondering if I shouldn't just shut the computer off and leave. I wasn't going to find anything this way.

Then I thought of Angie again. She wouldn't give up so easily, would she? I took a tour through Priscilla's other directories to see if any rang a bell.

How had I missed the directory called ENEMY? Excited, I pulled it up, but was instantly disappointed to find it was blank. She'd told me that *Sleeping with the Enemy* was the title of her next book, but there was nothing in the directory. Maybe she hadn't even started it, and that's why she'd seemed a little uneasy when we talked that night at my house several months ago. I could imagine her publisher pressing her to get another book done, and her being afraid to admit she hadn't gotten further than a title.

Unless I was completely off-base. Maybe that wasn't her new book at all, but just an idea for one.

I exited and recommenced my search, and this time I caught something far more interesting: FROME. Could it be *Ethan Frome?* That was the book they found in her car!

This was it for sure.

But I felt crushed when I went into the FROME directory. There was only one document in it, a title page:

## THE ETHAN FROME MURDERS

### *by Priscilla Davidoff*

The date on the file was only a few weeks back. Was this another new book? Why hadn't she mentioned the title to me? Unless it was the same book and she'd been experimenting with different titles? But why separate directories, then?

Or was it that *Sleeping with the Enemy* had been finished, but deleted, and Priscilla was just beginning to work on this one, and that was why she had a copy of Wharton's paperback with her when she died? It must have been inspiration, I figured, or a talisman of sorts.

But what the hell could it mean? I felt almost crazed now. Here I was, the one person in the world who'd read more about Edith Wharton than anyone else, and Wharton's best-known (but not best) novel looked like it was a major clue in a murder, and I couldn't figure it out.

I stared and stared at the screen. Then it occurred to me that Priscilla might have done more, much more than just create a directory and do a title page. And maybe everything in this directory had been deleted by whoever killed her. Which meant someone intimately aware of what she was writing about . . .

I looked down at my hands. Had the Campus Police checked for fingerprints? If not, then I had probably blurred any prints on the keys. Unless the killer had worn gloves.

If these were two separate books, Priscilla *couldn't* have killed herself, I thought with conviction, remembering what Stefan had said about her book coming out in the summer. She not only had the rush of that one, she had a claim on the future. She wouldn't have killed herself with a new book calling to her. No matter how despairing she might have felt about her career, the idea of a new book was a doorway to something better, a real promise of change and engagement. Didn't I know that from living with Stefan all these years? Whenever he was depressed, a new project always pulled him out. He knew it; I knew it. Sometimes in those dark moods, he'd snap at me when I suggested working on something new, but he always gave in to his own need to create and the inner certainty that work would pull him through.

I turned off the computer and tried going through Priscilla's desk and file cabinets, but there was nothing connected to this future book— no file folder labeled anything like *Ethan Frome*. I felt crippled by my lack of information: I didn't know who Priscilla's writer friends were, the name of her agent, or even her editor. All that might help me find out about what she was supposed to be publishing next.

The desk phone rang, startling me, but I didn't dare pick it up, and the volume must have been down on the answering machine because I couldn't hear if anyone was leaving a message.

Just as I was wondering about turning up the volume setting, I heard a key in the front door.

What if this was the mystery figure Mrs. Lorraine had spotted on those evenings? Or was it the murderer?

I was frozen to my seat—or Priscilla's seat, actually. I couldn't get up or make a sound.

I looked wildly around the room. Through the half-open blinds I could see that the small window had a storm window on it. There was absolutely no way I could escape through it quickly, or escape at all. I was trapped.

There was nowhere to hide. What could I use to defend myself? There was nothing in sight I could grab as a weapon—no heavy bookends, *nothing.* Could I reach for the phone and quietly dial 911? Was there time?

No. I heard footsteps.

Terrified, I swiveled in the chair to face the door, unwilling to be surprised by my fate.

Detective Valley appeared in the doorway, shaking his head.

I sighed heavily, feeling myself deflate, feeling the pulse beat in my forehead, the sweat in my palms.

We stared at each other. I asked, "Are you going to arrest me?"

"Why? For being an idiot? For interfering with a criminal investigation and trespassing in broad daylight? Give me a break. I've got more important things to do with my time."

I flushed.

"How did you get in? The lock wasn't jimmied. Was it that old bitch across the street? She give you a key?"

I was afraid to answer and get Mrs. Lorraine in trouble, but my silence was incriminating enough, and Valley nodded sourly.

Then something occurred to me. "I thought Campus Police only had jurisdiction at SUM."

"We do, normally. You're just lucky we're working with the Michiganapolis police on this one. Okay, Sherlock," he said, leaning on the doorframe. "Did you find anything us dumb-ass campus cops couldn't find?"

Now I felt a little better. I reported on Priscilla's new book—maybe even two new books—claiming this as proof that she couldn't, wouldn't have killed herself. Despite the agony over Chloe DeVore, the book was bigger than that. "She was a *writer.*"

Valley sneered at me. "So what? We know she didn't kill herself. We've got real proof—the physical evidence." He described it to me almost exactly the way Angie had, and I tried to look surprised or at least attentive, so that he wouldn't know I'd heard any of it before.

But while he was talking, something occurred to me. If Priscilla had indeed been murdered, then the copy of *Ethan Frome* in her car was just a coincidence, wasn't it? There'd be no link with the copy of *The House of Mirth* at Chloe's side.

"What?" Valley asked. "What are you thinking about?"

I shrugged, feeling like Lucy when Ricky sensed she was up to no good.

"What else have you been doing?" Valley asked.

"Do you have the registration list with you? The conference list?"

"It's in my office. Why are you interested?"

"Well, we've been wondering—"

He cut me off. "Who's we?"

I decided not to mention Angie's involvement, though I wondered if he already knew, since she'd said she was going to call him. Was Valley testing me again? Okay, then, let him test me.

"I've been talking it over with Stefan. Is that all right?"

He shrugged and I explained that we suspected there might be people besides me and Serena at the conference who weren't registered, and maybe they didn't get fingerprinted.

Noncommittally, Valley said, "We could pursue that." Then he clapped his hands like a kindergarten teacher shepherding her charges from one activity to the next. "Time to go," he said, ushering me out.

At the door, I asked him if he had known I was there, and that's why he'd come in. Valley smiled.

"I left my card around and told the neighbors to report anything suspicious. You're suspicious." He held out his hand. "The key." When I started to protest, he said, "I'll get it to the old lady." Then he gave me a warning: "Stay out of this now. Next time, I *will* arrest you."

And then, precisely because I should have just gone quietly to my car and driven away, I didn't. "What's your first name?" I asked. "How come it's not on your cards, and you just introduce yourself as Detective Valley?"

Unexpectedly, Valley smiled. "It's pretty bad. I'm half Italian, and I was named for my grandfather, Salvatore."

"Jeez! The kids must have called you Sally or something gross like that."

Valley winced. I'd clearly guessed right. He stood there in front of

Priscilla's house, probably to make sure I drove away. As I opened my car door, Valley said, "Remember—cool it with the detecting."

Sheepishly, I assured him that I would. And then I drove a few blocks away to Serena's house to see if she had a copy of the registration list.

# II

Serena lived on a short, dead-end street lined with Tudors and colonials. I'd attended a party at her place once, and the pseudo-timbered exterior gave no sign that inside, the house was relentlessly black, white, and red in each room, and filled with gleaming glass and plastic furniture.

She opened the door, clearly surprised to see me. And I was surprised to see her wearing jeans and an oversized University of Michigan T-shirt. That was SUM's rival school!

Serena didn't invite me in, and she even held one hand on the door as if she suspected I might try to force my way in. "What's wrong?" she asked. "Another fatality at the conference?"

"I've lost my copy of the registration list."

"Why do you need it right now? What's the problem?"

I'd thought of the answer to that on the short drive over. "I'm not sure why, but Detective Valley wanted a copy."

Now she was really suspicious, and I didn't understand why Valley could have come over himself, or called. Are you his deputy?"

I was thrown by her interrogation. After all, wasn't I the official program chair and didn't I have a right to this information? But I recovered quickly. "Well, yes. I am his deputy, in a way. Remember how he had me sit in when he was questioning people Thursday night, after Chloe's body was found?"

Serena considered that thoughtfully, then nodded. "Sure. Wait here, I'll be right back." She closed the door, which made me think there was someone inside she didn't want me to see. It couldn't have been that her house was a mess and she was embarrassed.

Serena was back quickly with her copy of the list, which she had slipped into a manila envelope.

I thanked her and drove back to the Campus Center, once again grateful that the weather for the conference, at least, had been good. No, not just good, terrific. I wondered if Serena had been a bit prickly simply because she'd hoped to have some time alone away from the conference, and I'd intruded on her rest.

At the Campus Center, I wandered down the main hallway into the bar where I was supposed to meet Stefan and Angie, but they weren't there. I decided to hold off consulting the list until the three of us were together.

Connected to the Campus Center restaurant, the bar was completely covered in mirrors and dark gray velvet, making it look like a seventies love pit. At a glass-topped corner table, Devon Davenport and Grace-Dawn Vaughan were throning, as Wharton would say. They grandly waved me over. Vaughan was drinking something from a saucer-shaped champagne glass, and Davenport had what looked like a glass of Scotch.

"We've been trying to figure out these deaths," Vaughan told me cheerfully. "Are they connected or separate? If they're connected, how? Is there one murderer, and was that Priscilla, or did one person kill both women? And if there *are* two murderers, was the second one opportunistic—did he, or *she,* decide to link the deaths to confuse the police?" Grace-Dawn sighed with contentment, as if she'd just sketched out a plot complication in one of her novels.

I wasn't far off.

"She's working on a new book," Davenport growled, eyeing her affectionately. Hell, why shouldn't he be affectionate? She was always on the best-seller list. But there was something more between them: the comfort of a long-married couple, who seem oriented to one another in ways too subtle for outsiders to guess.

"Yes," Vaughan said breathily, tapping my hand. "But I may change the setting to a literary conference, and throw in some extra murders for spice!"

Grace-Dawn Vaughan wrote Big Books with far-fetched plots, shallow but showy characters, and improbable coincidences. I dreaded the way our conference would be transformed in fiction by a woman who could write about a character cutting her wrists after having lived "on the jagged edges of her broken dreams." Stefan had read me that line, howling, after getting one of her books from the SUM library when I told him she'd be attending the conference. Her writing was almost as florid and ungrammatical as David Baldacci's in *Absolute Power*.

"No offense intended," Grace-Dawn said to me carefully, "but I think the conference in *my* book will have to be a little more exciting, I mean in the choice of writer. Edith Wharton isn't very sexy, is she? My God, have you ever seen that picture of her where she looks positively strangled by all those pearls—well, of course you have, you've written about her—and she's got no lips? No lips at all!"

"Damn straight," Davenport said, and I had no idea what part of her remarks he was agreeing with.

I wondered if Grace-Dawn was going to mention Wharton's lip lack when she explored Wharton's passion and pain.

"What do you think about a Marianne Williamson conference? It could be sexy and spiritual!"

Davenport laughed. "She doesn't even write her own books! At least get somebody who can write, for crissakes."

Vaughan wrinkled her nose. "Like Jane Smiley?"

"Forget it. Smiley has no sex appeal. You might as well get Barbara Bush."

"Don't be mean. Barbara Bush wrote a *lovely* book."

"One book," Davenport said. "Short conference."

Vaughan objected. "But Dee-dee, think of the appeal! The patriotism!"

"What would the professors say about her book?"

"If they can make up nonsense about Edith Wharton, Barbara Bush shouldn't be a problem."

"Granted. But Bush is a hag. And people have already forgotten her." Grace-Dawn nodded. "Okay."

I didn't mention that Mrs. Bush had written her book with a dog, because I wasn't sure if that would make Grace-Dawn's imaginary conference more or less appealing.

"Madonna wrote a book," I offered. "With pictures."

Grace-Dawn squinted at me. "Yes, I saw it, and it has too much sex."

Davenport frowned, as if doubting that could be possible, and I wondered if this interplay between them was some kind of postmodern lounge act. They couldn't be serious, could they?

"Listen," Davenport said to me, without preamble. "I heard you've been nosing around to find out who did it. Don't bother asking who told me. That's not the point. There's no fucking way I could have killed either Chloe DeVore or Priscilla Davidoff, if you're thinking I did it. Right after the reception and before we had to do those speeches, Grace and I dived into the bar here for a quick drink—a real one, not that pissant stuff you had at the reception. Grace wanted to stop at the crapper before getting to the auditorium, so I gave her a head start and had another."

Grace-Dawn smiled at me as if to say, Isn't his crudeness adorable?

"The bartender remembered me."

Well, I didn't doubt that. And I wondered how many drinks they'd actually had. Alcohol might explain Grace-Dawn's attempted flights of fancy in her keynote speech, and Davenport's belligerence in his.

Was he bluffing, though? I couldn't check that with Valley after he'd warned me to mind my own business, could I?

"Anyway," Davenport rolled on, "I wanted Chloe alive. I wanted her new book. The memoir. I know, I know, that's not what I said to Detective Shmuck, but who cares. I don't tell my business just because somebody asks me."

Grace-Dawn frowned, busying herself with her cocktail napkin, and I assumed she was jealous of Chloe, and maybe even alarmed that Davenport had admitted lying to the police.

"Even if we couldn't bag the hardcover, we could still go for the paperback rights."

"Yes," Grace-Dawn said, looking up as if taking a cue. "And I was planning to spoof Chloe in my new book. *So* much more satisfying than killing her for real."

I'd been silent all through this strange interchange, but now I asked Davenport, "You wanted to publish Chloe DeVore's memoir *and* publish a book by someone satirizing Chloe DeVore?"

Davenport said, "Sure, why not? We'd clean up! Think of the coverage!"

I glanced from Davenport to Grace-Dawn, both looking very sincere in their insincerity. I decided that Davenport wasn't bullshitting me, and that he certainly didn't have as good a reason to kill Chloe as I'd thought. Neither did Grace-Dawn, unless it was to keep Davenport from signing Chloe. Maybe, as his obvious favorite author, she was jealous and threatened, fearful that someone like Chloe, "the one who got away," could displace her. But that wasn't rational, since Chloe had never maintained best-seller status.

Stefan would probably say, "When is murder rational?" Jeez, I'd said something like that myself.

"Okay," I said to Davenport. "What about Priscilla's death?"

Grace-Dawn took my arm and said, "Frankly, I think the two murders are just the work of some maniac—probably a homosexual, since they hate women as a rule, you know."

Furious, I yanked my arm away. "That's ridiculous. That's an outdated stereotype! I'm gay and I like women! Lots of women!"

"Then you're obviously different," Vaughan sniffed. "Though yelling at me is hardly the way to prove it."

I was about to start shouting when Davenport muttered, "Calm down," as if Grace-Dawn had merely expressed a peculiar taste in sandwich spreads. "Chloe's murderer is either Crane Taylor or Gustaf Carmichael. That's what I think."

"Why?"

"Nothing to it. Not everybody knows this, but Chloe was married to Taylor when she did her first book, and the divorce was bad news. For them, I mean. They kept it quiet. So then the two of them end up here by chance years later—so why not off her? Hell, I'm surprised she didn't kill him first. Hey, maybe she was trying to and he got the upper hand."

"And Gustaf Carmichael," Grace-Dawn prompted.

Davenport shrugged his burly shoulders. "Simple. The guy teaches at a shitty branch campus of the University of Ohio, never got a better job. You think he wouldn't blame Chloe for nuking his first book in the *New York Times*? That review finished Carmichael," he said casually. "His book sold three hundred copies. Nobody wanted to touch him after that."

I was persuaded by this last argument, because I knew very well that promotion and moving to another school are impossible without major publications, and I also understood the depth of humiliation an author can suffer from a very public bad review. Stefan still raged about a bad review in *Chuppah,* the pretentious, pseudointellectual liberal Jewish quarterly claiming to "marry Jewish tradition and contemporary inquiry."

Grace-Dawn called the waiter over, and ordered another champagne cocktail, offering to get me a drink, but I passed. "My theory is that they did it together," she said. "Carmichael and Taylor both killed Chloe."

"I'll tell you who else looks funny to me," Davenport said, downing the last of his drink. "That Jones fart and the leather jacket babe. They've been acting shifty since Chloe was killed, and all that yelling in public, maybe that's a cover. Maybe they've been making themselves conspicuous so nobody's going to think they're suspects."

Grace-Dawn nodded eagerly, enjoying Davenport's theorizing. He was right about finding Jones and Gallup suspicious—they worried me, too.

"Wait a minute," I objected. "What are their motives? And what would they have wanted to kill Priscilla for? If you start suspecting conferees who're odd or suspicious, everyone's a suspect."

Davenport grinned. It was an unpleasant display of very white equine teeth. "You got that right, kiddo. Authors may be scum, but you professors, you're roadkill. You wouldn't believe the morons who've been hitting on me here, trying to pitch me half-assed book ideas. Like they even have a clue for what makes a book sell."

Davenport and Grace-Dawn exchanged a loving glance. They clearly had the secret, and were an unbeatable team. And I suppose they were: seven best-sellers and 223 million copies of her books in print.

Given all Davenport's blustering and bluntness, I asked myself if he might not be doing exactly what he had just accused Van Deegan Jones and Verity Gallup of doing: making himself conspicuous in order to throw sand in people's eyes. I was saved from any more diatribes when Stefan called to me from the entrance to the bar. I joined him and Angie at a nearby table out of Davenport's and Grace-Dawn's sight line. I had the waiter bring us all coffee.

"So?" I said.

Angie and Stefan both looked tired and disappointed. They had learned nothing today. Angie said she'd left a long message for Detective Valley, "But I haven't talked to him. It's so frustrating."

"Well, get this," I said. I told them about retrieving the registration list from Serena, and finding the Wharton-related book title on Priscilla's computer before that.

Angie repeated it: "*The Ethan Frome Murders.* Yuck."

Stefan blinked a few times. "You went to Priscilla's house? You stole a key and—"

"Borrowed a key. Borrowed."

"But what if Valley had found you?"

"Actually, he did." I felt cocky now, since Valley hadn't arrested me.

Angie shook her head, clearly impressed by my pluck. "This is awesome," she said. "I wish I'd been there instead of trailing around looking at shrubs and eavesdropping on nothing."

"It's not great. He's a felon," Stefan said, obviously forcing himself to speak quietly.

"Stefan, that's not important. What's important is that Valley's convinced that Priscilla was murdered. So where does that leave us?"

"Let's check out the registration list," Angie suggested, and I pulled the two stapled pages from their envelope and set them down on the table where we could all see. We slowly matched names and faces, and came up with seven people who'd been attending sessions but weren't down as registered: me, Stefan, Serena, Bob Gillian, Joanne Gillian, Devon Davenport, and Grace-Dawn Vaughan.

Angie asked me, "Why didn't the two main speakers register?"

"It's a courtesy to cover a speaker's registration fees."

"Oh."

"But when I was waiting for you two, I was sitting with Davenport and Vaughan, and they spent a lot of time trying to convince me that they're innocent. And they put the blame on Gustaf Carmichael, Crane Taylor, Van Deegan Jones, and Verity Gallup."

Angie clapped her hands together. "This is like a movie!" she exulted. "What if fingerprints and registration don't have anything to do with who killed Chloe and Priscilla? We're back to where we started." The prospect didn't faze her at all. Was it the coffee?

Stefan mumbled something.

"What?"

He wouldn't look at me. "This is pointless. We split up for the afternoon and all we've done is waste time."

"It could be worse," I said.

"How?"

"In mystery movies, when people split up, somebody usually disappears or gets killed."

Angie smiled, but Stefan was not about to let me shake him from his mood. "There has to be something we can accomplish. The answer has to be in the Edith Wharton books they found at the scene of each crime. Those are the only real clues."

"Look," Angie said, pointing. "There's our detective."

Valley was walking down the hallway and he stopped at the door when he saw us. He seemed to be debating a point, and then must have decided, because he came right over to our table.

"Professor Hoffman, you may be onto something with the fingerprints/registration business. I'm bringing another detective with me to ask all the people at dinner who aren't registered to step outside so we can double-check whether their fingerprints have been taken."

I slid my hand over the list on the table, but Valley saw me, and said, "I guess you know who they are, too." He left before I could think of anything to say.

DINNER SEEMED AN edgy affair, perhaps because there was a rumor going around that the conferees might have to stay beyond the end of the conference Sunday morning, since the Campus Police hadn't solved anything.

Serena snubbed me when Stefan, Angie, and I entered the dining room, as if she knew we suspected her. Van Deegan Jones and Verity Gallup were whispering to each other once again. Devon Davenport and Grace-Dawn Vaughan seemed very pleased with themselves, and were sitting at a table with Gustaf Carmichael and Crane Taylor. The Gillians arrived, and I bristled at the way they both stopped in the doorway as if expecting some kind of ovation, or at least attention—like Queen Elizabeth and Prince Philip.

"Maybe they're practicing," I whispered to Stefan.

"What for?"

"For when Joanne's governor of Michigan, and Bob's her consort."
Stefan looked like he wanted to puke.

Watching the Gillians smugly make their way to a table, I said, "How did I ever imagine Bob Gillian could be likable?"

Now, that made Stefan smile. "Nick, you're a very enthusiastic guy. Sometimes it's about the right things, sometimes it isn't."

"I was right about you," I said, a little defensively. "Wasn't I?"

Angie beamed at the two of us as if she were a matchmaker pleased with her work. I wondered briefly if she might be gay, or have a gay brother or friends. She was so relaxed around the two of us, but maybe it was just progress. At the same time that some students on campus seemed incredibly intolerant of all minorities, others tended to be very matter-of-fact about homosexuality.

Suddenly, Joanne Gillian stood up and loudly proclaimed, "Let's have a moment of silence." The attempt at solemnity was undermined by rolls being brought out by the waiters and waitresses from the kitchens through the service entrance at the back of the room. "A moment of silence for those who have left us," Joanne added sententiously, in her best I-speak-to-God voice.

Amid much embarrassed sighing and chair scraping, silence fell on the room for a minute, as everyone followed her lead and stood, except Devon Davenport, at first, until Grace-Dawn yanked at his arm.

"Amen," Joanne said, and I wondered what her private prayer had been.

We all sat down as relieved as if we'd been standing for hours, and I despised her for having turned Chloe's and Priscilla's deaths into an opportunity for a studied act of pretentious religiosity.

The dull salad was followed by more acceptable gumbo, the food animating everyone more than I would have expected. Maybe people were glad to have had a break to tour the campus, sleep, screw, plot against their rivals. The entrée was good—a vegetarian lasagna with real kick to it—and I felt myself beginning to unwind.

But it was all pretty hopeless. The two deaths would go unsolved just like crimes in a big city, I wouldn't get tenure, and we'd begin an impossible job search, but somehow it didn't matter anymore. I was burned out by all the worrying and commotion.

Stefan must have been feeling better, though, because he started teasing me, telling me that he'd planned a surprise dinner for me when the conference was over. "You deserve the best after all this."

I didn't object.

"But, Nick, if you ever agree to organize another conference, I'll put you on bread and water, and start an enemies list."

The others at the table seemed amused, but vague, as if they couldn't or didn't want to follow.

"Wait," I said. *"Enemies."*

Everyone stared at me.

"Stefan, come on!" I rushed out of the dining room to find the nearest and quietest corner. Stefan had followed, looking as perplexed as if he thought I might finally have snapped.

He sat right by me on a couch with a view of the dining room doorway. "What's going on?"

"Priscilla told me a few months ago that her new book was called *Sleeping with the Enemy.* And when I checked her computer, she had a directory called ENEMY I forgot to tell you about. It was empty, just like the other one. I thought the title was a reference to the Julia Roberts movie, and it probably is, but what if it was something much more personal? What if it's about the killer? I mean, whoever became the killer—whoever killed Priscilla, and Chloe. I don't know if that was really her new book and someone deleted all the files, or what. But it was definitely important if it had its own directory."

Stefan chewed all that over a little, and asked, "You're saying that Priscilla was sleeping with someone who was an enemy. What kind of enemy?"

Feeling a little dizzy, I closed my eyes. The answer suddenly seemed as stark as fresh footprints on a snow-covered driveway. "Who would her enemy be?" I asked. "Who would she despise that would feel the same way about her, at least publicly?"

Stefan shook his head.

"Someone at SUM who's politically conservative, and opposed to everything she believes in, right?"

Stefan looked thunderstruck. "Joanne Gillian? That's impossible! She's not gay."

"Oh, it's better than that. Bob Gillian."

"Impossible—he's a guy."

"Exactly. The 'enemy' to some lesbians, and some feminists. That part might have been a little joke for Priscilla."

"This doesn't make sense."

Leaning towards him, I felt my face growing hot with conviction. "It makes total sense, Stefan. Remember Angie said they didn't find fingerprints on the granite tile Chloe was killed with? Bob likes to carry those driving gloves with him. He could have slipped them on before killing her, and then shoved them back into his pockets. They're that really thin leather—nobody would notice because they wouldn't take up any room. And they wouldn't leave prints."

Stefan frowned, unconvinced.

"Come on, Stefan, this has to be it. Who would have time to kill someone right out there in the hallway where they might be discovered, and then wipe the granite tile off so thoroughly it was clean?"

"Nobody," Stefan said, blinking.

"That's right. Nobody. But you wouldn't have to if you were wearing gloves. Why's Bob here at the conference, anyway? Joanne wants to be on the scene because she thinks it's Sodom and Gomorrah, but why would he need to be here? He's been stalking them, stalking Chloe and Priscilla."

"Wait a minute. You don't have a motive. Bob could have done it, he could have killed both of them, but why?"

He had me there. "Maybe Priscilla wasn't exaggerating. Maybe he really is evil. Maybe Joanne's the loudmouth, but he's the one who's really dangerous. I mean, all that niceness when I was first getting to know him. It's just like Hamlet says: 'One may smile, and smile, and be a villain still.' Let's go back inside. I want to watch him. And I think I should talk to Valley."

We quickly returned to our table, but just as we sat down, Valley appeared at the door to the dining room, followed by a tall, curly-haired, dark-eyed woman in a drab suit. I figured she was his "other detective."

I didn't get a chance to talk to him because he said, "I'd like to see the following people outside, please." He read from a list: "Joanne Gillian, Robert Gillian, Serena Fisch, Devon Davenport, Grace-Dawn Vaughan, Nick Hoffman, and Stefan Borowski."

Davenport groused, "Can't this wait until we're done with dinner?" Grace-Dawn clucked with annoyance.

Serena Fisch challenged Valley: "What the hell is this all about? You've talked to us already. I don't have anything more to say!"

"We want to get your fingerprints to check them against the books found next to Chloe DeVore's body, and Priscilla Davidoff's."

Davenport reluctantly got to his feet, cursing about "half-assed cops" and "hick towns." Grace-Dawn was at his side as he headed from their table, head high as if she were Mary, Queen of Scots facing the ax. The other people Valley had designated began to stand and leave their tables, some looking anxious or frightened. Don't ask me why, but even I felt uncomfortable, as if somehow I might get framed for killing Chloe or Priscilla.

Heading towards the door with Stefan, I heard Joanne Gillian behind me suddenly let out an anguished cry of "NO!"

I whirled around to see Bob Gillian leap from his chair and race to the service door, crashing through. There was a jagged, brutal clamor of shouting, struggling, dishes breaking, trays falling. Valley and the woman detective didn't even stir. I watched their aplomb with astonishment, until the service door flew open and a tall, muscular, uniformed Campus Policeman shoved Bob Gillian back through the door, his arms pinned behind his back.

In the hushed, expectant room, I was transfixed by the scene, and reached out to touch Stefan as if to ground myself.

Bob Gillian's left side was slathered with what looked like key lime pie.

"I think I'll skip dessert," I said.

Just then Bob kicked back at the Campus Cop, getting him in the knee. The cop let go, doubling over in agony, and Bob ran straight for the door, cannoning right through Valley and the woman detective, who rushed over to help the injured cop while Valley tore after Bob. Stefan and I ran after him. We heard a crash of some kind down the hall and followed it.

Bob Gillian was on his back in the same hallway where Chloe had been killed, wrestling wildly with Valley near a ragged heap of those granite tiles. There was blood spattered on the floor and his clothes.

"Get a doctor," someone called from behind me, and I turned to see a mass of conferees gaping at this new spectacle.

Bob somehow dragged himself to his feet and lunged at Valley, who finally stopped him cold with a very professional-looking right to the chin and a quick left. Bob collapsed on his ass, gasping.

The woman cop burst through the crowd and yanked Bob's hands behind his back, then handcuffed him.

Valley turned and saw his audience. His suit was torn and bloodied, and dotted with some of that pie, but he grinned at all of us. "He tripped." Valley pointed. "He tripped on those tiles and cut himself."

"It's all her fault!" Bob screamed as Joanne Gillian pushed through the crowd and approached him. She froze. "*She* did it!" Bob shouted.

Joanne tried to look innocent, but Vivianne suddenly leapt out of the throng and shouted "Assassin!" She smacked Joanne repeatedly across the face before Joanne started fighting back. The two women fell grappling to the floor, cursing in French and English. Valley watched, breathing hard and looking exhausted.

Stefan rushed over and swept them apart. Valley announced he was arresting Bob and read him his rights. Then he turned and asked the wild-eyed, red-faced Joanne to come along for questioning.

"I'm calling my lawyer first, and then the governor!"

Valley wasn't intimidated. "You can call from the station."

"Detective Valley," I said, "did you suspect him?"

Valley grinned. "Nope. But I hoped showing up and starting to take more prints would smoke out the killer. It worked." And with that, the strange procession left the Campus Center.

Weeping, Vivianne fled, to the ladies' room, I suppose.

Stunned, we all trickled back to our tables, and dinner resumed, but in a roar of speculation and excitement.

"I was right!" Angie said at our table. "I think. But what if Bob Gillian was afraid of being fingerprinted because he has a criminal record that could sabotage his wife's political future? Don't they say she might run for governor? And what if her husband's fingerprints aren't even on the book they found with Chloe DeVore?"

Stefan chimed in with his own objection. "How can Bob's fingerprints be on the book if he was wearing gloves when he killed Chloe? Isn't that what you assumed, Nick? That he wore his racing gloves? And if he was wearing them, why would he try to escape? Wouldn't he be sure he was safe?"

I heard the questions, and heard myself say, "I guess he just panicked." I was sitting there in a stupor, too dazed to even touch my coffee, working on the motive. I felt sure that Stefan and Angie were wrong about us jumping to conclusions, and that Bob was obviously guilty because he'd made a run for it, but why?

Dinner continued for most of the conferees with as much festivity as if they were at a wedding and had just seen the bride and groom drive off to their honeymoon. No, it was more intense than that. There was an almost prurient undertone, as if the guests had also gotten to secretly watch the consummation. What a show!

It completely eclipsed the entertainment scheduled for after dinner. I'd arranged for the chair of the Theater Department, Vic Godine, to do a dramatic reading of Wharton's delicious short story "Xingu," a satire of culture vultures. A Wharton fan, Vic had a rich round voice that matched his rubicund tenor's body, and he gave the story every bit of nuance it needed.

But the performance fell flat—how could anything follow up a dramatic arrest? We all scattered when the reading was over, incidentally proving what Wharton had observed in *The Age of Innocence,* that "Americans want to get away from amusement even more quickly than they want to get to it."

I woke from a drugged and dreamless sleep to find Stefan sitting in the bedroom with a broad and easy smile. He looked almost like a goofy lottery winner.

"Why are you dressed already?" I asked.

"I went to get the paper. Look." He held the *Michiganapolis Tribune* out for me to see the enormous headline, "BOB'S BOMBSHELLS," over an article that took up the entire front page. "It's like something from the *National Enquirer.*"

"Read it to me!"

He did, and I luxuriated under the covers while scandal broke over me in lavish waves.

Bob had confessed to killing both Chloe and Priscilla. He had lured Chloe to the dark hallway and killed her because she'd had an affair with Joanne when they were both students at Smith. He claimed he was afraid Chloe was going to write about it in her memoirs. He arranged for Joanne to find the body, so that no one would suspect her.

And Bob killed Priscilla because she was blackmailing Joanne. Priscilla had demanded Joanne Gillian change the Board of Trustees' position on domestic partner benefits for gays and lesbians, or she'd reveal that she was having an affair *with Bob—and with Joanne.*

Stefan would look at me every now and then to catch my reaction. "You were right," he said. "You were more than right, if it's true. And you're also *bouche bée.*" He laughed.

"Please, no French before breakfast! I don't know that one. What's it mean? Bouche Bay sounds like some vacation spot in Maine."

"Your jaw's hanging open," he explained. "Shall I go on?"

"Yes I said yes I will yes." Nothing less than Molly Bloom's rhapsodic voice seemed fitting for such wild revelations. Stefan finished the article with gusto.

So if Bob Gillian was telling the truth, then Priscilla was not only sleeping with a man, but with a man she had said she detested.

Stefan was less astonished, and very logical. "Priscilla wouldn't want anyone in the lesbian and gay community to know she might be bisexual. It would bring her a lot of flak. They'd say she was betraying the cause and all that."

Though I'd figured out that Bob was the murderer, elements of the case didn't make sense to me. "But what about sleeping with Joanne! She's Michigan's own Jesse Helms, she's the Antichrist! And Priscilla told me she loathed them both! She even criticized me for trying to be nice to Bob. Was it a cover?"

Stefan had an explanation for that as well. "Of course she'd have to hide an affair with someone who publicly bashed gays and lesbians at SUM."

"Okay. But I still don't understand how she could sleep with *Joanne*—and when could they have met?"

Stefan figured that Joanne and Priscilla had probably first encountered each other at a Board of Trustees meeting, or when the task force got going. "There are some people who are attracted to women or men precisely *because* they're the wrong person, and cruel."

"That's sick!"

Stefan disagreed. "It makes sense emotionally."

Well, who was I to argue a point like that? And then something came back to me from the first time Priscilla and I ever talked about Bob and

Joanne Gillian. She'd said that even if members of SUM's gay and lesbian task force had slept with their opponents, nothing at the university would have changed.

"Was that a Freudian slip?" I asked Stefan. "Or did she decide right then she was going to sleep with Bob and Joanne to shake everything up? Or had it already happened?"

"I don't know, Nick. But this might not make Priscilla into a villain at SUM for gays. If people think she was killed because she was trying to get the Board of Trustees to change its position, she might end up being seen as a martyr for gay rights, despite how she went about it."

"Saint Priscilla? That's a stretch."

"Well—you're probably right. The whole situation does make domestic partner benefits at SUM feel even murkier than before."

I suddenly slapped my hand to my head. "Stefan! *Ethan Frome!* It's all about a triangle. Ethan, his wife, and Mattie, the girl who's their servant. No wonder Priscilla was fascinated by that novel enough to think of using it somehow for a mystery. It's a story of being trapped, and guilt and shame. It's so dark and twisted—just like her own story!"

I showered and dressed quickly and we headed off to the Campus Center for the last conference breakfast, where I was greeted like a hero at the door to the dining room. People crowded up to shake my hand and congratulate me on the conference. They praised the panels and the speakers and the food.

No one mentioned the murders or the arrest, but that was clearly what had excited them. Sweet Angie was there practically bouncing off the walls. "I can't believe we were so close to death!" she said over and over.

I marveled at her youth.

Before I could even sit down, Gustaf Carmichael and Crane Taylor stopped me to say that they were thinking of having another joint conference of Wharton scholars, less formally, to see about healing the wounds that had been caused by the open dissension at the conference. What could I do? I gave them my blessing.

Then they asked if I'd like to chair the conference since I'd done such a marvelous job on this one.

"I couldn't possibly," I said. "I'm booked through the end of the century." When Carmichael started to speak, I added, "And beyond." That quashed any further recruiting.

As breakfast began, Verity Gallup and Van Deegan Jones rose. "We have an announcement," Jones said, looking very serious. A buzz went around the dining room and I wondered what the hell was going to happen now.

"Yes," Verity said. "We're both resigning from our respective Wharton societies."

There were gasps from the conferees.

"We're getting out of Wharton studies entirely," Jones said, and now the room sang with gossip. Jones took Verity's hand. "I'm taking early retirement. We've fallen in love here at this—" He choked up a little. "At this wonderful conference."

Stefan kicked me under the table.

"We're getting married," Verity said with a proud grin. "And we're moving to Santa Fe."

They sat down, still holding hands, and there was an immediate uproar of protests and applause—for the marriage, for the retirement, for their both quitting their positions as society presidents. Instantly, I could sense factions form across the room as Wharton scholars started quietly electioneering, surveying their chances, calling in favors. Would there be one society or two—or more? The only unhappy people in the room, that I could tell, were Gustaf Carmichael and Crane Taylor. They looked disgusted and confused by the turn of events, the announcement dimming their shot at being Wharton peacemakers.

Vivianne slipped into the empty chair next to mine at that point and started apologizing for her behavior the previous night. "My code has always been *Sois sage, sois chic,* and I am mortified to have displayed such bad manners at your conference."

Stefan asked her if she knew anything more about what Bob said.

Vivianne nodded. "I believe that Priscilla drove to the Gillians' home distraught, terrified she would be arrested. Mr. Gillian took her home, and they parked in the remote lot because he was trying to calm her down. Priscilla grabbed the gun she kept in her glove compartment for protection and said she wanted to kill herself. He saw his opportunity to get rid of trouble, and pretended to try taking the gun away, but pointed at her instead, and fired."

The story came out with impeccable smoothness.

"How do you know all that?" Stefan asked.

Vivianne smiled. "Do you remember the woman detective last night? She and I have . . . spoken since then."

Fast work, I thought.

"But what about Chloe's memoir? Wasn't Chloe going to reveal the publisher she'd chosen at the end of the conference? Did she tell you who it was?"

"There was no memoir. She was just making trouble, making publicity."

Astonished, I brought up the supposed bidding war between publishers. Was that phony? What were they going to bid on?

"Her name," Vivianne explained. "And scandal. Monsieur Davenport has said that writers are scum. Well, I say publishers are fools."

Stefan and I wanted to applaud.

Vivianne rose, nodded to both of us, said, *"Au plaisir,"* and left.

A latecomer to breakfast announced to the room that he'd heard on the radio that Joanne Gillian had denied her husband's allegations and was filing for divorce, citing "drug abuse and sexual perversion." Joanne Gillian planned to hold a press conference later that day.

More tumult.

Angie was craning her neck, trying to take it all in. "This is just so awesome—it's so cool—it's awesome."

Serena waltzed by just then and said gently, "Give it a rest, babe."

A waiter came up to me, one I didn't recognize. "Are you Dr. Hoffman? You are? Well, the other day, when we were cleaning up here, someone on the staff found a paperback they figured must belong to someone at the conference." He handed it to me, saying, "Sorry I forgot."

It was a copy of *The House of Mirth,* and when I opened it up, Priscilla's name was written on the inside flap. Her missing copy.

"She must have dropped it somewhere," Stefan said.

"But what about the copy in the hallway where Chloe was killed?"

Angie shrugged. "We might not ever find out who it belonged to or how it got there." She sounded as thrilled as if she were a Bermuda Triangle fan.

Van Deegan Jones and Verity Gallup started to leave the room hand-in-hand. At the door, they turned. Verity said loudly, "Why don't you all go home and live real lives?"

That seemed a more than fitting way to wrap up the conference.

But when they were gone, I rushed out after them. They turned, amused at my haste, eyebrows up in a silent "Yes . . . ?"

"What did you have against Chloe DeVore? There was something personal, wasn't there?"

They looked at each other and shrugged as if to say, Why not tell him?

Looking markedly less affectionate, Verity said, "Chloe was a good friend of a prominent French publisher interested in doing a French translation of my first book. Chloe said the project would be a waste of time." She stiffened and Jones slipped an arm around her.

"And you?" I asked him. "Why did you dislike Chloe DeVore?"

Jones was as welcoming as someone on *60 Minutes* being invaded by a camera crew at his place of work.

"She knew something about me that no one else did," he said stiffly. "A cousin of mine was an ex-lover of Chloe's—" He broke off and now it was Verity who offered him comfort, slipping both arms lovingly around his waist. "It's not at all widely known that . . . my mother was a Jewess," Jones brought out at last, eyes down.

"Jewess," I repeated, understanding at once how shameful that would be to someone claiming patrician status, claiming descent from Edith Wharton, who herself was of fine old Dutch and English stock, and not exactly philo-Semitic herself.

"None of that matters now," Verity said, grinning, and Jones perked up.

I left, glad to be rid of them both.

WHEN STEFAN AND I got home, I began pulling off my clothes to take a long hot bath, but Stefan said, "Start packing. We're going to the cabin."

"We can't. We both have classes tomorrow."

"So we'll drive back early. Pack. Now. And stay out of the kitchen."

I'd wanted to escape all weekend—so why not do it? I felt chilled by the odd good-byes at the Campus Center: each conferee said they'd never been to such an exciting academic conference before.

Exciting? It was like a Reverend Moon mass wedding during a hurricane.

While Stefan did mysterious things in the kitchen, I threw clothes and toiletries into the leather Gladstone bag he had bought me for my last birthday because I'd always wanted one. I closed shades, put some lamps on timers, and was ready to go in under half an hour.

Stefan lugged out two large coolers and some grocery bags, and wouldn't tell me what was in them. We sped north. It's a dull drive straight up Route 27 through St. John's and Mt. Pleasant because everything's so flat. But further north, the ride becomes more scenic and you move through farmland and rolling hills.

We blasted Annie Lennox's "Diva" and Bronski Beat, feeling like teenagers running from their parents.

Heading northwest to Lake Michigan at Grayling, you're in a hillier part of the state, like another world, with dense woods and picturesque lakes. The conference dropped from us like sweat off a whirling dervish.

We were free, and I felt incredibly relaxed by the time we drove down the three-mile dirt road near Norwood just south of Charlevoix. Well screened by poplars, white pines, and hemlocks, our gem of a cabin was right on the lake, with two hundred feet of beach on a deep half-acre site. The setting was even more private because we never invited anybody—there simply wasn't enough room for guests. Two-thirds of the space was the open kitchen and living room; the rest was a cozy bedroom and bath with a sunken whirlpool tub.

We turned up the heat and settled in very quickly because I wanted to make the most of our half day here.

I love being by Lake Michigan. I don't care that it's not the ocean—it looks plenty big to me, since I can't see the other side, and it has waves. Even better: there aren't any jellyfish or sharks.

"So what's for dinner?" I finally asked. "You have to tell me now."

Stefan grinned and laid out the menu: sweet potato and foie gras ravioli; butterflied leg of lamb stuffed with spinach, mint, and orange zest; roasted garlic potatoes; a bottle of 1990 Vieux Telegraph. Followed by Grand Marnier ice cream in white chocolate shells and a 1988 Dom Perignon. He whipped out an ice bucket and started filling it for the champagne.

"No wonder you had to pack so much stuff. You really love me, don't you?"

Stefan nodded gravely. "It kills me that you're still thinking about last year, and Perry Cross."

I looked away. "Well, it still hurts."

"As much as before?"

I met his eager, melting glance. He was on the point of tears.

"No," I said confidently. "Much less all the time."

He sighed, looking relieved and grateful.

The phone rang, and we both glared at it, letting the machine take the call. It was Serena. "Nick! Nick! If you're up there, you have to turn on the TV! It's Joanne Gillian! She's having a press conference at her *church*. It's priceless!"

We didn't take the call, but it got us both curious, and we switched on the TV—luckily we had cable here—and tuned in a Lansing station.

I was amazed to see a room full of cameras and reporters. Facing a tangle of black microphones, Joanne sat at a small table in front of a gory silk-screened Crucifixion scene. She wore a modest white blouse and black suit.

"That's so tacky," I said, taking Stefan's hand. We were sitting very close.

"The banner or the clothes?"

"Both."

We hooted as the woebegone, pale Reverend Gillian began her statement. "Ladies and gentlemen of the press and people of Michigan, I come before you as a victim. I have been lied to, duped, cheated, and viciously maligned by my soon-to-be ex-husband, a dope fiend, a transvestite, and an evil, evil man who stole my heart and my trust, and kept me a prisoner for years. I couldn't escape because I loved him. I trusted him. I was sadly wrong."

The phone rang and I absent-mindedly picked it up, riveted to the screen.

"Professor Hoffman?" It was a reedy teenage voice I thought might belong to one of my students. But why would a student call me up here?

"I'm with the *Detroit Free Press* and I'd like to interview you about the murders at your conference. Could you give me some background?"

"Who is it?" Stefan whispered.

"Some reporter." I was so busy watching Joanne Gillian's twisted, anxious face, I didn't think of hanging up.

"Professor Hoffman, let's start with you telling me a little about Edith Wharton."

"Edith who?"